SIGNED: ANONYMOUS

"This is the second threatening letter," Helma said. "It might be smart to cancel the reunion."

"We can't cancel, Helma!" Ruth exclaimed. "We already bought crepe paper. The letters are a big joke, that's all. Why let some creep who's probably angry because he didn't get elected class president ruin a great party?"

"I'll agree to proceeding," Helma said, "but with caution. Only the foolhardy disregard threats."

Praise for JO DERESKE'S
debut mystery
MISS ZUKAS
AND THE LIBRARY MURDERS

"If you enjoy a light-hearted mystery, you're in for a good time."
Toronto Sun

. . . Appealing . . .
is straightforward,
tongue in cheek . . .
p a popular following."
nchair Detective

"A quick read . . . RECOMMENDED"
Montgomery Advertiser

Other Miss Zukas Mysteries by
Jo Dereske
from Avon Books

MISS ZUKAS AND THE LIBRARY MURDERS

Miss Zukas
AND THE
ISLAND MURDERS

JO
DERESKE

AVON BOOKS ◆ NEW YORK

MISS ZUKAS AND THE ISLAND MURDERS is an original publication of Avon Books. This work has never before appeared in book form. This work is a novel. Any similarity to actual persons or events is purely coincidental.

AVON BOOKS
A division of
The Hearst Corporation
1350 Avenue of the Americas
New York, New York 10019

Copyright © 1995 by Jo Dereske
Published by arrangement with the author
Library of Congress Catalog Card Number: 94-96360
ISBN: 0-380-77031-8

First Avon Books Printing: April 1995

AVON TRADEMARK REG. U.S. PAT. OFF. AND IN OTHER COUNTRIES, MARCA REGISTRADA, HECHO EN U.S.A.

Printed in the U.S.A.

RA   10   9   8   7   6   5   4   3   2   1

For K., K&B and pb

CONTENTS

CONTENTS

❧ *chapter one* ❧

THE LETTER

On Friday, when the letter arrived, Miss Helma Zukas was seated at her desk in the overcrowded workroom of the Bellehaven Public Library.

On her desk blotter lay a week-old newspaper article listing ten books a local group, calling themselves Save Your Kids, demanded be withdrawn from the library collection. Two of the books, including Madonna's *Sex*, weren't even owned by the library, although twenty-three patrons had requested them since the article appeared in the *Bellehaven Daily News*.

In her precise penmanship, Helma Zukas listed the remaining eight books, intending to research their publishing histories for a possible well-documented rebuttal to Save Your Kids.

It was the second week of February and the third day of a relentless cold rain that had blown inland off Washington Bay.

Bellehaven, Washington, a temperate city where the inhabitants grumbled that snow was about as likely as sunshine, was saturated. Mists clung to the hills and obscured the Cascade range behind the city; the ground squished; water seeped through concrete walls; buoyant hairstyles wilted flat. And in the library, the heating system ran hot and cold.

The wind rattled a roof fan and Helma Zukas buttoned the top button of her green wool sweater and pulled her hands inside her sleeves.

Miss Zukas, although possessing a sense of fashion, was not a follower of fads. She wore a touch of pink lipstick but no eye makeup. Her ears were not pierced, nor were her nails tinted with any polish but clear. Not that she was without indulgences. Barely visible from beneath the hem of her green dress was the lacy edge of a teal satin slip that matched other intimate apparel she ordered from a very expensive catalog that arrived wrapped in plastic in her mailbox.

"Fan mail!" Eve sang out, swooping into Helma's cubicle as if she were on roller skates. She dropped a haphazard stack of mail into Helma's empty desk tray, her eyes sparkling. "Pretty cruddy day, huh?"

Helma glanced at the rain spattering dully against the library's windows. "You sound almost happy about it, Eve."

Eve, the youngest librarian on the staff, was in charge of the fiction collection. She lived above a pizza parlor with her boyfriend and thrived on pizzas customers ordered and then neglected to pick up.

"I have this fantasy," Eve said, dropping her voice and pushing back her yellow curls, "that if this stuff would only keep up, certain people would run screaming back to their homeland."

Eve meant Ms. Moon, the new library director, hired from California last year by the library board in their stated effort to import "new blood" into the Bellehaven Public Library system.

Eve pointed to the Save Your Kids article on Helma's desk and stuck out her lower lip. "Why ban Little Red Riding Hood? What did *she* ever do?"

"I believe it was the wolf who did it," Helma said. "But don't worry, she's safe. Fortunately, the Constitution's still in effect."

"Yow!" Eve yelped and jumped farther into Helma's cubicle, rubbing her hip.

"Whoops, sorry," Curt, one of the pages, apologized, grinning widely as he pulled a loaded book truck to the side of the aisle. "There's not enough room back here to get through."

"Yeah, sure," Eve told him. "Likely story."

Curt shrugged and continued on his way, still grinning.

Eve leaned close to Helma. "You'll never in a million years guess who I saw coming out of the pizzeria last night."

"Is this gossip, Eve?" Helma asked.

Eve giggled. "I hope so."

"I really don't care to listen to gossip."

"Then I won't tell you, but picture two of our unlikely comrades gazing moonstruck into each other's eyes." Eve batted her own lashes in an exaggerated flutter. "And that's all I'll say." She waved her hand and singsonged, "See ya!"

Helma straightened the stack of mail Eve had delivered. Two of their comrades? There were six librarians and it wasn't Eve or Helma so that left . . . Helma shook her head. It wasn't any of her business. She slipped an M&M from the Chinese enameled box on her desk to her mouth, discreetly holding it beneath her tongue, and opened the first envelope: an ad for noiseless pencil sharpeners. She dropped the brightly colored brochure into her wastebasket.

Curt was right; there really *wasn't* enough space in the workroom. On one side, cramped cubicles for four of the six librarians were arranged against the wall, one after the other, separated by low bookshelves. At the end of the workroom, Ms. Moon, the director, occupied the only office with a door and located next to her was the awkwardly small librarians' lounge. At the opposite end of the room, George Melville's cataloging staff struggled to create order out of overloaded book trucks, stacked cardboard boxes and haphazard labeling stations, not to mention the disarray caused by the ongoing card catalog conversion to computer.

The next envelope held an interlibrary loan request that should have been routed to Mrs. Carmon. Helma jotted Mrs. Carmon's name on the envelope and set it aside.

In the cubicle beside Helma's, Patrice, the social science librarian for whom the staff had thrown a retirement party last fall before she changed her mind and returned, spoke on her extension in a coaxing, soothing voice.

Helma wasn't listening—not at all—but she couldn't help but catch the word, "Binky." Every morning and again after lunch, Patrice phoned home and talked to Binky, her French poodle, over her answering machine. "He won't eat his dinner if I forget," she'd once explained.

The next piece of mail was a legal-sized envelope with Helma's full name, "Miss Wilhelmina Cecelia Zukas," typed above the Bellehaven Public Library's address. There was no return address. The reverse of the envelope was blank, a clean white expanse.

Helma pulled her desk lamp closer and squinted over the circular, smudged postmark. That was odd: the letter had originated in Scoop River, Michigan.

Scoop River, Michigan: Helma's hometown. Certainly Aunt Em wouldn't have typed a letter to Helma. Aunt Em's letters arrived on pale blue stationery, in a tidy, thin script with equally spaced letters in lines that veered neither up nor down.

Helma swiftly slit the envelope with her letter opener. A single folded sheet dropped onto her blotter.

Neatly centered without greeting, date, or signature was a block paragraph of print.

It's been twenty years. The Scoop River/Hopkins Class D Conference basketball game was a LIE. It wasn't accidental death. It was MURDER. You promised to bring us together again. You PROMISED.

Helma turned the page over and checked inside the envelope. There was nothing else, only that lone paragraph, printed from a computer. Murder? Scoop River had lost a basketball game so badly the writer classified it as "*murder*"? If Helma remembered correctly, Scoop River had frequently been "murdered" in sports, but how did that involve her?

The workroom's lights flickered and the workday buzz eerily ceased like a caught breath.

"Better switch off your computers," George Melville the cataloger cheerily called out from his cataloging corner, stroking his beard. "If we fry these babies, the city will take it as a sign from God we marched too rashly into the twentieth century."

It's been twenty years, the letter read.

Twenty years since the basketball game? Helma had rarely attended basketball games. All that noise ricocheting in such a confined space gave her a headache.

And what did *You promised to bring us together again* mean? It sounded cultish or counterculturish, or even Nixonish, and Helma couldn't imagine promising any such thing to anyone, anywhere.

. . . bring us *together.* Us: it had to be a contemporary, a classmate, perhaps.

And *MURDER.* Perhaps the writer *wasn't* referring to basketball . . .

"Oh, Helma," a melodious voice interrupted. "Did you listen to those tapes I left by the herbal tea? Don't you just love the joy in Swami Rashti's voice? He's so childlike, so inspiring."

Ms. Moon, the library director, smiled serenely, holding her arms so her earth-toned clothes draped, reminiscent of robes. Here in the rainy Northwest, Ms. Moon, who claimed her given name was May Apple Moon but please call me Ms. Moon, was always tan as if the San Diego sun had been permanently etched into her skin.

Ms. Moon cared deeply about the image of the library and librarians and had even published two definitive articles, with footnotes and extensive bibliographies from the voluminous literature on the subject, in highly respected professional journals. She encouraged those who wore glasses to exchange them for contact lenses and to wear what she called "personal power" clothing. "Smile, smile," she liked to exhort. "Let the warmth of your inner librarian shine through."

"Thank you," Helma Zukas told Ms. Moon, "but I'm rarely inspired by anyone being childish."

Ms. Moon's pale brows gathered in concern. She clasped her small multiringed hands to her breast. "Hostility blocks beauty from entering your soul, Helma. Have you read *Releasing Your Angry Child*?"

Over Ms. Moon's shoulder, Helma saw George Melville, chin in hand, blatantly watching. He slowly lowered one eyelid in a wink. George called Ms. Moon a "vessel of all things current."

The lights flickered again and Helma slipped off her sweater, slid the sleeve cuffs into the pockets and draped it over her chair before she picked up the interlibrary loan request. "Excuse me. I accidentally received mail that belongs to Mrs. Carmon."

"*Embrace Your Rage* is another healing experience," Ms. Moon called after her.

"Try *Embarrass Your Page*," Curt the page mumbled without looking up from his book truck as Helma passed.

Surprisingly few people browsed in the library's large L-shaped public area. Rainy days brought them in but if the weather turned severe, patrons scurried for the safety of home. Rain streamed down the tall windows and the banks of overhead lights had been turned on against the dreary day.

Helma pondered the anonymous letter as she pushed in chairs and removed books left haphazardly on the tables, standing them on book trucks for the pages to reshelve.

The letter was meaningless, a sick mind's idea of a joke. *Murder*? Basketball and promises she had supposedly made twenty years ago? She plucked a Snickers wrapper from under a table and tossed it precisely into the middle of a wastebasket. She would do the exact same thing with the letter. Anyone too cowardly to sign his or her name to a letter wasn't credible enough to be taken seriously.

She was just reaching for an old 1952 Bellehaven High School annual lying splayed on a chair seat when she remembered.

She knew what the letter writer was referring to, what it was Helma had promised to do.

Long ago, could it be twenty years? Yes, nearly twenty years ago, Helma Zukas had promised to organize the Scoop River High School twenty-year reunion.

❦ *chapter two* ❦

SORTING
IT OUT

Holding the bag containing her good shoes and three professional journals close to her chest, Helma Zukas dashed across the parking lot and up the outside staircase to the third floor of the Bayside Arms, splashing water with each step. There was an elevator but whenever possible, Miss Helma Zukas avoided elevators.

The Bayside Arms was a plain three-story apartment building with balconies off each apartment that overlooked Washington Bay, affording spectacular views of sunsets and the San Juan Islands. When Helma Zukas moved into the newly built Bayside Arms fifteen years ago, apartments on the bay had been considered desirable but still within the reach of those who *didn't* have high paying jobs and expensive cars.

Now, there were new, fancified, postmodern and, well, architecturally *silly* apartment buildings and condominiums sprouting up all along the bay, with correspondingly astonishing prices.

On the third floor, rain rolled off the roof in sheets, backing up the gutters and spilling onto the landings. As she ran past 3E, Helma caught a glimpse of Mrs. Whitney in her chair by the window, her white hair, pink cheeks, and plump flowered figure bright spots of color in the gloomy day.

The *Bellehaven Daily News* lay in a sodden lump in front of Helma's door. "Oh, Dos Passos," she murmured as she unlocked the door to 3F. Her paper rarely made it into the newspaper holder beside her door. How many times had she caught the paperboy standing beneath the apartment building and pitching newspapers onto the landings?

She set her bag on the floor and leaned back outside to pick up the pulpy mess. As was her habit, Helma glanced around her apartment before she took another step inside.

First the kitchen: dishes washed and put away, counters cleared, floor spotless, rugs in place. The dining area and living room, decorated in beige-pinks and creamy greens. A potted Chinese elm stood beside a root-bound fern. Magazines: *Time, TV Guide, American History, Good Taste*, overlapped evenly on her coffee table. Sometimes, when Helma didn't recognize the grocery checker, she bought *People* magazine, but that she read in her bedroom.

There were two bedrooms in Miss Zukas's apartment. Her own was decorated in a soothing color scheme, similar to her living room, but the second bedroom, Helma's "back bedroom," held a riotous mixture of colors and textures, a repository for gifts that didn't quite suit Helma's taste. "Now *this* room I feel at home in," Helma's friend Ruth had said once, kicking off her shoes and dropping onto the bed, which was covered by an overbright South American bedspread from Helma's mother. "And I'm honored you'd even hang one of my paintings in here."

A dark shape on the balcony caught Helma's eye. It was that cat again.

It sat calmly in front of her door, peering in with golden eyes that showed no curiosity, only arrogant cool regard. Its drenched fur emphasized its gaunt black body and torn ear. Either a spot of white fur or a circle of bald flesh shone beneath its chin.

Miss Zukas froze, meeting the cat's gaze. A shiver ran down her arms. Cats reminded her of snakes, the way they slunk around where you least expected them, speculatively watching, categorizing every living being as harmless, dangerous, or edible.

She knew how it managed to reach her balcony three floors above the ground: up the fir at the corner of the building, onto the roof, and from there an easy descent into Helma's territory.

Cautiously, Helma moved forward, the wet newspaper still in hand. She unlatched the glass door and in one swift movement, opened the door and threw the newspaper, landing wide. The cat leisurely stood and jumped onto her railing.

"Shoo!" she said. Low but meaningful.

The wet cat regarded her for a moment and then surefootedly leapt across the three-story drop to Mrs. Whitney's balcony.

Good riddance. Animals weren't allowed in Bayside Arms, at least they hadn't been when Howard Marble was manager. But Howard had fled the rainy Northwest for Arizona and now there was a new manager, an overweight man in his thirties named Walter David, who wore baseball caps and instead of keeping a car in the manager's parking place, kept a motorcycle with an anatomically exaggerated, buxom redhead painted on the gas tank.

Helma drew her drapes against the night, removed the mysterious letter from her purse, and opened it. The rain beat with steady monotony against her roof.

Why an anonymous note to remind her she'd promised to coordinate the reunion? To catch her attention with its novelty? And why bring up a twenty-year-old basketball game? And the reference to murder, *that* was totally incomprehensible.

Cousin Ricky still lived in Scoop River. Helma involuntarily grimaced. She wouldn't put anything past Ricky. But this wasn't his style. Too tidy. Cousin Ricky was more the blue-crayon-on-lined-paper type.

After dishes and Tom Brokaw's six o'clock news, Helma glanced at her watch. Seeing there was still an hour before her shift at the crisis center, she pulled her Scoop River High School annual from her bookcase where it stood between her baby book and her library school textbooks.

Fifty-two members in her graduating class. She slowly turned the yearbook's pages, scrutinizing each black and white senior picture. It was curious: they didn't really look *young*, more like they were out-of-date, unformed, and yes, even interchangeable.

High school hadn't been particularly *un*happy. Her memories weren't *bad* memories, except for that incident with Geoff Jamas. Helma had been voted class treasurer during her senior year but her name hadn't even been whispered as a possibility for homecoming queen.

Here was Dora Durbas, with whom she still exchanged Christmas cards. There Roman Fonszelvitcz, the dentist's son who thought he was destined to set the world on fire; what had happened to him?

Helma barely glanced at Geoff Jamas's picture, her jaw clenching as she quickly flipped the page.

A class reunion. Twenty years and not once had anyone made an effort to reunite the fifty-two classmates. Who knew how far they'd all scattered? Helma was too busy to organize a reunion for people she hadn't seen in twenty years. And how could she do it from 2,500 miles away, anyway?

She closed her eyes, momentarily overwhelmed. If she took a nap . . . No. She sat up, shut the blue embossed annual harder than she intended and set it on her coffee table.

At seven forty-five, Helma was back on the road driving along the dark curve of the bay between the Bayside Arms and downtown Bellehaven. She drove with both hands on the steering wheel, at ten o'clock and two o'clock, the way she'd learned in driver's training, her right foot tentative on the gas pedal, prepared to instantly shift to the brake. Plumes of water sprayed up from passing cars and her windshield wipers snicked back and forth, throwing off shimmering lines of rain. Approaching headlights were ringed, like round rainbows.

Every Friday evening from eight o'clock until midnight Helma volunteered at the Bellehaven Crisis Center, answering telephone calls from desperate people.

A year ago she'd read a moving article about professionals who volunteered their skills to their community. She then attended a meeting in the Bellehaven Community Center, a meeting Helma believed was being held to explain the numerous volunteer opportunities in Bellehaven.

Instead, she'd found herself sitting in the front row of the crisis center's first night of intensive training. Miss Zukas, who sometimes believed in the serendipitousness of life, stayed.

Helma was even more convinced she'd been right in staying when she recognized the similarities between manning the reference desk at the library and the phone desk at the crisis center. It all came down to soothing the public while you searched for whatever answer they demanded.

Once, at the crisis center, when she'd been asked by a furtive whispered voice, "Who killed John F. Kennedy?" she'd automatically answered, "You want the Warren Commission Report, 364.1524, third tall stack on the left, second shelf from the bottom." Realizing her lapse, she'd tried to apologize but the caller had thanked her profusely and hung up.

But usually, the calls were from truly desperate and deserving people: men who'd lost their jobs, mothers with children and no place to go, the old and lonely. Or sometimes girls who thought their lives had ended because it was Friday night and they didn't have dates.

With these people Helma was as efficient as she was on the reference desk. "Of course we'll find you a place to stay." "I'll tell you where the food bank is located." "Let me connect you to a counselor." "What can I do to help you?"

But as in the library, occasionally even Helma was taken aback by the demands people made.

This Friday night was no exception.

"Is that place one of those kinds where you have to pray just so you can spend the night?" a homeless caller asked after Helma gave him the mission's address.

"I believe they have a service after dinner, yes."

"I won't go there. Find me somewhere else."

"I'm afraid tonight there aren't any other available places."

"Well, it's your job to find me another place. I'm not listening to no prayers."

"This isn't a job. I'm a volunteer."

"I don't care what you are. I won't listen to no prayers. I might as well sleep in the street."

"Yes, I suppose you may as well," Helma said in her silver-dime voice and hung up, quickly glancing around to be sure the night supervisor hadn't heard.

The calls slowed down after eleven and Helma spent her free time listing the names of her graduating class in Scoop River, Michigan. She stopped at forty-two, remembering the name of David Morse.

David Morse, the sports star who was supposed to have graduated with them but hadn't. He'd died their senior year in an automobile accident. She tapped her pencil, wondering.

When Helma's doorbell rang Saturday morning, she rose from the floor without using her hands, allowing herself a single, satisfied sigh. Exercise had its rewards.

A distorted face from the nose down pressed too close to the peephole. Bright red lipstick, silver dangling earrings nudging the shoulders of a black wool coat. A fuchsia scarf.

Ruth.

"What took you so long? It's freezing out here and I'm in a hell of a mood." Ruth slapped her gloved hands together and stepped inside, the top of her bushy hair brushing the door frame. A damp, cold draft swirled in with her.

"I didn't know you were coming by." Even after all these years, Helma preferred to prepare herself for Ruth's company. She glanced down into the parking lot for Ruth's aging Saab. "Where's your car?"

"It committed suicide on the Chester Street hill. Very fitting for the frigging day I'm having. Can I call somebody to come bury it, and maybe bum a cup of coffee?"

"I only have instant coffee, but go ahead. I'll put on the kettle."

Ruth unzipped her two-inch-heeled boots and kicked them off, then shrugged out of her coat, revealing green tartan pants and a deep purple, nearly black turtleneck. Helma intercepted Ruth's damp coat on its way to the floor, avoiding the side that was tweedy with gray cat hairs.

"The devil designed today, end to end," Ruth grumbled and stepped into Helma's living room, heading straight for the glass door to the balcony.

Helma's curtains were open, the dark opaque shades that protected her furniture from the sun were rolled up. Still, in order to see what she was doing Helma had been forced to turn on her lamps, despite it being eleven in the morning.

The skies loomed a mass of gray, mimicking the rough water on Washington Bay, obscuring the islands. More rain approached in misty steel columns between Bellehaven and the islands. And more behind that. Relentless.

"Nasty day," Ruth continued, standing in front of the door with her hands behind her back. "Damn nasty. Why'd I ever move to this sodden excuse of a city?" She shrugged and turned. "You won't believe . . . Helma! What are you doing?"

"I'm reorganizing my fiction collection." Stacks of books lay scattered around her living room, piled on her couch and chairs. "Alphabetically by author."

"Oh horrors. You don't mean to tell me that before this they were *haphazard* on your shelves!"

Helma removed Scott, Spark, Steinbeck, and a copy of *A Midsummer Night's Dream* from her rocker and sat down. "Actually, they were in a modified Library of Congress system, arranged within nationalities, and collections separate. It'll be easier this way."

"Gads, yes." Ignoring Helma's glance, Ruth perched on the arm of the couch, eyebrows drawn together, one leg swinging. "My car's just the frosting on the cake. I met *her*."

"Met who?" Helma asked patiently. Ruth's dramatic flair often got in the way of simple declarative sentences.

"What do you mean, '*who?*' Kara Cherry, that's who, as if even God could believe that's her real name, the new pseudo art critic and features editor for the *Bellehaven Daily Nuisance*." Ruth made a face, stretching the corners of her mouth downward.

"I have a hunch you weren't impressed," Helma said. The *Bellehaven Daily News* had, with some ceremony, announced its newest employee who stated in a determinedly upbeat article that she saw her position as a "mission of encouragement and empowerment to Bellehaven's community of *true* artists."

"It was mutual. She comes to my waist and wears a size two, one of those nasty little itty bitty people who chew kneecaps for entertainment. She took one look at me and asked, 'Just how tall are you, anyway?' and from that point it was all downhill."

"Is she reviewing your show next month?"

Ruth nodded morosely. "I can hardly wait. She's a paleface who makes cutesy fake Indian jewelry and calls it 'my art.'"

"You haven't given her a chance," Helma told her. "You're being too pessimistic."

Ruth bit one of her paint-stained nails. "I detect a certain glumness in you as well, Helm."

"Helma," Helma automatically corrected, as she always did and which Ruth ignored, as she always did. "Do you know what happened twenty years ago next summer?"

"Haven't the slightest. Do you?"

"We graduated from high school."

"No kidding? Are you sure it's *twenty* years ago? Dear old Scoop River High." Ruth hummed a few bars of the chorus and broke into: "SO: GO! FIGHT! SCHOOL OF RIGHT AND MIGHT!" brandishing her arms like a cheerleader, which of course she'd never been.

Ruth had taken a more circuitous route from Scoop River to Bellehaven than Helma. Helma had accepted her job at the Bellehaven Public Library fresh out of library school, sight unseen. Ruth had hitchhiked to Santa Fe with a musician, then a few years later moved to Seattle with another artist, whom she discarded—"He was too jealous,"—and nine years ago ended up in the growing arts community in Bellehaven, where the rents were still affordable and the scenery as beautiful as Seattle's had once been.

Helma and Ruth had been uneasy friends since fourth grade when Ruth's non-Catholic parents sent her to St. Wynden's elementary school, in a forlorn hope that the nuns could either instill or enforce a little discipline.

From that day forward, whether it was marching two by two in front of Sister Mary Martin into their fifth grade classroom or proceeding up the aisle to receive their high school diplomas, Ruth and Helma had been joined by their place in the alphabet: Winthrop and Zukas.

Helma distractedly opened *Idylls of the King* and fanned the creamy pages. "I volunteered to arrange our twenty-year class reunion."

Ruth leaned forward. "When?"

"Twenty-one years ago. In the cafeteria at the first Commencement Planning Committee meeting. Presided over by Michael Petronas."

"Well, you can just rest easy and forget it. You're not responsible for whatever you volunteered to do at seventeen. Seventeen's not even the age of consent."

"I volunteered to do it and I meant it."

"'An elephant faithful one hundred percent.'" Ruth jumped up as the kettle burped and whistled. "Whoops, I'll get it."

Helma vaguely listened as Ruth made her coffee, with, as usual, far more commotion than necessary. Everything Ruth did seemed to simply *be* more than necessary. Her clothes, her voice, her appetite. And her paintings: big, untidy, too bright, and too many colors; but other people, people Helma didn't know, sought them out, even commissioned work from Ruth.

Ruth opened Helma's refrigerator and rooted around. "Any care packages from your brother lately?"

"They're not care packages," Helma said. "They're Bruce's idea of necessary food staples."

"Well, tell Brucie to send more of those Lithuanian koogie potato things, would you?"

"*Kugelis*," Helma corrected.

"Right. So what's the plan?" Ruth sat down and pointed her steamy cup at Helma. "Are you going to trundle back east to little old Scoop River, armpit of Michigan, and throw this shindig in the fire hall? Hang blue and gold crepe paper and play old forty-fives? Maybe give old Stanley Rybauskas a bottle of whiskey to play his accordion?"

After living fifteen years in Washington, "back east" was still too vague a term for Helma to bring herself to use. Anything east of the Cascade Mountains was "back east," said with a touch, just a touch, of dismissal, as if all life worth living existed between the Cascade range and the Pacific Ocean.

Helma removed a coaster from the stack she kept on the end table and set it in front of Ruth. "I haven't decided. Maybe I can find someone in Scoop River to help me. Do you remember David Morse?"

"Don't *you*?" Ruth shook her head sadly. "The athlete dying young."

Helma nodded. "It was a one-car accident, wasn't it? Did it have anything to do with a basketball game?"

"Not *with* one, but after one. Why?"

"Could it have been the Scoop River/Hopkins Class D Conference game?"

"Of course it was."

"Are you sure?"

"Yes, I'm sure, Wilhelmina Zukas. I avidly followed basketball, remember? It was the one arena with boys consistently taller than me. He was a charmingly youthful but conceited basketball star interested only in girls the size of Kara Cherry and it was a tragedy and all that, but what does David Morse have to do with the Scoop River class reunion?"

Helma gave Ruth the anonymous letter she'd received at the library. Ruth opened it, frowned over it, and read aloud:

"It's been twenty years. The Scoop River/Hopkins Class D Conference basketball game was a LIE. It wasn't accidental death. It was MURDER. You promised to bring us together again. You PROMISED."

Ruth tapped the letter against her knee, looking up at Helma's ceiling. "Too weird. Murder? I'd ignore it if I were you. I always ignore my anonymous letters."

"No, I promised. But if the letter writer is referring to David Morse, why would he suspect David had been murdered?"

There hadn't been many deaths among the young when Helma was growing up and each one occupied a potent black pedestal: the bicyclist in the hit-and-run incident, the car-train crash, the boy who fell off the pickup. David Morse slipped through her memory: tall, dark, the kind of boy who, even in a school as small as Scoop River, probably hadn't spoken two words to Helma once he'd realized girls were attracted to him and he had his choice.

Ruth shrugged. "It seems like there'd have been rumors back then, doesn't it? I only remember the usual, 'oh-what-a-shame' garbage."

Ruth was right. Scoop River thrived on rumors, carrying them from generation to generation. All Helma's life, hearing her last name had elicited embarrassing wild tales from older people about her supposedly Communist grandfather, or her father and his brothers' and sisters' escapades.

"Can't you do some library inter-something or other and get the *Scoop River Herald*'s articles about David's death?" Ruth asked.

"Interlibrary loan," Helma said. "Although Ms. Moon now calls it 'Resource Sharing.' The paper's probably on microfilm."

"Scoop River's light-years away, isn't it?" Ruth said. "I haven't been back in at least fifteen years. No reason to."

Ruth was an only child and her parents were dead. When asked, Ruth shook her head sadly and explained her father had been killed in a drunk-driving accident when she was a teenager, failing to mention he'd been the drunk driver.

"Back to the reunion," Ruth said. "This won't exactly be a cheap undertaking."

"Actually," Helma said. "There *is* some money. I still have charge of the class bank account."

Ruth sat upright and turned wide eyes toward Helma. "You're kidding. Money still exists from all those car washes and cake sales? Weren't you supposed to turn that in when we graduated?"

"I invested it."

"Invested it! That was sneaky."

"There was no stated rule against it," Helma pointed out. "At the time there wasn't enough money to purchase an appropriate class memorial."

"Hey, wouldja look at this," Ruth said, picking up the Scoop River annual on Helma's coffee table. "Mine went in the garbage about nineteen and a half years ago." She flipped through the pages. "All these names: Asauskas, Durbas, Gimbutas, Kantinski. Lugans everywhere. I'd forgotten."

"Lugan is derogatory," Helma pointed out, which Ruth already knew. "The correct term is 'Lithuanian.'"

"Oh, *excuse* me: Lith-you-anians."

"Wilson Jones!" Ruth exclaimed, and gave the picture a hearty kiss. "Oh, these clean young faces. Did we really look this virginal?"

"Some of us actually were," Helma reminded her.

Ruth found her own picture. "What a puss!" she screeched.

"Watch out, Picasso!" it read beneath Ruth's photo. Wide mouth, too much makeup, challenging eyes burning from beneath her bushy hair.

Next to Ruth: Wilhelmina Zukas. Helma's white blouse had a gold circle pinned to its round collar. Thankfully, unless she remained in the sun too long, those few freckles had disappeared. "Order and sensibility guide her way," it read beneath Helma's photo.

"This picture of you could have been taken last week, Helma. Even your hair's still the same."

"Thank you," Helma said.

"Ah, here he is," Ruth said, "right where he belongs: last and least."

Cousin Ricky. Yates Richard Zukas, Helma's tormentor, the enemy of her youth. Helma pursed her lips to keep them from curling. The quote beneath Ricky's photo was blacked out because Ruth had snuck into the galleys the night before they were due at the printer and changed Ricky's saying to "Picking his nose on his way to Hell." No one but Helma knew Ruth was responsible and Mr. Carson, the principal, after conceding he'd never discover the culprit, had drafted the Future Homemakers of America club to shuffle through all the annuals and individually cover up the damage with black Magic Markers.

"Who'd a thunk it? Fifty-two people who lived in each other's pockets during their formative years and twenty years later, they're lucky to be reduced to Christmas cards." Ruth paused, swinging her leg, and then asked casually, "You never hear from Geoff Jamas, do you?"

Helma and Ruth knew most of each other's secrets, but Geoff Jamas was one subject they never touched upon.

"No," Helma said stiffly.

"Mmm," Ruth murmured and sipped her coffee.

Rain splattered against the windows. A tattered wind sock, blown from somewhere else, caught on the railing of Helma's balcony before it tore loose and disappeared. Helma thought she caught a glimpse of black but when she looked for a lurking feline shape, nothing was there.

Ruth set her coffee on the *House of Mirth*. "Helma, I've got it! It's perfect! I have the answer! If you're determined to pull off this reunion, why not have it here instead of in Michigan?"

"Here? But we graduated there."

"No, listen. Half of our honored classmates have probably never even traveled outside Michigan. Remember how people got confused when they realized they were trapped by all those Great Lakes? Invite them here. It'll be a cultural experience. They'll talk about it for the rest of their lives."

"It would be too expensive," Helma argued, but suddenly visualizing her classmates in Bellehaven, where Helma lived, where *she* felt comfortable, in *her* territory. Not having to return to Scoop River in time or place or memory. "There is the bank account, but . . ."

"How much moola is there? Maybe you could offer scholarships or awards or something."

Helma went to the oak file cabinet in her hallway and pulled out the folder labeled, "Scoop River HS Account." She handed it to Ruth.

Ruth opened the folder and took out the top, most recent statement. Her eyes widened. She whistled through her teeth. She held one hand to her heart. "My God, Helma Zukas, this is unbelievable. All this from cake sales and sock hops?"

"Car washes, too."

"Car washes, too," Ruth repeated distractedly. She thumbed through the statements. "Who did the investing for you?"

"I did it myself. There's a wide range of excellent investment materials in the library."

"Microsoft, Beatrice, Vanguard." Ruth whistled again. "Weren't you ever tempted to clean out the account and go to Tahiti or something?"

"No. It's not my money."

Ruth looked wistfully out at the gray rain and shook her head. "Tahiti, at least," she said. "You could fly every classmate out here, buy crepe paper streamers and pointy hats, and some naked guy to jump out of a cake, besides," Ruth said. "What do you say? I'll bet more people would show up for a reunion here than in Scoop River."

"It *would* be easier to plan it here," Helma allowed.

"Listen, Helma," Ruth said, raising her right hand and intoning. "I promise, if you have the twentieth Scoop River High School reunion here in Washington, I'll volunteer as your able assistant. Anything you want me to do I'll do without bitching or complaining. I'll lick stamps and string crepe paper and use my considerable artistic talent to draw cute little name tags. I'll smile at people who called me 'Beanpole.' I'll restrain myself from killing Ricky. Think about it. It would be fun. Really."

Ms. Moon didn't use the term "staff meeting." She preferred "Harmony circle."

The rectangular table in the staff lounge had been exchanged for a circular table and during each meeting

Ms. Moon sat in a different spot, claiming to "alternate the group dynamic."

A hand-lettered sign over the coffee pot read:

**When a librarian delights in greeting the Public with "NO,"
Away from the reference desk he or she must "GO."**

And on the staff bulletin board hung Ms. Moon's latest find: a magazine ad for an investment company, portraying a librarian in glasses surrounded by a confusing assortment of printed investment resources. Beneath the ad Ms. Moon had written the offending company's address. "Complain about *your* image!" she'd jotted in red pen. The sweater the librarian model wore was exactly the style Helma had been searching for, and Eve had pronounced the model's sensible shoes, "cool."

"They've done it again," Roberta Seymour said as she entered the room, red-faced. She slapped a folder on the round table next to Helma and dropped into her chair.

George Melville, Helma, Eve, Patrice, and Roger Barnhard, the diminutive children's librarian, all sat waiting for Ms. Moon to join the meeting.

"They, they, they," George Melville said, rocking back in his chair and gazing at the ceiling. "The omnipotent 'they.'"

Eve giggled.

"Who are 'they' and what have they done?" Patrice asked.

Roberta Seymour pounded one thin fist on the table. She was the newest librarian, half-time Washington state history librarian and half-time genealogy specialist, her position partially funded by the county's rather militant genealogy group.

"That . . ." she sputtered. "That saboteur has clogged the drains in the men's room with rolls of toilet paper again. Water all over my floor."

Roberta's "official" desk was fourth against the workroom wall after Eve's, but she also kept a genealogy office of sorts in the old audiovisual closet on the lower level near the public restrooms. "This is the second time this month." She looked at Helma meaningfully. "I want something done about it."

"I suggest you discuss it with Ms. Moon, then," Helma said.

Roberta glanced toward Ms. Moon's office and lowered her voice. "But we need some *action* on the matter. I understand you and the chief of police are close. Can't you talk to him?"

Miss Zukas raised a hand to her forehead. She felt the heat rising in her cheeks. "Who said that? They were misinformed. You were misinformed. Chief Gallant and I are merely acquaintances. I hardly know him. That's all. We've never . . ."

"Maybe an alarm of some kind," Roberta interrupted. "Or a surveillance camera."

"A surveillance camera in the public *restrooms*?" Eve asked.

"This kind of behavior *never* happens in the women's restroom," Patrice said, brushing cookie crumbs from her bosom. "Never."

"Do you think it's due to lack of imagination?" George Melville asked her, bending so close she pressed into the back of her chair, her arms braced against the table.

Helma glanced around the table. Who had told Roberta she and Chief Gallant were "close"? It was untrue. Totally untrue.

"It's chronic," Roger said. "Every year or two some kid thinks he's being original, plugs the drains a couple of times, makes a mess, then forgets it. There's no sense in trying to stop it." He shrugged. "These things end. They always do. Everything has a life of its own and then it inevitably ends. You think it's fine and wham, it's over. Right between the eyes. Life and death . . ." Roger trailed off and looked glumly at his hands. Everyone stared at the children's librarian.

"Those tykes coloring in the picture books again, Rog?" George Melville asked in a surprisingly gentle voice.

Roger looked up and blinked. "Sorry. Just thinking out loud."

Eve passed a piece of paper to Helma. "Roger's wife moved out," it read. "I heard she . . ."

Helma crumpled the paper before she could read any more.

"What's that book, Helma?" George Melville asked.

Helma lifted her yellow note pad off one of the two books beneath it: *So You're Planning Your High School Reunion.*

"High school reunion, eh? Which one?"

"Twentieth," Helma told him.

"My twentieth was last year," Roberta said. "Be careful what games you plan. We played touch football and one of the guys dropped of a heart attack."

"Is that your high school annual?" Eve asked. "Can I see it?"

"Are you going back to Michigan?" Roberta asked.

"I'm thinking of holding it out here," Helma told her.

George Melville whistled through his teeth. "You still in touch with everyone?"

"Look at these clothes!" Eve squealed, pointing to a picture taken in the Scoop River High School cafeteria at the opening day of deer season dance.

"Only a couple," Helma told George. "That'll be the hardest part, finding everyone."

"Guys really wore their hair like that?"

"I can help," Roger said, showing the first flicker of interest.

"How?" Helma asked. "You've never even been to Michigan."

"I've been to Detroit."

George Melville leaned forward. "Tsk, tsk. Detroit's Detroit, not Michigan, like New York City isn't New York state."

"I'm on WorldWide Info. It's a computer network. I can find anybody's address and phone number. Just let me borrow your yearbook overnight."

"Did you hear?" Patrice interrupted. "The Save Your Kids group sent an amended list of books they want withdrawn. They traded Madonna's *Sex* for everything written by a Harry Miller. Do you think they meant Henry?"

"My aunt knows Cissy Moses, the head of Save Your Kids," Eve told them. "And she said Cissy Moses doesn't read fiction because it's all pretend. She only reads the dirty parts people mark for her."

"I used to do that," George volunteered. "In the dictionary. Pretty racy stuff in there."

Ms. Moon entered the lounge, arms akimbo, her golden face lit by a gentle smile. "I can tell this is going to be a successful circle today."

Behind one hand, George Melville pointed toward Ms. Moon and turned his finger in a circle of his own.

"Mother," Helma asked, balancing the phone on her shoulder so her hands were free to fold clothes fresh from her dryer. She stood in her living room, watching a ferry glide toward the mouth of the bay. "Do you remember twenty years ago when David Morse was killed?"

"Alice and Joe's boy. What a shame. He was an only child, you know. Alice was never the same after that, mourned herself right into the grave. It's a mistake to have a single child, I always say. You shouldn't fill your basket with just one egg. You're bound to get your heart broke one way or another."

After Helma's father died, Helma's mother, whose name was Lillian, moved from Michigan to Bellehaven at Helma's urging. She lived on the opposite side of town in a retirement apartment complex that had a reputation among the senior set as being a little "fast."

"Did you know his parents very well?"

"We were in VFW together. Joe liked his beer, especially after the boy died. His uncle married your grandfather's brother-in-law's sister. Twenty years difference . . ."

"Do you remember any rumors about the accident?" Helma interrupted.

"Well, let me see. Alice claimed David was too good a driver to lose control of his car like that." Lillian sighed. "But that's just a mother talking. We mothers never know our children as well as we think we do. By the way, have you heard from your brothers lately?"

The next day Roger proudly handed Helma a computer printout of twenty-one of the twenty-eight men's addresses and seven of the twenty-four women's addresses.

"Do detectives know about this?" Helma asked him, quickly scanning through the lists.

"You bet. Not that it was that difficult. Your class had some pretty unique names. What are they, Polish?"

There he was: Geoff Jamas. A Chicago address.

"Pardon?" Helma asked, looking up and folding the sheets in half.

"The names of your classmates. A lot of Poles?"

"Lithuanian," Helma told him, bristling a little, briefly recalling the year there'd been a fight between the predominantly Lithuanian Scoop River boys and the predominantly Polish Manistee boys. Even in America, the two nationalities couldn't resist the habit of living close to one another, affording them the opportunity to more conveniently continue ancient animosities as well as raid each other's restaurants and stores for the best ethnic food they grudgingly held in common.

Years ago, Helma's mother had told her Geoff Jamas was in Chicago, pausing so Helma could ask for the details. But she hadn't.

❧ chapter three ❧

PLANS IN ACTION

"So, what do *you* make of it?" Ruth asked, handing back the photocopies Helma had made from the microfilm of the *Scoop River Herald*. It was a month later, and Ruth stood inside Helma's cubicle in the library workroom, leaning against the wall.

"It seems straightforward." Helma read the twenty-year-old headline aloud: " 'Scoop River Basketball Star Killed in Wreck,' " and the first sentence beneath it: " 'David Morse, eighteen, was killed instantly when he apparently swerved on Hilltop Road and crashed his 1966 Volkswagen into a telephone pole, shortly after the Hopkins Scoop River Class D Conference game.' "

"But then, how often did the *Horrible* ever get anything right?" Ruth frowned and rearranged the combs that held back her hair. "I wonder why he swerved."

"What do you think of the last sentence in the adjoining article?"

"Didn't read it."

"It's about the basketball game itself." Helma read, " 'After Scoop River's loss, police were called to a fight outside the high school but the participants had scattered by the time police arrived.' "

Ruth shrugged. "They were a rowdy bunch, remember? And we were sore losers."

"I made a copy of David Morse's obituary, too. He had a fiancee, Patty Anne Sands. Did you know her?"

"Only by sight. She was a slutty type from Hopkins. 'Fiancee' is stretching it a little, I think."

Helma returned the photocopies, including the ghostly newspaper photos of the crumpled Volkswagen and David Morse's youthful face, to the folder marked MORSE, DAVID. The news of David Morse's death was twenty years old but Helma vividly recalled the horrified fascination that a member of *their* class—a boy their own age—had *died*, remembering that unbidden, deliciously scary chink in their sense of immortality, that elevation of ordinary teenager to Dead and Gone beyond reproach, beatified and protected by death.

"Supposing someone from our Scoop River High School class wrote the anonymous letter," Helma said. "Why involve me in a twenty-year-old death?"

"Because it's a joke? Or maybe they think one of our jolly classmates was involved?"

"Maybe. I talked to Dora Durbas last night. She still lives in Scoop River. She couldn't recall anything suspicious about David's death."

"You didn't tell her about the letter, did you? She'd broadcast it to the world."

Helma shook her head. All Helma did was mention David Morse's death and Dora's considerable curiosity was fully ignited. "I can ask around," Dora had eagerly offered, launching into a list of Who Might Know, before Helma managed to sidetrack Dora onto the subject of which classmates had gotten fat and which were divorced.

"She also had a few more addresses."

"Good old Mother Hen Dora. Is she tickled just pinker than pink about holding a reunion out here?"

"Actually, she's very enthusiastic."

"Told ya."

Of their fifty-two classmates, three were dead: two in auto accidents, one—quiet, timid, always-smiling Rhonda Parbutas—of a drug overdose. Five remained to be found. But the majority still lived within two hundred miles of Scoop River.

"You're putting in an appearance at my opening tomorrow night, aren't you?" Ruth asked. "A chance to see Bellehaven's cutting-edge art." In the next cubicle, Patrice raised her glasses and frowned at Ruth. Ruth grinned and waggled her fingers at Patrice.

"I'll stop by before my shift at the crisis center," Helma told her. She might not stay at the gallery very long, but Ruth *was* her friend.

"And if you can get close enough to stumble over that fine local art critic, Kara Cherry Pit, do me a favor and break her pencil."

"You mailed out all the reunion letters last week, right?" Helma asked, trying not to sound like she was checking up on Ruth. Ruth, surprisingly, had been true to her word; she'd addressed envelopes, listened to Helma's ideas without undue arguing, and had done whatever Helma had asked her to do. Helma didn't know how long before Ruth grew bored but she was determined to take advantage of this uncharacteristic compliance.

"Sure. I even livened them up a teensy bit."

"I thought we agreed they were fine the way I'd written them."

"They *were* fine. They only needed a smidgen of embellishment. Just a sec. I've got one right here." Ruth dug around in her pockets and pulled out a folded sheet of paper with a smudge of green paint across it.

> *Greetings Scoop River Tigers!!!*
> *Can you believe it, Twenty long years have passed since we bolted from Scoop River High for the great wide world.*
> *It's REUNION TIME and have we got a surprise for you!*
> *Our illustrious class treasurer, Helma Zukas (still single—all you single guys out there!), prudently invested all that Sock Hop and Car Wash money and now we can PAY your way to the great state of Washington for the reunion of a lifetime!*
> *Mountains! Oceans! Islands! A green you won't believe!*

Say Yes! Yes! Yes!

There's lots to talk about: the senior prom when the fire alarm went off, Mr. Hanson winning the lottery, the Scoop River/Hopkins basketball game.

Just say Yes! More details to follow.

"This isn't at all what I wrote," Helma said in dismay.

"But the idea's the same. Notice how I threw in the Scoop River/Hopkins game? That should pique somebody's guilt or curiosity, eh?"

Helma bit her lip and said nothing more. At least *Ruth's* name was signed to the letter.

With the toe of her red boot, Ruth prodded the cardboard records box sitting beside Helma's desk. "Is this all the reunion stuff?"

Helma nodded. "I can carry it back and forth from my apartment. I'm using the library's address instead of my own."

"Using the library's postal meter, too?"

"Of course not."

"I believe you, Helm. I truly do. Well, I guess I'll see what's happening in the real world. Don't forget to show up tomorrow night."

After Ruth left, Helma turned her back to the entrance to her cubicle and reopened *Get Your Reunion Hopping!*

"Excuse me, Helma," George Melville said, leaning over Helma's bookcases. "Two things. First, Eve's off telling a story in the kiddies' room so here's your mail. And second, I've got a deal for you."

"A deal?"

George nodded. "For your class reunion. Where are you holding it?"

"I haven't decided yet. The Elk's club rents out its facilities. There's also St. Alexander's gymnasium."

"A twentieth reunion calls for something more celebratory than a hall smelling of gym shorts. What do you say to an island resort? A friend of mine owns a small resort on Saturday Island. Very elegant back in the thirties. Lots of bigwigs, political intrigue, illicit romances, that sort of thing."

"I don't think we could afford that."

"No, listen. This is his last season. The land's being sold for condominiums so he's not booking in the regulars this year, just a few parties before the walls are pulled down. I know he'd make a real deal for a reunion party."

"Have you been there?"

"Several times. It sits on a tiny bay on the west side of the island. Beautiful cliffs, tide pools, seagulls, nice sunsets, sailboats and ferries passing in the distance. It'll wow your landlocked friends, I guarantee."

Miss Zukas rarely made decisions before investigating her options. "I'd be interested in learning more about it," she told George Melville.

"Here's the name and address. Tell Larry I told you to call."

GULL ROCK INN
SATURDAY ISLAND
CAPTAIN LARRY AND DIANA SCOTT, PROP.

She jotted the phone number in her address book and slipped the card into the ACCOMMODATIONS folder.

When it was time for Helma's stint on the reference desk she carried her mail with her to read between patrons.

Three people stood in front of the reference desk, awaiting professional attention.

"My daughter's in seventh grade and she has to write a report on the Seven Wonders of the World," the first woman in line told Helma briskly. She was well dressed, close to Helma's age.

Helma glanced behind the woman, then around the reference desk area. "Where is she?"

"In school, of course," the woman said with a touch of impatience.

"I'm sure her school librarian can lead her to some excellent sources," Helma said.

"You don't understand. Her report's due tomorrow and Melanie has ballet class tonight."

"And you're writing Melanie's report for her?"

"Ballet is Melanie's true love," the woman said stiffly. "There's a little party after class she simply cannot miss. It's a matter of priorities."

"I can see it is," Helma said. Parents who did their children's homework were far too common.

"If you could help me, please. I'm in a hurry and I don't have much time to spend on this. Teachers expect so much from youngsters these days."

After providing the woman with a bare minimum of ideas, Helma told the next man in line that she was sorry, the list in the *Daily News* was incorrect, and the library *didn't* own Madonna's *Sex*; and then she recommended *Middlemarch* to a woman who wanted to read only nineteenth-century fiction to put her in the mood to write a romance. Finally, Helma looked up to see Ruth standing at the desk, holding a copy of *Art in America* folded backward and a copy of *Money* magazine under her arm.

"I forgot to tell you. Remember Jorge, that travel agent I used to date?"

"Vaguely."

"About three years ago. The one who liked feet." A young man looked up from the card catalog in interest. "Anyway, it's about the reunion."

"You'd like to bring him?"

"Not particularly. But listen, he says if we figure this right he can get us a group rate on airfares for our dear classmates. Save a bundle. Whaddaya think?"

"What kind of commission would he charge?" Helma asked.

Ruth laughed her deep hiccupy laugh. "*I'll* take care of that department."

"We'd need to coordinate everyone's flight. What if . . ."

"Don't worry. We'll talk about it later. But you'd better take a look at this." Ruth thrust the copy of *Money* magazine in front of Helma. It was an article ranking the top one hundred jobs in America.

"See. Librarians are rated fifty-first. And look—your estimable career ranks at the bottom of the Stress and Strain level, below homemaker and hair stylist. So how come you guys don't smile and make nice all the time?"

The line at the reference desk was backing up behind Ruth.

Helma briefly scanned the article's columns. "If you care to leave it here, I'll peruse it for accuracy as to who did the ranking and which sets of criteria were used."

Ruth clutched the magazine to her breast in mock horror. "If it's in print, Helm, it's gotta be God's truth."

"Not necessarily."

"Oh, say it isn't so!"

Ruth's eyes twinkled. The man behind her drummed his fingers on the cover of the Chilton's manual he held.

"Ruth," Helma began, nodding meaningfully at the line behind her.

Ruth turned, still in her mock horror mode. "Oh dear, I'm holding up the dissemination of information. Sorry, all," she said loudly. "Gotta run."

During the next lull on the reference desk, Eve rushed past as Helma sorted her mail. Eve's face was painted with circular pink cheeks, black whiskers, and a black nose. "I could just eat up those kids," she called over her shoulder to Helma.

In Helma's mail was a letter addressed to her in care of the library. No return address and mailed from Scoop River, Michigan. With a feeling of *deja vu* Helma slit it open. The note inside was unsigned:

> *A reunion is NOT a good idea. People could be hurt, including you. I suggest you cancel it.*

Unbelieving, Helma read it over twice. She was being threatened. The writer was warning her not to hold the reunion and actually threatening her!

"Ma'am?"

An elderly man stood in front of the desk, pointing to a line in *Readers' Guide*. Helma stood. "Excuse me. It's imperative I leave the desk for a moment," she said and hurried to the workroom.

Beside her desk she opened the box of reunion files and pulled out the folder marked ANONYMOUS LETTER. She held the two letters side by side. They both had been printed by a computer printer, but with different print fonts and on different weights of paper, one an expensive high rag content, the other common perforated computer paper.

They might have been written by the same person using two different machines, but that didn't make sense. One letter reminded her of her promise to plan the reunion, to "bring us together," while the other threatened her, "suggesting" she cancel it.

"Excuse me, Helma, but is a phantom minding the reference desk?" Patrice stood on her side of the bookshelves, looking down at Helma over the tops of her glasses, shoulders squared, lips pinched.

"Of course not. I needed important information from my desk," Helma told her, adding the second anonymous letter to the folder and adding an "s" to the heading, ANONYMOUS LETTER. "Now if you'll excuse me I must return to my patrons."

For the next hour Helma answered questions automatically, deferring to her years of training and experience, while in her mind she wrestled with the two letters, both from Scoop River, each with a different message. Two different people who felt so strongly and oppositely about the same event, one claiming murder and requesting help, the other sending a warning. She pictured her classmates. None that she recalled fit either description, not from the Scoop River class she knew twenty years ago.

"Miss Zukas."

Helma looked into the crinkly smile of Chief Wayne Gallant. He bent slightly over the reference desk, relaxed, his eyes intent on hers.

Helma had obviously raised her head too quickly because she suffered the sudden sensation of tunnel vision, Chief Gallant's smile at its distant center.

"Hello. I mean, how may I help you?"

"Nothing really." He held up a copy of *Herbal Gardening Tips*. "Just stopped by to pick this up and thought I'd say hello. How have you been the past month? I enjoyed our lunch. Would you . . ."

"Fine. Everything's fine. I'm working here . . . still. I'm planning a high school reunion, the twentieth."

"I went to mine a couple of years ago. It might sound odd coming from a man but it was my observation that the men had aged more than the women."

"It's your business to be observant," Helma said.

His smile broadened and Helma felt her face flush. She glanced toward the magazine section. Thankfully, Ruth was gone. Ruth pounced on the most innocent contact Helma had with Chief Gallant more eagerly than Helma's own mother.

Helma thought of the anonymous letters. One of the letters *was* a threat, wasn't it? Certainly Chief Gallant had experience with anonymous threats. He'd have worthwhile advice for her.

"You haven't had any misadventures lately, have you?" the chief asked in a light tone. "Anything the police should know about?"

He was teasing her, referring to an unfortunate and entirely accidental relationship they'd shared a year ago during a local criminal incident.

Helma sat straighter in the reference chair. "Of course not, and I never withheld information, either."

He laughed and raised his hands. "I surrender. I thought we exonerated each other on those charges long ago."

"We were both doing our jobs."

"That's right, we were. I noticed your friend is having an art opening tomorrow night. Will you be there?"

"I may stop by, but I volunteer at the crisis center Friday nights," Helma told him.

He nodded. "I saw your name on their roster. That's a stressful job. I admire you volunteers."

Helma ducked her head modestly and saw that while they'd been talking she'd torn a patron's purchase request in half and in halves again until it was a clump of one-inch squares. She hastily dropped it in the desk drawer to reconstruct later.

Chief Gallant glanced at his watch. "I have a meeting in a few minutes but I hope we can talk longer next time." He gestured toward her sweater. "That blue brings out the color in your eyes."

"Blue is my favorite color," Helma said.

"Mine, too." The chief laughed. "That's fitting, isn't it? Take care now."

Helma smoothed her hands over her blue sweater and watched the chief stride toward the circulation desk.

"How go your reunion plans?" Roberta asked when she arrived at the reference desk to relieve Helma. "Do you have a theme?"

"A theme? No."

"Ours was 'Purple Passion.' Everything—and I do mean *everything*—was purple. Drinks, decorations, even the toilet paper."

"I'm searching for a place to hold the dinner and dance. George Melville suggested a resort on Saturday Island called the Gull Rock Inn."

Roberta Seymour coughed in a snort that exhaled through her nose. Her thin face blushed pink. "Excuse me," she said, blotting her lip. "Something caught in my throat."

"Have you heard of the Gull Rock Inn?"

Roberta fussed with the buttons of her blouse, her head down. "I spent . . . I mean, I recall reading about it. It was a well-known resort in the twenties and thirties, I think. Very romantic."

"That's what he said."

Roberta looked up, her face still becomingly pink. She smiled. "He did? George said that?"

"Yes, I think I'll investigate it."

Helma left her apartment early for her shift at the crisis center, allowing herself twenty minutes to attend Ruth's opening.

The Upper Crust Gallery had most recently been a bakery and on damp days was graced by a lingering odor of freshly baked bread. The gallery was long and narrow and packed with people who slowly moved past Ruth's bright paintings in a clockwise procession, holding plastic beverage glasses. Laughter and chatter filled the room.

Ruth, dressed in another of her self-concocted creations—this one lime green and blazing red—stood a head above most of the crowd. When she spotted Helma, Ruth beckoned, nodding meaningfully to her left. Helma squeezed through the crowd toward the area Ruth had indicated, wondering what she was supposed to see.

She glanced up at Ruth, who pointed downward into the crowd.

Then Helma noted the knot of people beside her, their heads inclined toward a tiny woman holding a leather-bound notebook. She wore mocassins and fringes and around her neck hung a silver figure that was a blend of Northwest native art and liquid-eyed children popular years earlier.

It had to be Kara Cherry and the silver figure must be what Ruth called Kara Cherry's "cutesy fake Indian jewelry." The roots of Kara Cherry's black hair were plain brown. Her sharp eyes were definitely blue and her nose pug.

"As an artist myself, I also understand what the painter is trying *not* to say," Helma heard her say before the inexorable crowd pushed her past.

And directly beside Chief Gallant.

"Helma," he said. "It's good to see you." He beckoned to the paintings. "I think your friend's outdone herself."

"She frequently does," Helma said.

"Can I get you a glass of wine?"

"No thank you. I'm on my way to the crisis center."

"Then how about a cup of coffee?"

Someone bumped against Helma and she, in turn, bumped Chief Gallant. He caught her by the shoulders and steadied her. Helma held up her wrist, pointing to her watch. "I have to leave. I'm sorry."

Chief Gallant put his hand on Helma's elbow and guided her toward the door of the gallery. The crowd magically parted and too quickly Helma was on the sidewalk. She gratefully breathed the evening air.

"Can I walk you to the crisis center?" Chief Gallant asked.

"I have my car," she said, turning and firmly shaking the chief's hand, wishing he'd stop smiling like that. "But thank you for the offer."

"You're most welcome," he said and she was aware as she walked down the street toward her parked car that he remained standing in front of the Upper Crust, watching her.

The sun had shone that day, and as Helma had observed on other fair-weather days, there were fewer desperate calls to the crisis center. She spent extra time with a young man who couldn't bring himself to tell a girl he cared about her romantically.

"What if she laughs?" he asked.

"Has she ever laughed at you before?"

"Well, no."

"Then I doubt she will now. Perhaps she wants to tell you the same thing."

"You think so?"

"I wouldn't be surprised. It can be frightening to trust other people with your feelings."

Between calls Helma perused the crisis center's small library. The only information she found on anonymous letters said, "Threatening letters, anonymous or from someone known, should never be disregarded. Authorities should be notified and the recipient should exercise extra caution while continuing his or her daily life."

"Did you *read* it?" Ruth shrieked in Helma's ear.

Helma pulled away the phone. "I can hear you, Ruth. Yes, I read it."

"Oh God, I want to die. No. I want to commit murder. What if people—*real* people—mistakenly believe she knows what she's talking about? Oh, that pint-sized pissant. I'll . . ."

"Ruth," Helma interrupted. "It was on page two of the second section. Not many people will even see it. The *News* is only a small-town paper. Besides, it wasn't that bad."

"Sssss," Ruth hissed. "She said my work was . . . 'barely controlled . . . overly influenced by Northwest languor.' What in hell does *that* mean? Can't she make up her miniature mind? It sounds bad to me."

"Ignore it. The people I saw were enjoying your show."

"Kara Cherry will *not* get away with this, this . . . impersonation of an art critic. I swear she won't. Just you wait and see."

❧ chapter four ❦

WORRIES

"**R**uth should be here any minute," Helma told her mother, glancing toward the door of Saul's Deli and hoping this wasn't one of those times when Ruth "just forgot." "Four and a half weeks until the reunion and nearly all the plans are set," she continued. "Statistically, the last weekend in July is the most likely time for sunshine."

"Mmm," Lillian said.

Helma glanced sharply at her mother. Lillian had been vehemently interested in every aspect of the class reunion, providing tidbits of information—"facts only," Lillian insisted. "I don't gossip."—about the families of each classmate Helma mentioned.

"Are you all right, Mother?"

Lillian put down her fork and looked at Helma with unusually wide and troubled eyes. "Something's happened, Helma," she whispered.

Helma felt a shiver at her neck. Something. Something bad. Cancer, death, financial ruin.

"What is it?" she asked, so shocked she forgot her mouthful of roast beef sandwich.

Lillian lowered her eyes. "It's a man," she whispered.

"What about a man?"

Lillian cleared her throat and looked out the window. "I met him two weeks ago. He just moved into the complex."

"You're dating him?"

Helma's father had been dead four years. As far as Helma knew, Lillian had shown no interest in another man. "Your father was quite enough, dear," she'd said once.

"Mother, there's nothing wrong with dating. In fact, I think it's a good idea. You're a healthy woman and Dad's been gone a long time."

Lillian exhaled and patted Helma's hand. "I'm glad you feel that way, Wilhelmina. That's why I'll have to cancel our dinner this weekend."

"Would you like to have dinner on Saturday instead of Sunday?" Helma asked.

Lillian twisted her hands together in front of her salad. "No, no. That won't work. You see, well, I'll be gone all weekend."

Helma pushed aside her plate and leaned across the table. "You're going away for the weekend with a man you've only known two weeks?"

Lillian faltered for the tiniest moment. Then her chin stiffened. "Yes, yes I am. We're going across the Cascades to a cabin he has in Roslyn."

Helma swallowed. She blinked.

"Hi, you guys. Sorry I'm late."

It was Ruth, in jeans and a sweatshirt and her hair pulled back in a frizzy knot. She set her lunch on the table. "You two look like you're into a heavy discussion."

"My mother's disappearing for the weekend with a man she's known for two weeks."

Ruth lightly nudged Lillian's shoulder with her fist. "Good going!" she said to Lillian.

"But she's only known him two weeks," Helma said.

Ruth shrugged. "No sense wasting time at your age, is there?" she asked Lillian.

Ruth and Lillian had always been polite to one another but it was no secret Lillian disapproved of Ruth's paintings and her untidy lifestyle with too many men and too little responsibility.

"Ruth's right, dear," Lillian said, smiling warmly at Ruth for probably the first time since Ruth, barefoot, wild-haired, and already taller than Helma's mother, had shown up at their back door after school one day when she was ten years old. "And at my age, the barrel's a lot emptier than it used to be, too."

Ruth laughed and saluted Lillian with a fourth of her club sandwich.

"I'm going to run along now," Lillian said, standing and pushing in her chair. "You girls have a nice lunch. I'll talk to you next week."

"Have fun!" Ruth called after Lillian.

Helma watched her mother step out of Saul's Deli and hurry down the street, an unusual spring in her step.

"Jealous?" Ruth asked.

"Of course not. But my mother is sixty-four years old. It just seems . . . unseemly."

"It's her life. But I want to show you what came in the mail yesterday." Ruth pulled a long white envelope from her purse and handed it to Helma.

"This looks familiar," Helma said. "Typed. No return address."

"And mailed from Scoop River," Ruth finished. "Another frigging anonymous letter. The booger's getting nasty. Read it."

" 'Do you know what color blood is?' " Helma read. "This is a threat, Ruth."

"It's probably not a reference question," Ruth said.

"That's not funny. This is the second threatening letter. We don't know what this person," Helma shook the page, "is capable of doing. It might be prudent to cancel the reunion."

"We can't cancel, Helma. We already bought crepe paper. Heaven help me but I'm beginning to look *forward* to it."

"It's irresponsible to put our classmates in danger. Whoever's writing these letters is unbalanced."

Ruth wiped her mouth with her paper napkin and shrugged. "These are kids' tactics: anonymous letters, vague threats. You just have the jitters." Ruth winked. "I know a certain chief of police who would probably bust his suspenders to help you figure this one out."

"He doesn't wear suspenders," Helma said.

"Oh, you know that, do you? But really, I don't see any reason to give these letters any credence. They're juvenile. Probably pranks by one of our charming classmates. Maybe Ben Kovas or, Zeus help us, your cousin Ricky. It'll all come out in the wash at the reunion."

"I don't detect a sense of humor here at all," Helma argued. "On the contrary. Somehow, all three of the anonymous letters are connected to David Morse's death. We could be responsible for a classmate being injured . . . or worse."

"You're paranoid, Helm. David Morse died in a simple accident. The letters are a joke, a big joke, that's all. Why let some creep who's probably pissed because he didn't get elected class president or make it with a cheerleader ruin a great party? That's coercion."

"I'll agree to proceeding," Helma said. "With caution. But if there's another letter, I *will* cancel the reunion. I've learned at the crisis center that only the foolhardy disregard threats."

"Then we'll be careful. Here, do you want this for your file?" Ruth asked.

Helma nodded and put the threatening letter in her purse. "What about the Gull Rock Inn? Did you confirm our dates?"

"I said I would, didn't I?" Ruth asked.

Ruth had taken over arrangements with the Gull Rock Inn and she was touchy about it. Helma was uncomfortable scheduling the class reunion at a resort she hadn't seen but one of Ruth's arty friends had seconded George Melville's opinion, saying the Gull Rock Inn was "beautiful, spectacular, to die for," and Helma had reluctantly given the responsibility to Ruth, whose interest was waning in the more pedestrian aspects of the reunion.

"What about the menus?"

"I'll send them over tomorrow."

"I gave them to you two weeks ago."

Ruth slurped the last of her frozen coffee drink through her straw. "The reunion's still a month away, Helma. You're acting like the planning part's more important than the event."

"Without careful attention to planning, this particular event *won't* take place."

"How many have promised to show up so far?" Ruth asked.

"Sixteen."

"Sixteen out of fifty-two? That's pretty pathetic."

"Out of forty-five, actually. Three are deceased, and four we couldn't find." Helma handed Ruth three of the acceptance letters.

> Well, well, cuz, aren't you the little organizer? I wouldn't miss this for, as they say, all the tea in China.
>
> *Ricky*

Ruth groaned. Of all the class, Helma's cousin Ricky was the one classmate Helma had hoped wouldn't attend. She should have known better. If Ricky believed there was anything he could possibly do to irritate Helma he'd make every effort to do it.

Ricky's and Helma's fathers had been brothers. Uncle Mick had died first, when Ricky and Helma were both nine, but his suicide had provided Ricky with an excuse for every shortcoming the rest of his life. Stuck at the end of the alphabet with Ruth and Helma, he'd tormented them with a single-minded viciousness that Ruth grudgingly called "brilliant."

"I thought he was getting married," Ruth said.

"Aunt Em said the bride-to-be postponed the wedding."

"Smart girl. Any word from Geoff Jamas?"

Helma shook her head and Ruth said nothing, squinting over the next letter.

> Oh Helma, I'm sooo excited to come to this reunion— on an island! Wheee! Sounds delish! The old gang together again! I'll take pictures until my brains fall out and I'll bring some old photos you're going to scream over! I can't wait to hug everybody to death!
>
> *Lolly Kuntritas*

"Oh Lolly, queen of superlatives. Is Fiona coming, too!"

"She confirmed last week."

Ruth's eyes brightened. "Lolly and Fiona. This oughta be good." Ruth rubbed her hands together and cackled like a witch. "I'll lay my money on Lolly, how about you?"

"I can't believe that twenty years later they'd still be bitter over teenage quarrels," Helma said, refolding her paper napkin.

"You can't? What about the sweet case of loathing and disgust you feel for your dear cousin, Ricky?"

"I wouldn't put it that strongly, and Ricky's a different situation. *You* still feel antagonistic toward Ricky."

"Right," Ruth said smugly, "but I'm happy to admit it."

I'm comin'! Tell Ruthie to get out her dancin' shoes!

Wilson Jones

Ruth shook Wilson Jones's letter. A sometime date of Ruth's, Wilson Jones had been one of four boys in their class taller than Ruth. "This letter is a guarantee we'll have a good time," she said. "Any teachers accept?"

"Miss Higgins."

"That's it? Miss Higgins is still alive? She must be ready for a spot on Willard Scott's birthday wishes."

"She said she's eighty-three. She's bringing her sister with her."

"I hope it's her younger sister. Why don't we send out one more letter to try and coax a few more out of the woodwork. You could include a list of who's accepted."

"That's a good idea, Ruth."

"Thank you."

Helma was uneasy. She lay prone on the carpeted floor of her living room, having just completed twenty minutes of vigorous exercise from the second edition of *Look Your Best at Any Age*. Her shades were drawn and the door was securely locked and bolted. She stared at her textured ceiling, thinking about the anonymous letters.

They were connected to David Morse's death after the basketball game twenty years ago, she was positive.

Helma rolled off her exercise mat and rose to her hands and knees, reaching for the reunion box. She pulled out the MORSE, DAVID file and reread the photocopied news stories.

The stories contained nothing but tragedy. A promising young athlete: engaged, with college and life ahead of him. Eighteen was young to be engaged but it wasn't that uncommon in Michigan. She wondered what had happened to David Morse's fiancée, Patty Anne Sands.

Helma drummed her fingers on the file box and considered it. Why not? It certainly wouldn't do any harm.

Directory assistance had no listing for a Patty Anne Sands in Hopkins. Helma jotted down the four other numbers under Sands. Hopkins wasn't any larger than Scoop River and all the Sandses were most likely related.

"I'm looking for Patty Anne Sands," Helma told the woman who answered the first number.

"Patty? Why?"

"I'm an old classmate of hers," Helma lied.

"She's Patty Brotsky now. Been divorced for years but she kept Bill's name anyway. His second wife's still on a tear about that, you can bet."

"Do you have her phone number?"

"It's in the book. Just a sec."

Helma thanked her, hung up, and dialed Patty Anne Sands Brotsky's number.

"Hello?" The voice was quick, sharp.

Helma wasn't sure why she did it; it was unlike her, but she lied again. "My name is Dorothy Gale and I'm looking for information on David Morse for a story I'm doing about teen death."

"Why are you calling me?"

"Your name is listed in the obituary as his fiancée."

"You're lying."

"I beg your pardon."

"You're with what's-her-face, the woman who called before, aren't you?"

"What woman?"

"Don't pretend. I'm telling you what I told that nosy bitch. Stay the hell out of my life. There's nothing in it for you. If you call me again, you'll regret it."

"What will you do?" Helma asked, genuinely curious.

"I'll tell," Patty Anne said. "And then see what happens."

"Wait," Helma said. "Who called you? What was her name?"

"Drop dead." And the phone crashed in Helma's ear.

Helma sponged off her exercise mat and rolled it up, thinking about Patty Anne Sands Brotsky. Beneath Patty Anne's threats and bravado, Helma had sensed panic. Patty Anne had been angry, but she was afraid, too. Afraid of "what's-her-face's" questions.

Helma thanked Mrs. Whitney from 3E for the napkin-covered plate of oatmeal cookies. The bottom of the plate was still warm.

"That's all right, dear," Mrs. Whitney said, smiling her cherubic smile. Helma and Mrs. Whitney had shared apartment walls for nine years. "You stop by tomorrow and I'll show you the pictures Debbie just sent of the grandchildren. Cute as peanuts."

As Helma closed the door, a fragrant cookie partway to her mouth, her phone rang. It was Ruth.

"Helm. Guess who I just saw on TV?"

Helma didn't play at guessing games unless she was certain of the answer so she waited for Ruth to tell her.

"Mr. Broder! Guess where he lives?"

Again Helma waited.

"*Seattle!* He's running for state legislature, can you believe it?"

Ralph Broder, their counselor and class advisor during their junior and senior years. He'd been removed from Scoop River after two years, subsequent to fighting in vain for reinstatement of a pregnant junior girl. Helma hadn't taken part but she recalled a futile student march in Mr. Broder's behalf.

It wasn't a surprise he'd ended up in Seattle. The Northwest was full of immigrants, especially from the Midwest. Her father had once said, "It's like somebody turned the country on edge and everything loose rolled west."

"I called his house for you," Ruth continued. "So he'll be calling you back tonight."

"Why me instead of you?"

"I didn't want to embarrass him. One of his last acts before he got booted out was catching me and Wilson fooling around in the typing room."

"And that would embarrass *him*?"

"It might. You make a better impression than I do, anyway. I've got a date so I'm out of here. Tell Mr. B. hi."

Helma hung up and ate two more oatmeal cookies, remembering how Ruth had joked with Mr. Broder, and with other teachers, too, almost like they were peers. Teachers had never spoken to Helma in that easy bantering fashion, despite giving her good grades and high commendations.

Helma's phone rang and she reached for it. Mr. Broder already.

"Is this Helma Zukas?"

He'd pronounced Zukas like it was spelled Zuckas so it wasn't Mr. Broder.

"This is she," Helma answered coolly. This was the time of evening when the phone solicitors called.

"This is Baker Road Veterinary. Your cat was brought in an hour ago."

"You must be mistaken. I don't own a cat."

"Your landlord said it was yours."

"Then he was mistaken. I don't own a cat."

"You're sure? It's a black male. White patch under his chin. Looks like it's been in a few scrapes."

"I believe it's a stray. I've seen it in the area for several months."

"All right then. Sorry to have bothered you."

"Just a moment, please. Why do you have it?"

"It was hit by a car in front of the Bayside Arms this afternoon."

"What are you going to do with it?"

There was a long silence. The veterinarian cleared his throat. "It has damaged hindquarters and maybe some internal injuries. If we can't find the owner we'll put it to sleep."

"Oh. I'm sorry but I'm not that person."

"Right. Have a nice evening."

Helma hung up. It might not even be the same cat who skulked around her balcony, spying on her. She couldn't be responsible for stray animals. It was the fault of people who didn't have their animals neutered. Too many strays, not enough owners, and unfortunately, harsh measures were occasionally necessary.

Helma thumbed through her reunion files, passing over the ANONYMOUS LETTERS folder, refusing to consider them now.

She'd discarded the THEME file. Instead of a theme, every one of which Ruth had sneeringly rejected, including "Come as you were," and "Western Luau," they'd settled on a simple saying to be printed on napkins and programs: "Twenty Years of Memories."

A thump sounded on Helma's balcony and she crossed her living room to peer through her sliding glass doors.

The scruffy black cat wasn't on her balcony. The thump sounded again and she spied her plastic watering can lying on its side, bumping against the balcony floor when the wind rose.

Helma stood gazing out at her empty balcony. She glanced across at Mrs. Whitney's. She folded her hands together, then unfolded them. She gave an exasperated sigh. "Oh, Faulkner," she said and opened the phone book, running her finger down the B's.

The phone rang seven times before it was picked up. Helma was surprised to discover her palms were damp.

"This is Helma Zukas. Do you still have that stray cat that was hit in front of the Bayside Arms?"

"Yes, yes, we do. He's still hanging on. I was just preparing to . . ."

"Do you feel he can be repaired?"

"I think so. He's a tough character. It may be expensive."

"Please do what you have to. I'll pay for it."

The veterinarian's voice rose in obvious relief. "That's good, very good. I'll get right to work and let you know how he comes out."

"Thank you."

The sun had set and the sky above the islands was still rosy when Mr. Broder called. A sailboat, its mast outlined by lights, motored toward the marina across the bay. Helma opened the balcony door to allow the salty air into her apartment before she picked up the phone.

"Helma Zukas!" Mr. Broder said, his voice rich with the old warmth she remembered. "What a surprise! Do you live in Washington?"

"A hundred miles north of Seattle. Bellehaven," she told him. "A friend saw you on television tonight. I have a special request."

She told him about the reunion on Saturday Island, briefly telling him who had already confirmed.

"I'm honored. Scoop River was my one and only foray into education and your class is vivid in my memory. I could probably make it Saturday night, how would that be?"

"Remember, this won't garner you any votes," Helma reminded him. "Ruth and I are the only Washington residents and we're not even in your district."

Mr. Broder laughed. "Perhaps in the future I'll be in a situation where you *can* vote for me."

"Are you giving me privileged information?"

"I might be."

"Do you know I had to walk through a wild-eyed bunch of picketers to get in here?" Ruth asked when she dropped by the library with print estimates for the reunion program. "I felt like I was on my way to an abortion."

"The Save Your Kids group. They're demonstrating because we won't withdraw books they deem offensive," Helma explained.

"Oh. Can I get a list?" Ruth held up her hand. "Just joking. So what did Broder say?"

"He'll come to the dinner Saturday and spend the night."

"You're a miracle worker, Helm. Is there time to put it in our last letter?"

Helma nodded. "And this time I'll write the letter. Seventeen class members don't exactly make a full reunion."

"Who's the seventeenth? Last I heard there were only sixteen."

"Roman Fonsilwick."

"Who?"

"The former Roman Fonszelvitcz."

Ruth groaned. Helma pulled Roman's letter from the ACCEPTANCES folder and handed it to Ruth.

Helma:

My wife Jean, who is a well-known East Coast news reporter, and I will be attending the class reunion. Of course we'll be paying our own expenses. Perhaps you can use my allotted amount for some of our less fortunate class members.

I've come a long way since Scoop River but I've never forgotten my beginnings. Should you need help with wine choices or such, don't hesitate to call on:

Roman Fonsilwick
BA, MA Econ, MENSA

"What's MENSA?" Ruth asked.

"An organization for the mentally superior," Helma explained. "You have to pass an intelligence test to join."

"No lie? Roman must have had a ringer. Remember the time his mother tried to get his chemistry grade changed?"

Helma's phone buzzed. She raised her finger and answered it.

"Miss Zukas, you can pick up your cat tomorrow," the young voice told her. "Dr. Lawrence said he'll need care for a few weeks but he should fully recover."

"No. You've made a mistake. I was only paying for his surgery. You can send him to the shelter to be adopted."

"One moment, please." The line went dead.

Ruth's eyes widened. She sat on the edge of Helma's desk. "Whose surgery?" she asked. Helma shook her head.

Dr. Lawrence came on the line. "Miss Zukas. I'm afraid the shelter doesn't take animals in your cat's condition. You can take him in after he recovers but in the meantime, he needs to rally from his trauma."

"I haven't room for any type of cat, neither sick nor well."

Ruth snickered and pulled a face at Helma.

"You took responsibility for this animal, Miss Zukas," the doctor said firmly. "He'll be ready to go home tomorrow."

Helma narrowed her eyes at Ruth and said, "Thank you very much. Someone will be in to pick him up."

Ruth took the phone from Helma and hung it up. "What have you *done*, Helm? A cat?"

"It was hit by a car and the veterinarian was preparing to dispose of it. I thought you could take it until it recovers. Then it can go to the animal shelter."

Ruth shook her head, still grinning. "Sorry. You know Max. Another cat in his territory and he'd tear it to pieces."

Helma tapped her pencil on her desk blotter. Who else was there?

"You're stuck, my friend. But fear not. I'll guide you through the mysteries of cat ownership."

Helma shook her head. "I don't *like* cats, Ruth. You know that. I don't want this cat or any other cat. Where would I even put it? And what about a . . ." she grimaced. "A cat box."

"What's the greatest invention in the world?" Ruth asked.

"What does this have to do with a cat?"

"No. Really. What's the greatest invention in the world?"

"Some people say the zipper."

Ruth nodded sagely. "Right. Now picture an invention that rates right up there with the zipper, only in the world of cats."

"I don't have a clue what you're talking about."

"Clumping kitty litter!" Ruth said triumphantly. "It's a miracle. Truly. No more cat boxes to change. It's revolutionized millions of cat owners' lives. You'll love it. In fact, I'm going to go buy you some right now." Ruth stood up. "I'll buy *everything* you need, and tomorrow I'll go with you to get your new little kitty cat from the vet's. Oh what fun!"

Helma glumly watched Ruth sweep out of the work room, her stride full of the joyful purpose of a missionary.

"What's your cat's name?" the pony-tailed receptionist asked, pen poised over a set of hospital-looking forms.

"He's not my cat," Helma told her.

"She means she hasn't named him yet," Ruth said from behind Helma. "Write down Boy Cat Zukas for now."

The veterinarian's office smelled like animals and disinfectant. From behind closed doors, a dog barked.

The receptionist pushed the form toward Helma. Helma swallowed at the total and pulled out her checkbook. The receptionist smiled in approval. "I'll get him for you."

"Can't you take him, Ruth?" Helma tried one last time.

"Nope. You'll learn to love the little fella in no time."

The receptionist brought back the cat carrier. Two green eyes stared balefully through the barred side. She held out the carrier to Helma. Helma stepped back and Ruth took the case.

"Careful," the receptionist said. "He's a teensy unhappy."

The cat hissed and Ruth tsk-tsked at him, carrying the case away from her body.

Helma unlocked the trunk of her Buick.

"You can't put him in there," Ruth said. "This is a living, breathing creature, not a bag of groceries."

Walter David, the building manager, was watering the

thin strip of lawn beside the Bayside Arms when Helma and Ruth got out of Helma's car.

"Glad to see your cat made it," he said, lifting his Seattle Mariners cap and wiping his forehead. "Thought he was a goner for sure, lying out there in the street like an old sock."

"I was under the impression animals weren't allowed in the Bayside Arms," Helma said.

"Don't sound so hopeful," Ruth murmured beside her.

Walter David shrugged. "Cats are okay. I've got a Persian myself."

"You're putting him out here?" Ruth asked incredulously as Helma led her onto the balcony.

"He's an outdoor cat," Helma said with certainty. She pointed to the bed she'd made in a box tipped on its side. The covered plastic litter box sat beside it, the opening discreetly turned away from Helma's door. Matching bowls of food and water sat in front of the cat bed.

Ruth set the carrier down by the cat bed and opened it. The cat's left hindquarter was shaved and bandaged, a patch on his belly was shaved and a row of neat black stitches marred his pink and gray flesh.

"Geez. He isn't much to look at, is he?" Ruth said.

The cat looked up at her, blinked and then looked up at Helma, staring coolly into her eyes for several seconds before it awkwardly stood and climbed into the cat bed, curled into a circle with its left leg extended and promptly fell asleep.

❧ chapter five ❧

JULY:
DAY ONE

"**P**ick me up, would you?" Ruth asked. "I'll be ready. I promise."

Helma agreed and hung up the phone. The sun had crossed over the roof of the Bayside Arms and was just reaching its long rays into her apartment. She pulled down her shades, shutting out the gleaming bay and sun-spotted islands.

Boy Cat Zukas sat on her balcony glowering in at her. She firmly unrolled the door shade and he grumpily meowed. He was healed; not even a limp remained. So why didn't he just go about doing whatever stray cats did? Helma was unaware of his habits when she wasn't home but when she was, there he sat, gazing in at her in sullen regard. She wasn't about to allow him inside her apartment, *that* was certain.

"Stop feeding him," Ruth had advised.

Helma did and the next day he sat hunkered on the mat by her balcony door, crunching—audibly *crunching*—the sleekly feathered body of a house finch. After discarding birdless wings and stray feathers three times she went back to filling his bowls with food and water. She removed the cat box with its miraculous clumping kitty litter but when Boy Cat Zukas took to sleeping in

53

her flower pots she pulled his cardboard bed out of the recycling bin and returned it to her balcony.

Laughing voices filtered in through her screened windows and Helma closed those, too.

Thanks to Ruth's friend Jorge who liked feet, nine of the twenty-two attending the reunion were arriving on the same flight from Seattle. At least they were arriving on a sunny day. That should get the reunion off in the right direction.

The others, including Roman Fonsilwick and his East Coast wife, were making their own way to Bellehaven, hopefully all in time to catch the 11:20 ferry to Saturday Island tomorrow.

Helma checked her mirror one last time. Her peach sweater matched her peach and white cotton dress and was adorned by the very same circle pin she'd attached to her collar for her senior picture.

At her carport, Helma walked once around her freshly washed and waxed Buick, moistening her finger to remove a smear of dust on the chrome front bumper before she got in.

Ruth lived and painted in a converted carriage house behind a stately Victorian house on what was called "The Slope." The long-established section of Bellehaven was older, greener, and shadier, where ferns grew larger than shrubs, and ivy tended to creep over and subdue in a decidedly gothic manner whatever didn't move fast enough: fences, garages, electric poles.

As Helma drove up, Ruth stood waiting in the alley, framed against a tumble of laurel gone wild. She wore a brilliant blue overlong skirt and a brightly patterned shirt, the whole outfit hanging with too much fabric yet somehow managing to look risqué with her strapped high heels, deep eyes and bright lipstick. She was eating an oatmeal creme pie out of a Little Debbie box.

"Everybody will recognize you from a mile away," Ruth said, splaying her long legs to fit under the dashboard.

"Why do you say that?"

"Here you are driving your graduation car, looking like it did the very day your proud parents presented it to you."

"There's that scratch on the left fender," Helma reminded her.

"I should be so lucky." She held out the box of Little Debbies. "Want one?"

Helma shook her head.

From the streets on the slope, Washington Bay shone beneath them, sparkling and shimmering bright blue. Ruth pulled out her sunglasses and said in a deep voice, "Plans are laid for revenge on Kara Cherry, dog's breath art critic."

"Is it legal?"

"Helma Zukas! Of course it is. What do you take me for?"

"Then explain your revenge."

"I don't think so. You'll have to wait until my opening in Seattle." Ruth rubbed her hands together like a villain, smiling gently.

For the third year in a row, Ruth was participating in an autumn show at a small but "artistically important" gallery near Seattle's Pioneer Square. But this year it was her own show, all her own work, not shared with two other artists as in previous years.

"So tell me again who's coming in on this plane," Ruth said.

"Miss Higgins and her sister, Dora Durbas, Wilson Jones, Fiona and Lolly . . ."

"Ah, Fiona and Lolly. I wonder if they're gnashing their teeth at opposite ends of the plane, plotting against each other. That'll be good fireworks, for sure."

"Forrest Stevens," Helma continued, "and Michael Petronas."

"That only comes to eight."

Helma took a deep breath. "And Ricky."

"And Ricky," Ruth repeated. "Spawn from hell. Cretin of the deep."

Ruth craned her neck as they passed the meadow being bulldozed for the new mall—materializing despite vociferous local protests—watching a gigantic yellow machine jerk and butt at a pile of rocky dirt the size of a house. "Do you think that even as we speak they're up there clapping hands and singing 'Michael, row the boat ashore'? Maybe doing rounds of 'One hundred bottles of beer on the wall'?"

"I just hope everything's in place. You did reconfirm our plans at Gull Rock Inn?"

"Nothing to worry about, Helm."

"Helma."

"Everybody else is showing up tonight?"

"That's correct. Oh, I nearly forgot. Amanda Boston called last night. She's arriving tomorrow morning in time to catch the ferry."

"Amanda? Gorgeous Amanda. I wonder if she's gone to fat. Funny she'd come when she couldn't bother participating in anything during high school."

"She *did* only live in Scoop River a year. It was hardly time to become acquainted."

"Yeah, but she was a little weird, too. Remember that time she went catatonic in government class and Mr. Broder had to haul her out?"

"I don't recall the incident as being quite so extreme."

"*Everything* was extreme back then. Speaking of the extreme past, I had a postcard from Paul."

"Where was he?"

"Still in Minneapolis." Ruth toyed with the window crank and sighed.

Usually, Ruth left her men without a backward glance, but there'd been something about quiet Paul from Minneapolis who'd landed in Bellehaven for a month to research flash-frozen fish products that had unaccountably caught Ruth's attention, leaving her momentarily and uncharacteristically melancholy whenever she mentioned him.

Ruth leaned toward the windshield and scanned the sky. She pointed toward a distant speck. "I bet that's them. Oh happy days."

"Two of these people might be responsible for the anonymous threats we've received," Helma reminded Ruth.

"Are you still worried somebody's gonna jump out of the woodwork at us? Forget it. I told you it was just a joke. Before this weekend is over, we'll know who it is, if we're lucky."

"Or unlucky," Helma murmured, thinking of the anonymous letter she found most disturbing: "Do you know what color blood is?"

Ruth and Helma stood at the single gate in the Bellehaven Airport watching the little Horizon commuter plane being coaxed to a stop. It was the type of plane where only children could stand in the aisle.

Beside Helma, as they watched the passenger door open downward to form its own staircase, Ruth grew taller, straightening her spine, lengthening her neck, and squaring her shoulders. Helma had watched Ruth perform this same optical feat since they were ten. Ruth, when she was uncertain, attempted to vanquish dissent, ridicule, or argument through the intimidation of sheer bulk.

But Helma was nervous, too. Except for Ricky, she hadn't seen a single person on that plane in twenty years, people who at one time, long long ago, she'd known as well as her own family.

First from the plane descended a tiny, white-haired woman in sensible shoes and a blue suit. Two of the ground crew helped her to the tarmac where she turned to look back at the plane, expectancy clear on her wizened features.

"It's Miss Higgins," Ruth said. "Should we be hiring a nurse?"

"She said she was bringing her sister," Helma reminded Ruth.

Ruth laughed, hooted really. "*A* sister, anyway."

An equally wizened and similarly shaped woman cautiously descended the steps. The two men reached for her and lifted her to the ground, skipping her over the bottom two steps. She was a nun. Her veil and habit were short and her white hair was visible but Helma knew nuns and Miss Higgins's sister was definitely a nun.

Behind them, in pastel blue polyester and tennis shoes, only a little plumper, her pink-cheeked face as determined and sensible as ever, came Dora Durbas, student Volunteer of the Year three years running, former president of

Future Homemakers of America and the "Sew Sew" club. Dora addressed and corralled Miss Higgins and her sister even as her foot touched tarmac. Taking each sister by an arm, Dora headed for the terminal, moving like a woman who was accustomed to herding reluctant beings of one kind or another.

"Helma!" Dora Durbas called, letting go of the nun long enough to wave, and a belated beat later, slightly less enthusiastic, "Hello, Ruth."

Dora Durbas pressed Miss Higgins forward, patting the old woman's stooped shoulder. "You remember Miss Higgins, of course. Latin I, II, and III. And this is her sister, Sister Bernice."

A flash of annoyance pricked Miss Higgins's trembling smile. She pressed her thin hand into Helma's. It felt breakable and Helma held it gently. During fifty years of teaching, Miss Higgins had held office in every teachers' organization and won every teaching award the Scoop River school system had to offer.

"Ah, my star pupil," Miss Higgins said, rapidly blinking damp eyes. "She caught onto ablative case more quickly than any student I ever had," Miss Higgins told Sister Bernice. "And her verb declension was *pluperfect*."

Sister Bernice beamed at Helma. "*Amo, amas, amat, amamus, amatus, amant*," she recited rapid fire. "Please, call me Sister Bea."

Ruth coughed and Miss Higgins stiffly raised her head until she peered up into Ruth's face. "And Ruth," she said, her hand still in Helma's. "You're taller."

"You might be smaller," Ruth suggested.

"Oh yes, oh yes," Sister Bea agreed, bobbing her veiled head. "You start to shrink down after a certain age. The spine compresses."

"Then there's still hope I'll someday reach normal height," Ruth told her.

"Well now," Dora Durbas broke in. "This is nice but let's not wear ourselves out after that long flight. We'd better sit for a while." And she ushered Miss Higgins and Sister Bea toward the plastic seats.

And then Helma was surrounded by faces and bodies that mingled past and present, that wavered before her eyes, dropping pounds, erasing wrinkles, plumping cheeks, adding hair. Youthening until the past was more real than the present and each of them was recognizable as they'd been twenty years ago.

"Ruthie!" Wilson Jones cried, "the love of my life!", lifting Ruth in his arms and twirling her around, the two of them towering over everyone else.

Wilson Jones had made it through high school by the skin of his teeth, with no intent of going an inch beyond graduation. Jolly, troublesome, a football star, who with a little more grace, might have been a basketball star, too. Once Wilson Jones had donned a Richard Nixon mask and roared his motorcycle through the halls of Scoop River High School during fifth period, in one door and out the other.

Wilson's curly dark hair had thinned but he was still big-boned and broad-shouldered, his tapered body now thickened to a rectangular block emphasized by narrow legs. He wore short sleeves and as he whirled Ruth, Helma saw the crude self-inflicted tattoo on his forearm that had caused his suspension from the football team for two critical games: his own initials, WJ, inside a heart.

"Helma, honey," Wilson Jones cried, releasing Ruth and smacking a kiss loudly on top of Helma's head. "You're still just as cute as a button."

"Hello, Wilson," Helma replied, fighting the sense that she was spinning in circles: too many colors, too many voices, not enough air to breathe. "You haven't changed much either."

Michael Petronas laughed and before Helma knew it, she was enveloped in his arms, smelling aftershave, a rush of happiness at the old sound of Michael's generous voice.

"Helma, congratulations," Michael said. "Nobody else would have had the forethought to invest the class's money like you did. I couldn't have come without your stipend."

Despite his beard, Michael Petronas was still the same, Helma saw at once. Lean, flat stomached, earnest-eyed. Always solid, "nice," a word that caused Ruth to roll her eyes, but a concept that had more meaning—and more desirability—as adults than during their brief teen-age years, when "nice" was synonymous with boring and meant teacher's pet, student council president, and obedient son.

"I love it! I love it!" Lolly Kuntritas squealed, stamping her feet and clapping her hands, a vision of pink and blonde and ripe, barely-contained flesh.

Just like twenty years ago, Lolly Kuntritas giggled and twittered and hugged and wore mostly pink clothes that were too tight or too short or too . . . pink.

Lolly squeezed Helma's arm, flowery perfume settling over them. A brown beauty spot Helma didn't recall dotted Lolly's cheek. "My camera!" she shrieked in Helma's face. "It's in my luggage. I'd *die* for it right now!" and before Helma could answer she'd twirled to Ruth and plucked at Ruth's shirt. "This color is yummy on you, Ruth. Yummy yummy."

Lolly had loved boys and Helma supposed that now she loved men. In high school, Lolly hadn't recognized boundaries, or going steady or privacy or that she might be disliked or unwelcome or that people might tire of her company.

That she might make enemies, like Fiona Kamden, Lolly had been totally unaware.

At the edge of the crowd, far from Lolly, stood Fiona Kamden, more finely drawn, but then weren't they all?, who fussed with her carry-on and smiled nervously, waiting to be acknowledged. Her vibrant chestnut hair, which had always hung loose to her waist, was now cropped short in a cut they'd called a "pixie."

During their junior year, Lolly Kuntritas had slipped away from a party with Fiona's date and ever after, Fiona had referred to Lolly by the first syllable of her last name.

"Fiona," Helma said. "I'm happy you could come after all."

Fiona thrust her hand forward. It was icy cold and pulled away too quickly. Fiona nodded briefly and said in her soft, brisk voice, "It was necessary. I hope it works out. Thank you," and then grew flustered and took a step back from Helma, shrugging her thin shoulders as if the words issued from her mouth were as baffling to her as they were to Helma.

Also standing apart was Forrest Stevens. He'd been the science "egghead," the kind of boy who wore glasses before kindergarten and always carried too many books, who laughed a second too late or too soon and talked overlong about things like geometric theorems and electromotive force, and who was tolerated more than accepted and rarely even good-naturedly teased.

Now Forrest Stevens's temples were silvered. He stood slender and tall, dressed like men in one of those black and white ads in *Vanity Fair*, a slight smile on his face.

"Forrest," Helma said, holding out her hand.

"Hello, Helma."

"You came all the way from Florida," she said. "I'm glad you could get away from your practice. Should we be calling you Dr. Stevens?"

"No, no. Here I'm just Forrest. One of the old gang."

Helma looked around and caught her breath. It was disorienting, disturbing in a way. But they were arriving. The weather was beautiful, reservations were in place, menus had been approved, decorations were packed in boxes and ready to go into her trunk for the ferry to Saturday Island. Her worries were silly. It would be a well-executed and successful reunion, she could feel it.

"*Kaip gyvuoji?* Aren't you forgetting me, cuz?"

Helma turned at the familiar intonations and went dizzy at the sight of cousin Ricky. She hadn't seen him in years and he'd filled out, gained a sprinkling of gray hair. It wasn't fair, not in the least that someone like Ricky, the scourge of her youth—so closely resembled her father and Uncle Mick. The bright blue eyes and hawkish nose. Even the grin he made by raising one corner of his mouth. It wasn't fair at all.

Ricky went on, not waiting for her to answer, even if that had been her intention.

"Long time no see," he said, jangling coins in his pockets.

"Isn't it."

"Hey, sorry I missed your dad's funeral last year."

"That was four years ago," Helma told him.

"Yeah. Well, I already had a ski weekend booked at Boyne Mountain. Can't pass up good conditions, you know. Mom said you all held up real good. By the way, in case she mentions it, Aunt Em sent you some *kugelis*, but the plane food was so bad I ate it on the way here." He looked around at the chattering, laughing group. "Can't believe *you* pulled this off, cuz."

"What do you mean?" she asked and instantly regretted it.

Ricky shrugged. "It isn't like you were one of the 'insiders' in high school, is it?"

"Aunt Em said your wedding was postponed," Helma said.

"Didn't work out. She was too young."

Ruth leaned between Helma and Ricky. She and Ricky stood eye to eye. "If you're looking for someone unable to see through you, Ricky dear," Ruth said sweetly, "you'll have to resort to animals."

"Yeah, and what's your excuse, Stretch?"

Ruth's hands balled into fists. "Just stay out of my way," she said through gritted teeth, "or we'll finish that fight we began in the back of the band room."

Ricky raised his hands and pursed his lips. "Oooh, ooh, I'm so scared." He turned his back on Helma and Ruth and said to Lolly, "Well, Lolly Dolly, what say we chat about our blast of a past?" Lolly giggled and hugged Ricky.

Helma stepped away from the group. "Attention," she said in her professional voice.

Everyone, including the baggage handler and the people at the ticket counter quieted and gave her their undivided attention.

"Forrest Stevens and Michael Petronas are renting cars and I have my car. So we'll divide into three groups. There are reservations for everyone at the Sun Break Motel near the ferry terminal."

"This will be like the senior trip we got gypped out of," Wilson Jones said, looking pointedly at Ricky.

"Tomorrow morning there will be a tour of the Bellehaven Public Library at 9:00 a.m.," Helma continued, "and our ferry to Saturday Island leaves at 11:20. We'll go as foot passengers and the Gull Rock Inn will arrange transportation. In case you forget any of this you'll receive a packet of information when you register at the Sun Break Motel."

"She's so organized," Sister Bea said, shaking her head in admiration.

"You should have seen the papers she turned in," Miss Higgins replied. "Always done in ink, too."

"When's everybody else showing up?" Lolly asked.

"Mostly tonight. Mr. Broder's flying to the island tomorrow night."

"How many of us will be here?"

"Twenty-two."

"Out of fifty-two?" Ricky asked.

"That's right," Helma said firmly. Ricky grinned that grin and Helma looked away.

"Well then, let's make like a library and book," he said.

They divided up in the airport parking lot. Miss Higgins, Sister Bea, and Dora Durbas got into Helma's car. In a flurry of noise, Ruth—giving Helma a quick wave—, Wilson Jones and Lolly piled into Michael Petronas's rented red Trans Am.

"Comfy back there?" Dora Durbas, sitting with her purse on her lap, asked Miss Higgins and Sister Bea. "Seat belts fastened?" Helma's car smelled of lilac and lavender.

Miss Higgins turned and looked out the rear window at the red Trans Am. "They look like a racy bunch in that car, don't they? Wouldn't it be fun riding with them?"

As she pulled away from the airport, Helma checked her rearview mirror. Over the two gray heads she could see the laughing faces in the Trans Am behind her.

Sister Bea and Miss Higgins watched out their windows with intense interest, commenting on the Victorian homes, the white-capped mountains, the pervasive greenery, and the well-tended gardens.

Dora adjusted her seat belt and settled into her seat like a broody hen. "So this is Washington state," she said. "It looks more modern than I expected." Dora leaned forward and said in a low voice to Helma, "I almost called you two weeks ago."

"You found another address?"

"No, do you remember when we talked about David Morse's death?"

"Yes."

"His girlfriend. She's dead, too."

"Patty Anne Sands died? David's fiancée?"

Dora nodded, her lips pursed and her eyes shining in the way of those who enjoyed being the bearers of unexpected news.

"She didn't just die, though. She was murdered."

"Murdered! What happened?"

Dora glanced at Miss Higgins and Sister Bea to be sure they weren't listening. She held her hand to her mouth, blocking their view of her lips, and leaned her pink face still closer to Helma, constrained only by her seat belt. "They found her body in a motel in Detroit. She'd been strangled. I heard there were, you know, *gimmicks* in the room."

"Gimmicks?"

"Certain underwear, leather, like that."

"Why was she in Detroit? I thought she lived in Hopkins." Helma inwardly blanched, realizing she'd given away that she'd talked to Patty Anne, but Dora was too involved in her tale to notice.

"Nobody knows. There were rumors that she took 'trips' sometimes."

"Oh my, look at that dahlia garden!" Miss Higgins said.

"Funny, isn't it?" Dora asked. "Both of them dead? I mean, funny-odd, not funny ha-ha."

"Odd," Helma agreed, stopping her Buick at the stop sign onto Fairview Drive. "Very unusual."

Patty Anne Sands was dead, murdered. By whom? Did the anonymous letter-writer know? Who was the "what's-her-face" Patty Anne had mentioned, the other woman who'd called Patty Anne and asked questions about David Morse's death?

Helma had a sudden thought. "Did you phone Patty Anne Sands after I talked to you?" she asked Dora.

Dora sat back, pressing her hand to her chest. "Me? I hardly even knew her." She nodded toward the street. "Aren't you going to go? It's clear."

Helma pulled onto Fairview Drive, unexpectedly lurching forward, stalling, then quickly restarting the engine, as Miss Higgins and Sister Bea issued soft little "ooh's" of alarm in the backseat.

She glanced in the rearview mirror again at the cars behind her. Could one of them be carrying a murderer?

chapter six

TABLE TALK

"**R**uth, I have to talk to you," Helma said the moment Ruth joined her in the carpeted hall outside the ornate door of the Sun Break Motel's Orca Room. Helma held extra reunion programs. Ruth held a whiskey sour.

"Sorry I'm late," Ruth apologized. "Got to talking old times. Anybody here yet?"

"No, but it's about Patty Anne Sands, David Morse's fiancée. I . . ."

Ruth held up her hand. "Forget all that for one night, okay? Let's just have fun. Everybody looks good, don't you think? Few more pounds, little less hair. I bet Lolly's had her eyelids lifted. Her butt looks a little suspicious to me, too."

"But . . ."

"Right." Ruth squeezed Helma's arm and pointed as Wilson Jones, his curly hair glistening, entered the lobby from the elevator, his blocky body adorned in new jeans and a shirt with a definite Western flair. Wilson moved in that slightly stiff, self-confident gait of ex-athletes.

"Where's the Orchid Room, honey?" Wilson Jones asked, touching an imaginary cap and winking at the dark-haired woman behind the desk.

"That's 'Orca,' as in whale, you goon," Ruth called. "And open your eyes or you'll trip over it."

Helma gave up trying to tell Ruth about Patty Anne Sands. At the moment, she doubted Ruth would pay any attention if Helma shouted it out: Patty Anne Sands has been *murdered*.

"Ruthie," Wilson said. He grabbed Ruth around the waist and they clumsily danced a polka down the hall and back. "You look as juicy as a candy apple. Why didn't I marry you?"

"Sheer stupidity on your part, definitely," Ruth said, straightening her skirt.

"Who *did* you marry?" Helma asked.

Wilson held up his left hand. There was a slight indentation but no ring around his ring finger. "A sweet little girl from Oklahoma. Michigan was too damp for her and Oklahoma was too far from good fishing for me. She broke my heart."

"If anybody's heart got broken, Wilson," Ruth said, "I'd lay odds you did it."

Wilson's face sagged to serious planes, instantly older. "Maybe, but leaving my two girls, that about killed . . . that was tough." He shook his big head, then clapped his hands together and brightened. "So what's on the agenda tonight? Rehash old football games? Tell fish stories? I've got some Academy Award winners."

"Tonight's fun is free form," Ruth told him. "Just a casual dinner with the eleven of us who've shown up so far, menu gleaned from the terrific Pacific, orchestrated by Miss Helma Zukas."

"Speaking of games," Helma said. "Do you remember the Hopkins basketball game our senior year when David Morse was killed?"

"Miss Subtle," Ruth mumbled beside Helma.

"Dave the Caveman? Yeah, I remember. Damn shame. He was good."

"Was there anything unusual about that night or the game or David?"

Wilson Jones frowned and looked at the ceiling. "Not really."

"Anything at all," Helma prompted.

Two waiters passed, pushing a trolley laden with hors d'oeuvres. Wilson reached out and plucked up a shrimp puff.

"I spent a lot of time on the bench that game. Football was more my thing, remember? Dave could make impossible baskets, miracle rebounds. But that night, he was off."

"What do you mean?"

"Well, Dave had this natural grace, you know: slip between players, real fluid on his feet. The guy never tripped." Wilson's eyes went wistful. "The night he got killed, he was ramming his way up and down the court like a maniac. No grace, just hell bent to make baskets, like he'd kill any guy who got in his way."

"He was angry?" Helma asked.

Wilson shrugged. "Maybe. You know, he was kind of a hot head off court. Liked a good scuffle now and then."

"Do you know who he might have been angry with?"

"I can think of a few guys. He and I had a go-round at halftime over the way he was hogging the plays. Told him if we lost the game it was his fault. I still feel bad we didn't clean it up before he died. Hey, what are you girls up to? Why the grilling?"

"We're not girls," Helma said.

Ruth squeezed her free hand into one of Wilson's jeans pockets, and Wilson's eyebrows raised. "Just nosy. Come on. Let's go sit down and have a drink."

A moustached waiter approached Helma, diffidence in every move. Something had gone wrong, Helma knew instantly. "Excuse me, Miss Zukas. We've had a mechanical failure of the divider in the Orca Room."

"I trust this won't affect our dinner. We've had reservations for two months."

He fairly bowed. "No, ma'am. Not at all. Dinner will be as scheduled. However, there's also a dinner party at the opposite end of the Orca Room."

"Which you can't separate us from because of the mechanical failure," Helma finished for him.

"Yes. I'm terribly sorry. It's a large room and the other group is already dining so you'll have the room to yourselves shortly."

"What group is it?"

The waiter adjusted his red cummerbund, looking

embarrassed. "An organization called The Formerly Fat."

Helma followed him into the Orca Room. Beautifully set with white linen, silver and stem ware, was the Scoop River table with Ruth and Wilson huddled at one corner. Across the room, eighteen people sat at a table under a banner that read "We're in Charge!"

Helma recognized a library patron who was notorious for checking out so many books at a time she brought a wheeled wire cart to carry them all. Two waiters busily set plants in a row where the divider should have been, creating a symbolic barrier. The Formerly Fat group didn't seem unduly loud or raucous.

"Ask if they mind our playing orchestrated versions of twenty-year-old hit tunes," Helma instructed the waiter.

Dora ushered in Miss Higgins and Sister Bea, seated them at the end of the table, aligned the already straight table settings, and left to find decaffeinated green tea for Sister Bea. Sister Bea helped Miss Higgins untangle her necklace from the buttons on her sweater.

Helma sat beside Ruth, who was curiously watching Dora. "Doesn't she know school's out and playing Miss Brown-nose won't win her an *A* anymore?"

"Dora's always helped other people," Helma said.

"Especially if she can push them around."

"That's not fair."

"But it's true," Ruth said, turning her attention back to Wilson.

Helma couldn't argue with that. Dora had been a "club girl," who'd excelled at organizing the fumbling, the inept, and the directionless into after-school knitting groups, charity drives, and postdance cleanup crews.

"Beautiful country," Sister Bea said. "I hope heaven is this gorgeous," and she laughed naughtily.

Lolly entered with her arm through Forrest's. "Imagine, you in medicine," she was saying, gazing up at Forrest through supplemented eyelashes, her eyeshadow as bright as a tropical bird's. "Are you as rich as those doctors who live on Lake Michigan?" Lolly had put up her streaky blonde hair and changed into a pink low-cut top and white pants.

Ruth leaned over and whispered to Helma, "That bra makes use of the highest principles of engineering. Cleavage like that does not exist in nature."

Ricky dropped into a chair catty corner from Helma, and although she tried to ignore him, she couldn't shut out his voice. "Has anybody else noticed how people in this part of the country have skin the color of library paste?"

"What color's that?" Lolly asked.

"Ask my cousin Helma, here," Ricky said. "She's intimate with the stuff."

"Oh you," Lolly said, playfully slapping his arm.

Fiona was the last to arrive. She slipped in almost unnoticed, her eyes puffy as if she'd been napping, and sat next to Sister Bea. Helma noticed Fiona still had the habit of tensing one corner of her mouth in a spasm of twitches.

"I'd like to propose a toast," Michael Petronas said, standing and raising his glass of wine. "To Scoop River."

"Scoop River," they repeated, clinking beer bottles, wine glasses, and coffee cups together.

"*Carpe diem*," Miss Higgins said.

Across the Orca Room, the Formerly Fat, smiling, clinked their water glasses in a toast of their own, chanting, "We're in charge," then raised their glasses to the Scoop River table.

"Aren't people nice?" Lolly said, waving to the Formerly Fat.

Helma raised her own glass. "And to those who couldn't be with us tonight."

"Yeah," Ruth added. "Like the dead ones."

Glasses clinked again. Was it Helma's imagination or was there less enthusiasm in this toast, fewer eyes meeting?

Waiters entered from the kitchen, bearing plates of asparagus salad with citrus vinaigrette.

Ricky took a bite, then called to the waiter, "Do you have any Thousand Island dressing, something with a little more 'chunk' to it?"

Ruth and Helma exchanged quick glances. Helma studiously looked down and cut up an asparagus tip, refusing to give Ricky the satisfaction.

The entree was grilled salmon with a shrimp sauce accompanied by roasted potatoes with rosemary, and sauteed spinach. Baskets of warm sourdough bread sat at each corner of the table.

It was perfect. Helma mentally added a generous tip for the kitchen staff.

"You know," Lolly said brightly, "I like seafood best when it has breading on it, the crispy kind."

"And deep fried?" Ruth asked. "With French fries and catsup?"

"That's *right*," Lolly squealed. She poked at a shrimp. "This is kinda naked."

"Did you ever eat at Armedo's next to the bowling alley back home?" Wilson asked the table in general. "They *really* gave you a lot of food for your money."

"Too bad there isn't any gravy for these potatoes."

"Has this bread gone off? It tastes sour."

Helma hastily stood. "Why don't we go around the table and each relate our experiences since graduation."

"How I spent my life," Michael commented.

"All right, you go first," Helma told Michael.

"Okay. Get ready to be impressed, everybody. I teach high school English. One of the guys in the trenches who'll probably never reach administrative heights and I'm not so sure I want to anyway," Michael said with the familiar old modesty. He scratched his chin through his beard. "My wife Gail, who isn't here because she's leading a workshop in Lansing, teaches second grade. We have a son and a daughter, both hitting puberty and not enough bathrooms. Other than that, no complaints."

Wilson Jones stood abruptly. "Whoa!" he said, grabbing his chair to keep it from falling backward. "I've given it my damnedest, but I can't make a living trout fishing, so I'm selling insurance right smack dab in the heart of downtown Scoop River. I watch anything that resembles football, and I'm looking for a new woman unless Ruthie will take me back."

"Dream on," Ruth said.

Wilson grabbed his heart in mock pain and sat down. "I'm wounded, Ruthie girl."

Ruth leaned over and, with a loud smack, kissed Wilson on the cheek. "Better?"

"As you know," Forrest Stevens said in a soft, slow voice, "My career is medicine. My wife's a dancer and we have an adopted daughter."

"Hey, Doc," Ricky said. "Remember when you were the class geek? Do you give a break to old buddies?" Forrest smiled but didn't respond and Ricky took over. "I'm a free man, unencumbered. I hit Las Vegas a couple times a year. The world's my pearl and life's grand. No complaints here."

Ricky still lived with his mother and as far as Helma knew, hadn't held a steady job his entire life.

Lolly wiggled on her chair and before she stood, hiked up the bodice of her shirt with both hands. "I'm still in Scoop River, too. I've had two disastrous but pretty fun marriages and if Ruth doesn't want you, Wilson, I'm game."

Wilson raised his beer bottle to Lolly.

"Oh," Lolly continued. "I work in a day care center." She shrugged. "I don't have any kids. The equipment just didn't work the way it was supposed to, I guess."

Helma had the prickly sensation she was being watched. She glanced around the table and caught Forrest Stevens regarding her. Before she could read the expression on his face, he lowered his head and neatly snicked a potato in half with his fork and knife.

Dora Durbas took a sip of water followed by a deep breath before she rose. "I still live in the same house in Scoop River that Bob and I bought from his parents right after high school but Bob and I got divorced two years ago and that's probably his excuse for not showing up at this reunion." Dora held her hands tightly at her waist as if they might move without her consent. "He didn't want to be in the same room with me. He can't stand being in the same town; that's why he moved to Cadillac. It wasn't a very friendly divorce but I'm coping well and so are my two daughters." She sat down with a slightly dazed expression on her face.

Fiona didn't stand. The corner of her mouth twitched.

"I'm married," she said in a low voice Helma strained to hear. "And I'm a paralegal."

"Ooooh," Lolly gushed. "You poor thing."

"Lolly, sweetie," Ricky said. "A paralegal's a nonlawyer who does all the lawyer's work."

Lolly covered her mouth and giggled, her breasts pulsing, rocking from side to side and bumping between Ricky and Forrest while Fiona glared at her.

"Excuse me, Miss Zukas," the waiter said, bending low to Helma's ear. "There's a phone call for you."

Helma followed him to the house phone in the lobby.

"This is Helma Zukas."

"Helma! I'm glad I found you. This is Donald Westright."

Helma couldn't think. Who was Donald Westright?

"*Mister* Westright," he said. "Your old government and history teacher."

"Mr. Westright? Are you here in Bellehaven?"

"Not currently, but I intend to be if there's still time to crash your reunion. I apologize for not answering your invitation. I was out of town and then just couldn't catch up with myself."

"Please. We'd love to have you."

"Wonderful. I just finished a meeting in Denver but I can catch a plane to Seattle and drive up to Bellehaven in the morning. I have your program right here in front of me. The ferry's at 11:20, right?"

"That's correct."

"I know I can make it. Did everyone on this acceptance list you sent me make it?"

"There are eleven here now. Most are coming in later tonight and tomorrow morning."

"Great. I don't expect any problem getting there."

"We're looking forward to seeing you."

"Not as much as I am. Tell everyone hello."

Helma hung up. This was good news. She stepped from the phone cubicle and nearly bumped into Forrest Stevens.

"Sorry," he said. "I was looking for the restrooms."

"I think they're the other way."

"Thanks," Forrest said. He pushed his glasses up the

bridge of his nose and stood there. Helma waited for him to continue.

"Thanks," he repeated, and headed off in the opposite direction.

Helma watched, remembering how Forrest, the math whiz and now *doctor*—lost in computation—had accidentally been locked in the high school library once, missed by his parents before he realized himself what had happened.

In the Orca Room, the orchestrated version of "Please Come to Boston" was playing and Ruth and Wilson Jones were arguing over which of them had got in trouble for copying the other's government test.

"You'll be able to ask," Helma said.

"What?"

"You'll be able to ask Mr. Westright. It was he who just phoned. He's arriving tomorrow."

"Mr. Westright?" Michael asked. "I heard he was on the East Coast at some private school."

"Remember those stupid Quiz Bowls he tried to initiate between the schools?" Ricky asked. "He'd select his favorite students—"

"You never had to worry about *those*," Ruth interrupted. "He was looking for *smart* students."

"Ditto," Ricky replied.

"And remember his pipe?" Wilson asked, pulling his mouth downward in mock sophistication, striking a pose.

"He was trying to look older," Helma said.

Lolly giggled. "We all were."

"I wasn't," Miss Higgins said.

Michael turned to Miss Higgins. "Nearly fifty years you taught at Scoop River. What was so special about our class that inspired you to come all the way out here for the reunion?"

Miss Higgins touched an arthritic finger to her chin, thinking and tipping her head to the side. Light reflected off her glasses, hiding her eyes.

"Our brilliant minds?" Forrest prompted.

"No," Lolly said. "It was because we were simply unique and unforgettable."

"I came because I was invited," Miss Higgins said. "I

always do. Well," she conceded when she saw their disappointed faces, "some of you *are* more memorable than others."

"Which of us and why?"

"Oh, I'd never tell you *that*. That wouldn't be nice at all."

Under cover of their chatter, Helma glanced at each person at the table, wondering. How easy was it to hide that you wrote anonymous letters or that you might contemplate, threaten, or even commit murder? As her gaze landed on Forrest, she had the sensation that an instant before she looked at him, he'd been studying her. He took a sip of wine and nodded to a teasing comment from Lolly.

The door was held open by a waiter and another couple entered the Orca Room. Helma thought they must be members of the Formerly Fat, so dazzlingly were they dressed, as if they belonged to the recently transformed. He in a beautifully tailored summer wool suit, she in a white silk dress and pale fur wrap, pearls at her throat and earlobes. Certainly, they were neither Bellehaven nor Scoop River.

The table went silent in appraisal and approval. The couple glided toward the Scoop River table and Michael Petronas stood.

"Roman," Michael said. "Roman Fonszelvitcz."

"Fonsilwick, it is now," he said.

It was Roman. Helma closed her mouth.

"He *has* come a long way," Ruth said to Helma. "I swear he's even taller. Do you think he's wearing lifts?"

Everyone at the table was rendered subdued in the presence of a classmate in whom they couldn't detect the past, who'd escaped, not just from his old name, but to another realm.

Roman extended a manicured hand to Michael and smiled a polite businessman's smile. He said the correct pleasantries, noncommittally warm, as if possessing the capacity to mentally dismiss whoever he was talking to in the blink of an eye.

"I'd like to present my wife, Jean," he said to the group, pronouncing her name in French.

"John?" Wilson Jones asked.

"*Jean*," Roman replied, palatizing the *j*.

Jean, the "East Coast news personality," was stunning. Large dark eyes, aquiline nose, and full lips. She smiled almost shyly, nodding around the table.

"Sit down," Michael invited.

Roman declined. "Thank you but we had dinner in Seattle and we're suffering a little jet lag. Please excuse us while we catch up on our sleep. We'll meet you in the morning. It's good to see everyone."

The Orca Room, including the Formerly Fat group, was silent, watching the impeccable couple, as Roman, with his hand lightly on his wife's back, guided her out of the room.

When the door closed behind them, the group exchanged glances. Lolly was the first to speak. "Zhon," she said dreamily.

"I'll bet her mother didn't call her that," Ricky said.

"They're a vision," Miss Higgins said, smiling at the Orca Room door. "*Mirabile visu.* And to think I nearly failed Roman for taking a test with irregular verbs written on the inside of his wrist."

"*Eo, fio, fero*," Sister Bea provided.

Miss Higgins nodded.

At ten o'clock, Miss Higgins began to droop. She turned to Sister Bea. "I'd better get some rest. It's 1:00 a.m. my time."

Sister Bea, who'd been in an animated discussion with Michael Petronas about the sudden secular popularity of Gregorian chants, nodded in disappointment.

"I'll walk you to your room," Helma volunteered, and Sister Bea brightened.

Miss Higgins and Sister Bea's room was on the first floor toward the back of the Sun Break. "This is my last big trip," Miss Higgins said as she unlocked her door. "In October, Bea and I are moving into one of those snappy retirement apartments. The two of us together."

"She's leaving the convent?" Helma asked.

"Not exactly. Bea's going into semiretirement. Convents are poor, dear. They can't afford to support old nuns, but I'm tickled to have her back after all this time.

Our family's lived in Scoop River for over a hundred years, you know."

Miss Higgins turned on the light, illuminating the simple room. Helma, who had a sense about things, especially things out of order, stood at the threshold of Miss Higgins's room, her nostrils flaring, her eyes darting, while Miss Higgins cheerily chatted on.

Then Helma saw it: the drawn curtain across the room billowed and fell flat. She walked over and pulled aside the drape. The sliding glass door onto the tiny patio was ajar.

"Did you leave this open?" Helma asked. She pushed the door but it stuck, grating in its track.

"Of course not. Bea must have. She's getting old and she's . . . forgetful sometimes."

Helma finally got the door closed but it wouldn't latch. "I'll call the desk to have this fixed."

"Oh, don't bother them this time of night."

Helma peered through the glass into the night brightened by circles of yellow lamplight. Except for a car pulling sedately out of the parking lot, all was still.

"Your security is their concern and responsibility," Helma assured her. "I'll wash my hands first."

Helma approached the bathroom warily. It appeared spotless and in order. She stepped through the door—and frantically grabbed the towel rack as her feet slipped out from under her.

The towel rack loosened but held and Helma awkwardly regained her balance. She knelt down and felt the bathroom floor.

It was wet. No, not wet, but slippery. She sniffed her finger and smelled a sweet, slightly floral odor she recognized. On the sink sat a blue bottle of Nivea face cream. The floor in front of the door was slick with it.

Someone had wanted Miss Higgins or Sister Bea to fall. In their fragile states, either might have broken a hip—Helma glanced around the small porcelain and tile bathroom—or been killed.

With a towel, she wiped the floor until it was dry and then waited with Miss Higgins, sharply alert, for motel maintenance to arrive and repair the door.

❧ *chapter seven* ❦

TOURING

Helma waited until five past nine before she called Ruth.

"Huh?" Ruth grunted into the phone.

"Ruth, this is Helma."

"So?"

"So I'm waiting at the library to begin the tour."

"Waiting for what?"

"Waiting for the group. No one's here."

"I'm not surprised. Everybody was up too late."

"Aren't you coming?"

"Helm, why should I? I've seen the library's charms a hundred times." She paused. "What time is it anyway?"

"Nine-oh-five."

"I'd better get moving and pack a few weekend things. When's that ferry again?"

"Eleven-twenty. We need to talk, Ruth . . ."

"I'll be there, honest. It's coming together pretty good, don't you think? Last night was so great, especially after we got rid of that elevator music. Even the Formerly Fat got in on it. What a group!" Ruth was warming up, sleep falling from her husky voice, the decibels rising. "Either some of us haven't changed a smidgen, or the effect of being back together again has reawakened all those hormones. You know how people say they revert to being a kid three hours into a visit with their parents? Wilson

Jones told me the funniest story about . . ."

"I have to hang up now," Helma interrupted.

"Okay. You should have stayed last night, Helm. It was fun."

George Melville passed Helma as she stood at the glass doors peering into the hazy July air, and said, "I hope they show up. I wore my best tie for the occasion." He smoothed his tie so Helma could see the hulking gorilla emblazoning the pointed front.

Finally, at quarter past nine, a taxi pulled up in front of the library. Holding a coffee to go, Dora Durbas leapt out of the front seat and opened the rear door. Helma, relaxing her shoulders in relief, watched Miss Higgins and Sister Bea emerge, both intact and appearing rested.

As the women fluffed and straightened and rearranged on the sidewalk, Fiona Kamden stepped onto the curb, squinting as if the sun were too bright when actually it was partially dulled by haze. They each held a paper cup of coffee.

Helma studied Fiona. She stood tall but with a deliberate stiffness that accentuated her thin frame. Fiona had always been a person who moved sharply and with swiftness, not so studied as this.

Helma opened the library door for the four women.

"The taxi driver took us to a drive-through coffee shop," Miss Higgins said. "Can you imagine?" She held up her cup and said proudly, "We have these drinks called lattes." She pronounced it "laddies."

"Are the others behind you?"

"Oh my dear," Sister Bea said. "I believe we're the only ones. I didn't see any of your other classmates at breakfast this morning, did you, Ellie?"

"No, no. Not at all," Miss Higgins agreed sadly.

"Heaven knows how late they all stayed up last night," Dora Durbas added.

"Ruth's laughter woke me up about two," Fiona said. "Wilson Jones's room was next to mine."

Dora Durbas turned and gave Fiona a glance of reproval, nodding meaningfully toward Miss Higgins and Sister Bea.

Helma's little tour group oohed over the conversion process from card catalog to computer, smiled at the art in the children's room, and marveled at the video collection, growing more enthusiastic and louder the more coffee they consumed.

"I have a cousin—a man, I mean—who's a practicing librarian," Sister Bea said when she met George Melville. "He lives in Ohio."

Helma's concentration was marred by thoughts of slippery motel floors and broken bodies. She forgot to explain the checkout system and the automatic overdue notices. Finally, she skipped her planned demonstration of the computerized magazine index and drove the four women back to the Sun Break Motel. "The motel car will take you and your baggage to the ferry terminal," she told them. "I'll meet you on board."

"I took the *Badger* across Lake Michigan to Milwaukee during the storm of '58," Miss Higgins said. "Everybody got sick except me, even the deck hands. Lake Michigan's worse than the ocean when it's rough. The waves are closer together. Much worse."

"It should be a smooth trip today," Helma assured her.

"It doesn't matter to me. I just never get seasick. It's not in me. *Quod erat demonstrandum.*"

"Disgusting," Helma said when she spotted the velvety gray mouse head, not a speck of blood on its neatly severed neck, lying on her balcony doormat.

Boy Cat Zukas sat on her railing, licking his paw. His food dish was empty.

"Shoo!" Helma told him.

The cat lazily jumped across to Mrs. Whitney's balcony and resumed cleaning himself without another glance in Helma's direction.

Helma folded a square of paper towel in half and picked up the mouse head. Two children played on the rocks below the Bayside Arms, so she couldn't just toss the head over her railing. She carried it inside to her bathroom, turned her head as she dropped it in the bowl, and flushed the toilet. Then she filled Boy Cat Zukas's bowl with a heaping mound of dry cat food and set it on the balcony.

"This is the big weekend, isn't it, Helma?" Mrs. Whitney asked from her balcony. "That blue dress is very becoming."

"Thank you," Helma said. This was the first time Helma had worn the new shirtwaist in public. She always wore just-purchased clothing for an evening at home first, to remove its aura of newness.

Mrs. Whitney scratched Boy Cat Zukas behind his ears and he leaned into her hand, his purring audible to Helma. "Would you like me to feed your kitty while you're gone?"

"He's not my cat."

"Well, *he* certainly thinks he is. I'll put some tuna out for you, how would that be, Puss Puss?" Mrs. Whitney asked Boy Cat Zukas. The cat rubbed against her blissfully and opened his eyes to give Helma a cool glance. If Mrs. Whitney fed him, maybe he'd move to her balcony.

"That's kind of you, Mrs. Whitney. Thank you."

Helma's doorbell rang and she stepped inside, closed and locked her balcony door, and tested it twice before she answered the bell.

Ruth dragged in a bulging gym bag with a broken strap. Her legs emerged from a pair of red shorts, elongating her proportions like figures in seventy-millimeter movies compressed for television.

"You said you were going to the ferry with Wilson Jones."

Ruth shrugged. "Thought I'd stick with you. We're the promoters of this thing, aren't we?"

"That makes it sound like a circus."

"Exactly. Did anybody show up for your tour?"

"Four people."

"Oh. You need help carrying paper napkins or anything? Where's the painting I did for the door prize?"

"It's all in the trunk. But Ruth, I have to tell you about Patty Anne Sands."

Ruth looked at the ceiling. "Helma . . ."

"She was murdered," Helma said, cutting Ruth off.

Ruth dropped into Helma's rocker, her mouth open. "Murdered?" she repeated. "You mean, dead on purpose?"

Helma sat on the couch and stacked the magazines on her coffee table, then fanned them out again. "Dora Durbas said she was strangled in a motel room in Detroit."

"Who did it?"

"There are no suspects. Dora said there was paraphernalia in the room."

"Drug or sexual?"

"The latter."

Ruth blinked. "Detroit? Did she live there?"

"I talked to her last month and she was living in Hopkins."

"You talked to her? What about? Why didn't you tell me?"

Helma related Patty Anne's curious remarks.

"You mean she thought you were part of a conspiracy?" Ruth asked.

"Not a conspiracy, just in league with the other woman caller. She threatened to 'tell.' "

"And you think there's a connection between Patty Anne's death and whoever's been writing us those love letters?"

Helma twisted her fingers into a church and steeple and here's all the people. "It's too much of a coincidence. Patty Anne dies after her fiancée's death has been brought to our attention and after another woman has also contacted her about David Morse."

"Maybe that's the end of it, then. We haven't gotten any more threatening letters. Patty Anne Sands could be the final key to it all and with her dead, we're out of the picture, of zero interest, kaput."

"Then why would the letter-writer have wanted us to cancel the reunion? Patty Anne wasn't a Scoop River student."

Ruth ran her hands through her hair and tipped back her head. "Hell, I don't know."

"There is a possibility that . . ." Helma stopped. It wasn't fair to suspect Dora had called Patty Anne. Dora *had* denied it.

"That what?" Ruth asked.

"I might know someone who called Patty Anne Sands."

Ruth twisted her mouth and grimaced. "I hate it when you do this. Why don't you just come out and say it?"

"At this point, it's gossip. Besides, she denied making the call."

Ruth leaned forward and clapped her hands. "Dora! Dora called Patty Anne, trying to help you out, and got in over her head, didn't she? Heaven protect us from do-gooders. Let's quiz her."

"She said she didn't call," Helma reminded her.

"Which you don't believe."

"Let me be the one to talk to Dora," Helma warned.

"Sure. We can't worry about it *now*, anyway, can we? We've got our trusting classmates out here. The reunion's begun and we're on our way. Let's just go for it and be sharp for any developing nastiness."

"There's one more incident," Helma said.

"Another letter, after all?"

Helma told Ruth about Miss Higgins' motel door and the face cream on the floor of the bathroom.

Ruth frowned, chewing her thumbnail. Helma looked away, her arms prickling at the sound of teeth against nail.

"Maybe you're jumping to conclusions, Helma. The door could have been a result of sloppy housekeeping. Sister Bea might have spilled the stuff on the floor. She did leave dinner to get a sweater."

"Do you actually believe that?"

"I don't *disbelieve* it."

Helma gazed at her pointedly until Ruth raised her hands in surrender. "Okay, okay, so it's a little unusual to spread your face cream on the floor."

"Try to remember who else left dinner before Miss Higgins and I did," Helma told her.

"I didn't, that's all I know for sure. You left to answer the phone."

"Dora went searching for green tea," Helma added. "And I saw Forrest on his way to the restroom."

"Wilson and Ricky went to the john, too. In fact, Ricky

was in and out with all the beer he was tossing back. I bet he's wearing out his kidneys."

"Lolly left to repair her makeup and Sister Bea to fetch a sweater," Helma said. "Everyone probably left at least once."

"Maybe I'm slow, Helma, but are you suggesting one of our cozy group last night tried to hurt Miss Higgins?"

"Who else?"

"Why Miss Higgins? Revenge for a bad grade in Latin?"

"Unless she has some knowledge of David Morse or Patty Anne Sands."

Ruth pointed to Helma's kitchen clock. "We'd better get this show on the road." She picked up her bag and headed for Helma's door. "I'm not going to think about this anymore. It hurts my head."

"Have you noticed anything about Fiona?" Helma asked as she backed her car out of the carport, nodding briefly to Walter David, who was polishing his motorcycle.

"Only that she and Lolly haven't gotten into it yet. Why?"

"I just wondered."

"Helma dear, you never 'just wonder.' Now what's up?"

"I also don't make conjectures without facts."

"Since when?"

At the ferry terminal, Helma pulled her car into the number three lane behind a red convertible. It was still fifteen minutes until loading.

The white and green ferry was at the dock, its car decks empty, framing the blue day through its opposite end.

"Oh, look. There's the old gang." Ruth said, pointing at the knot of people standing by the walk-on bridge. "What a sweet-looking bunch of folks they are. Wholesome, white-bread America." Ruth opened the car door and said, "We've got time. Let's go chat with the new arrivals and see if we can pick out which one might be penning threatening letters for fun, or contemplating murder, or trying to dump old ladies on the floor."

"You're taking this too lightly, Ruth."

"No, I'm not. I just wanta see a little more proof—real proof—and I'll start worrying."

Helma assessed their classmates as she and Ruth walked toward them, their clothing bright Midwestern colors of pinks, yellows and blues, unlike the somber shades most Northwesterners preferred, or were driven to choosing.

Lolly's golden blonde head bobbed between Michael Petronas and Wilson Jones, thrown back in laughter Helma could almost hear. It was a gesture so familiar from their past that Helma again felt the slippage and mixing of times.

"It's difficult to believe any of our classmates . . ."

"Well, maybe Ricky," Ruth said. "But what do we know about how any of them turned out? We were babies in high school. Unformed plastic blanks . . ."

"*Tabula rasa*, as Miss Higgins would say."

"Whatever. Wilson's still cute, isn't he?"

"Fiona said you were in his room last night."

"Nosy little gossip. I was just showing him my scars."

Mr. Westright stood in the center of the group dressed, as Helma remembered him, in a tweed jacket, the stem of his pipe just visible from his pocket. He was in his fifties now and his face had settled into distinguished lines, his bearing the kind found in oil portraits. Helma guessed his light brown hair was now augmented by an expensive and well-fitting hair piece. He looked "academic," slightly rumpled, at ease yet in control, as if he might launch into a lecture on the parliamentary process or assign the Declaration of Independence for homework.

"Helma," he said warmly, taking her hand in both of his, smelling of spice and pipe tobacco. "Thank you for allowing me to arrive at the last minute like this."

"We're delighted you could join us," Helma told him. She turned to greet the other late arrivals: Sandy Snow, Joey Barnes, Mary Gimbutas. The greetings and exclamations over how much they each had or hadn't changed were growing automatic and wearisome and Helma felt the dizzying urge to take a short nap.

"Auto passengers, please return to your cars," a voice recommended over the loudspeaker.

"Go ahead, Helma," Ruth said. "I'll walk on."

The lines of cars snaked into the silver belly of the ferry, clanking and bumping as each vehicle drove aboard.

Helma directed the deck hand to place an extra car block under her front tire and found her Scoop River class on the open deck at the ferry's stern, watching the remaining traffic load. As was her habit, she took quick note of the location of life preservers and life boats.

The ferry was full; two lines of traffic remained behind to wait for the next ferry at two-thirty. Three children raced around the decks, holding pinwheels to the wind.

"This is the best idea in the whole wide world," Lolly told Helma. "You're absolutely a genius."

"Yeah," Wilson Jones said. "Can we get together and discuss some investment strategies?"

"I only followed advice I found in the library," Helma told him.

The ferry was loaded. The overhead walkway was pulled away. Helma glanced at her watch in approval. It was 11:19.

"These boats are the same at both ends," Lolly said, batting her eyes. "How do they know which way they're going?"

"You mentioned Amanda Boston," Michael Petronas said to Helma. "Wasn't she supposed to arrive this morning?"

Helma looked around at the group, then at the other passengers standing on the ferry deck. There was no sign of Amanda Boston, at least not in a form that Helma remembered.

"Maybe she's somewhere else on the ferry," Helma offered, "although she said she might be late."

"I'm surprised she's coming at all," Dora said, having torn herself away from Miss Higgins and Sister Bea, who sat by a window looking out at the silvery blue water, white and veiled heads close together. Dora was completely coordinated in yellow, from her yellow sneakers to her plastic earrings shaped like lemons.

"Amanda was such a weirdo," Lolly said. "Pretty and all that, but what a snob."

"She might have been shy," Fiona said. "Sometimes the two can look alike from the outside."

Ruth's head swiveled from Lolly to Fiona, anticipation lighting her eyes.

Lolly shook her blonde head and threw back her shoulders so her breasts thrust forward. "Not in my book," Lolly told Fiona. "A girl who won't talk to people who are trying to be nice is a snob, not shy."

Fiona's eyes snapped. "I'm surprised you even know the word, shy."

"At least I—"

"Michael and Amanda used to sit together in study hall," Dora interrupted.

They glanced over at Michael Petronas who was deep in conversation with Mr. Westright and Joey Barnes about the financing of public transportation.

"Men talk about the funniest things," Lolly said, fluffing her hair and turning her back on Fiona.

🌿 *chapter eight* 🌿

THE ISLANDS

Normally, just boarding the ferry carried with it a powerful sense of freedom. All Helma's concerns were stranded on the receding shore like gremlins forbidden to cross water. She breathed deep the evocative sea air, felt its moist breeze, wondering if this time, the gremlin had managed to board with her, hiding behind a familiar smiling face.

The ferry horn gave one long blast and a moment later, left the mainland behind, gliding in a stately fashion toward the rocky and tree-covered San Juan Islands.

Despite the haze it was a fair day and the ferry passed through flocks of pleasure boats whose occupants waved and honked. Tangles of bull kelp and driftwood floated past, and seagulls coasted off the bow, taking turns landing on the railings, their beaded black eyes alert for food.

The wind rose as the ferry entered the straits, whipping against the Scoop River classmates and gradually they retreated to the enclosed upper passenger deck where Dora Durbas had commandeered four green booths and several chairs on the starboard side near Miss Higgins and Sister Bea.

The constant vibration of the ferry's engines was as soothing as a train. Helma felt it through the bottom of her feet, and when she sat down.

Roman and his wife, *Jean*, both beautifully groomed and clad in white and beige natural fibers, sat apart from the rest of the class, perusing booklets on exclusive real estate—including complete islands—offered for sale in the San Juans.

Helma found her notes and rose to stand in the center of the group. "I'd like to explain what you're seeing," she announced. "There are over seven hundred islands in the San Juan archipelago, approximately two hundred of which are named. They are the granite remains of an ancient mountain range, ground down by time and glaciation. The San Juan Islands were named . . ."

"Stop! Stop!" Ruth cried, covering her ears.

"Time out," Wilson joined Ruth. "School's over."

Ricky held up his fingers like a cross against her.

Helma waved her notes toward the rocky shoreline of a small island they were passing. "Don't you want to understand what you're seeing?"

"What for?" Lolly asked. "It's pretty. I'm happy with that. Besides, I want to talk."

"We'll probably never come here again, anyway, Helma," Dora said, setting down a tray full of hot coffee from the shipboard cafe. "What's the point?"

"The point is simply to add to your store of knowledge," Helma tried. "Francis Bacon said, 'Knowledge is power.' "

"And ignorance is bliss," Ricky retorted, grinning proudly.

Ruth pointed at Ricky. "Then you must aspire to the sublime, Ricky."

Helma gave up. "Maybe later," she said, folding her notes in half.

Mr. Westright motioned her to come sit by him. "I'd like to hear about the San Juan Islands, Helma."

"You're welcome to read my notes then," she said, handing him the sheaf of papers.

He smiled at her. "It was the same story twenty years ago. The only surefire method is to threaten a test."

"I doubt if I'd be believed."

"Ah," he sighed, pointing to the east. "Is that Mount Baker?"

The pristine glacier-covered peak hung in the sky above the haze and misted blue hills. "It's a living volcano," Helma told him. "It steams sometimes in the winter."

"Beautiful. What a place to live. You'd expect residing in such surroundings would only engender peace and kindness, wouldn't you?"

"I wish it were so simple."

The ferry passed between rocky islands as random as pebbles scattered from a giant's hand. The tide worked, flowing in toward land, rising along the pale ringed edges of the islands and creeping up the rocky tidal beaches. Beyond, to the west, islands piled up behind islands into the distance, their colors fading from green to blue to miragelike violet.

"Are you happy living here?" Mr. Westright asked.

Helma had never considered that question and she studied the enormity of answering it. She must be; she'd lived in Bellehaven for fifteen years.

"I've lived here for fifteen years," she told Mr. Westright. "I miss Michigan's seasons at times. What about you? Are you happy in Massachusetts?"

"Yes. Yes, I am. My wife's from Massachusetts. I'm suited to life there, to the private school system. There are a lot of Lithuanians there, too, in the Boston vicinity, just like Scoop River."

"You weren't happy in Scoop River."

Mr. Westright laughed. "That's a kind way to describe it, Helma. I wasn't suited to Scoop River but it was a step forward in my educational career. I haven't been back in seventeen years, how about you?"

"Four years ago, for my father's funeral."

"I'm sorry to hear that. Am I right in assuming you haven't been married?" he asked.

"That's right."

"I'm surprised. Look. There's someone's fantasy come true."

The ferry passed a small round island where the evergreen trees grew down to the water, their roots tangling and squeezing between rock fissures. On a small cove of still water, a cedar house sat nestled among the trees, stilts holding it level on the steep slope. The passing ferry reflected majestically in its wall of windows.

Michael sat down next to Mr. Westright.

"I hear you've joined the world of education, too, Michael," Mr. Westright said.

"High school English, only in the public school system, 180 degrees from private education like you're in."

"We all have the same high goals," Mr. Westright said. "To educate our youth."

"Except you're paid substantially more to reach yours."

Mr. Westright nodded. "It's gratifying to teach the more . . . privileged students. What they learn, they have the funding and opportunity to pursue."

"You're saying wealthier students attend better colleges and have more lucrative careers?" Helma asked.

"That *is* true," Michael agreed. "And I'll stay in the public schools for the same reason: Bright kids deserve the best education possible, no matter their parents' income level."

"That's commendable, Michael," Mr. Westright said. "I admire your idealism."

Dora paused beside their booth, checking for empty cups. Michael set his on her tray and she bustled off. Helma glanced over at Miss Higgins and Sister Bea, who were happily chatting with a woman holding a toddler. If the face cream on the floor had been intended for one of them, shouldn't she take measures to assure their protection?

"Do you coach high school basketball, too?" Helma asked Michael.

Michael shook his head. "I play every Wednesday at the Y. That's the extent of it."

"A lot of people were surprised you didn't win a basketball scholarship," Mr. Westright said.

"I was good in a small town like Scoop River but mediocre out there with the big boys." He raised his hands as if he were shooting a basket. "We had some great games, though. Remember the team from St. Stan's? Always at the bottom of the heap because their coach made them cross themselves before they took a shot."

"Did you play the night David Morse died?" Helma asked.

"Sure I did. It was a conference game. Now *he* was a great player."

"Wilson said David acted like he was angry that night."

Michael frowned and smoothed his chin whiskers. "That's right, he did. I don't know why. He'd been owly for a couple of weeks."

"I remember that game," Mr. Westright said. "Because of the accident. Such a shame."

"The newspaper reported there was a fight afterward," Helma said.

"If there was," Michael said, "I missed it."

"Perhaps some people thought Scoop River should have won."

"We *all* thought that. It's tough to lose by one point."

"Losing's always tough," Mr. Westright agreed, "whether it's by one or thirty points."

A plastic bag of peanuts was passed hand to hand. Helma declined and lifted the bag over the back of the booth to Forrest Stevens who fumbled and dropped it in his lap, spilling greasy peanuts across his pants.

"Sorry," Helma said.

"My fault, my fault," Forrest replied, picking up peanuts, not looking at Helma.

A smaller ferry, the *Nisqually*, passed them going in the opposite direction, close enough they could see passengers drinking coffee in the lounge.

In the next seat, Wilson began, "Two ships . . ."

"Say it and you die," Ruth threatened.

Lolly got up from beside Forrest Stevens and headed for the restroom.

"Excuse me," Helma said, rising to follow Lolly.

As Helma entered the restroom, a middle-aged woman exiting from a stall met Helma's eyes, gasped, and stepped back inside the stall, closing the door. Helma heard the tick! of the bolt being drawn. She was so startled she stood staring at the sneakered feet facing wrong way around beneath the stall door.

"This is such a blast, Helma," Lolly said when she saw Helma in the mirror.

"Pardon?" Helma said, meeting Lolly's gaze in the glass.

"Forrest Stevens turned out to be a dream, don't you think? And a doctor, too. I wonder why his wife didn't come. Do you think they're splitting up?"

"He didn't include that in his reservation letter," Helma said. "Lolly, do you remember when David Morse was killed our senior year?"

Lolly turned, screwing her mascara wand back into the tube. "Sure, my cousin had a major crush on him. She'd have *died* for him."

Shivers raced up Helma's arms. "Patty Anne Sands?"

Lolly laughed and touched a pinky finger to the inside corner of her mouth, catching the dab of lipstick there. "No way. My cousin Barb. But David was so crazy about Patty Anne, Barb was totally invisible. She kept hoping Patty Anne would drop Dave but then," Lolly raised her eyebrows. "he goes and dies. What's a girl to do?"

"Why did she think Patty Anne might drop Dave?"

"Barb said Patty Anne was kind of, you know, loose. She liked to play games with the boys. Well, to be honest, Barb called her a ball breaker."

"She's dead, too," Helma said.

"Yeah. I heard. I got the picture she was doing some hot stuff." Lolly shook her hand like she was trying to cool it off. "Fun until you get caught. Poor Dave. Fiona's probably still mad at me over him."

"Fiona? Why?"

Lolly stuck out one hip. "It was back before Dave got to be hot property. Remember Donna Torkas's party?"

"I wasn't there."

"Well, anyway, I left with Dave. Fiona thought he was *her* date."

"That was Dave Morse you left with? *Was* he Fiona's date?"

Lolly shrugged and waved her hand in dismissal. "He brought her but it wasn't like she *owned* him, you know. Besides, Fiona was always looking for an excuse to be pissed at me, after I won that cheerleading contest—and a few other things. She has *no* sense of humor." Lolly considered Helma for a moment. "You've got such great eyes. They'd be dynamite with a little makeup."

Lolly left the restroom and Helma stood before the

mirror, taming the stubborn strand of hair behind her ear.

The stall door opened and the middle-aged woman emerged, an embarrassed smile on her face. "I'm sorry. You work at the public library, don't you?"

Helma immediately understood. Similar incidents had happened before. "And you have overdue library books?" Helma suggested.

The woman laughed. "And a guilty conscience. I get the same way when I cross the Canadian border. Ask me where I'm from and I'm ready to confess."

"I've read that's one sign of an honest person," Helma said.

Helma met Dora entering the restroom as she exited. "Dora," she said. "It's very considerate of you to take an interest in Miss Higgins and Sister Bea. They'd be a little . . . lost without you."

Dora beamed. "I try to be helpful," she said. She leaned forward and whispered, "Did you learn any more about David Morse's death?"

"Actually, if you have a moment, I'd like to talk to you about Patty Anne Sands."

"I'm in a desperate hurry right now," Dora said, already reaching for the button of her yellow pants. "Can we do it later?"

At Shaw Island, where the ferry landing was operated by Franciscan nuns, Sister Bea waved down to a young nun in a brown habit and black tennis shoes working the ramp controls. "Peace be with you," she called.

"And also with you," the young nun called back and then, in unison, the two nuns made the sign of the cross.

"That's spooky," Ruth said. "It's like a secret sign."

"It *is* a secret sign," Wilson Jones told her.

One of the tourists snapping photos of the young nun quickly turned his camera and caught Sister Bea leaning over the railing, her old face glowing with peace and satisfaction.

The ferry slipped past island after island: dull sheer cliffs and bony headlands, gentle meadows and porous sandstone banks, and spits that held houses surrounded by sea grass, with logs and driftwood caught against the narrow shores.

"Looka that!" Wilson Jones said, pointing to a blue and white fishing boat pulling a skiff. "I'd give up my old man's fly rod for a chance at that."

In one shadowed passage where there barely seemed room for the ferry to pass beside the green channel marker, a sculpture of a stylized man stood outside a log house, brooding over the passage's waters. Helma contemplated it as they passed, remembering the Lithuanian shrines her grandfather used to carve to stand sentinel at the edges of his fields.

"Saturday Island's next," Helma announced.

Their first glimpse of Saturday Island was of the smoky green trees that grew close to the rocky shore of the island's tiny black-watered harbor. The clefted hill behind it was densely covered with a forest of fir and cedar accented by ferns, tangled brush, and brilliant mosses. There were no buildings visible except for a tiny concrete structure next to the ferry landing. A single man stood by the ramp controls, smoking a cigarette and watching the ferry approach.

"Where are you taking us, cuz, the end of the world?" Ricky asked.

The ferry shuddered, nudging one of the pilings and sending two seagulls into flight as it docked, its reverse engine churning the water.

Only two bicyclists and two cars—one of them Helma's—and the assembled Scoop River high school class exited the car deck at Saturday Island. The other car and the bicyclists sped away up a narrow road that quickly disappeared into the dark trees.

Helma pulled into the lot next to the square building and parked a safe distance from a multicolored pickup with a rope tying the driver's door closed. A half-dozen older cars, battered and dirty, some the caliber of junkyard inhabitants, were parked nearby. She locked her car and joined the group beside the ferry ramp.

"I'll be in next week to bring back those books," the woman from the restroom called down to Helma from the passenger deck.

"Passing out overdue notices again?" Ruth asked.

Seconds later, the gleaming green and white ferry disappeared around the curve of the island and the Scoop River reunion class moved closer together in the sudden and complete silence: twenty-two brightly dressed, wide-eyed, expectant tourists and their luggage.

"Where's our bus?" somebody asked.

"They're late."

"These people live on this island and they don't know what time the ferry arrives?" Ricky asked incredulously.

The beefy dock attendant finished putting the sawhorse barricades in front of the ferry approach and reentered the concrete building without so much as a nod in their direction, slamming the door behind him.

Helma checked her watch. It was her practice never to wait longer than fifteen minutes for anyone or anything. Fifteen minutes was her limit. Period.

Roman unzipped a leather case and set up a tripod and camera, aiming it at a heron standing regally in the shallows at the edge of the harbor.

Fiona spotted a blackberry bush and she and Sandy Snow began picking them into an empty potato chip bag.

In the curious way names sometimes reflected people, Sandy Snow was pale, with hair the color of a sand dune, lashes and eyebrows that were nearly invisible against her skin, and barely defined lips. As in high school, she wore no makeup and the effect was still of pale, youthful androgeny.

"What are those trees?" Wilson Jones asked. "They look like they belong in a jungle." He pointed to the twisted coppery brown trees at the edge of the forest, their paperlike bark peeling off to reveal brilliant green skin beneath.

"Madronas," Helma told him. "They grow near salt water."

"Don't look like they'd be good for much, all twisted up like that."

"Where is this lodge, anyway?" Lolly asked. "Can we walk?"

"The owner said it was four miles from the ferry dock," Helma told her. "It's too far to walk. I'm sure they're just momentarily detained."

"Is this a junkyard?" Ricky asked, pointing at the older cars parked behind the dock attendant's building.

"Island cars," Helma explained. "Some islanders keep an old car to get around the island and a better car on the other side."

"These people are smarter than I thought."

"I'm sure they'll appreciate knowing that," Ruth told Ricky.

When Helma's watch showed fifteen minutes had passed, she entered the tiny concrete building. The man inside was bent over a chessboard, his brows intently drawn together.

"Excuse me," Helma said.

He held up his hand, cautioning her to silence without looking up.

She waited politely until she'd mentally recited three stanzas of "The Owl and the Pussycat."

"I'd like some information, please," she said in her silver dime voice.

He looked up and grinned, younger than she'd thought. "I wondered how long you'd wait."

"Was this a test of some kind?"

"Just curious. What can I do for you?"

"Someone from Gull Rock Inn was supposed to meet us and transport us to the resort," she explained.

"They're closed."

"You're mistaken. We," Helma pointed to her classmates, "have reservations for the weekend at Gull Rock Inn. All of us."

He frowned at the group as if they'd mysteriously materialized, and he fully expected them to vanish quietly from his territory.

"Well," he said, drawing out the word. "Two days ago, Bootie, who cooks up there, moved off-island. Word I had was the place was coming down so some California hot shot could turn it into getaway, time-share condominiums and aren't we natives just tickled pink about it?" He raised his voice and moved a threatening step closer to Helma.

"I don't know anything about *that*," Helma told him, holding her place, despite the odor of his cigarette breath.

"But I *do* know we have confirmed reservations at the Gull Rock Inn."

She glanced out at Ruth standing next to Mr. Westright, a half-head taller, making some point by waving her hands. Ruth had been in charge of the accommodations. Ruth had investigated the Gull Rock Inn. Ruth had assured her there was "nothing to worry about." So why was Helma, not Ruth, in here dealing with the absent transportation?

"Just a moment, please," she told the dock attendant.

"Oh-oh," Ruth said when she saw Helma approaching. "Problems?"

"Ruth, you did confirm our reservations this week when I reminded you, didn't you?"

Ruth drew herself taller. She inclined her head regally toward Helma. "Why?"

"Did you?"

"What was the point? I'd already sent the menus over. They knew we were coming."

"Has something gone wrong?" Mr. Westright asked.

"I hope not. I'll need to make a call first." She shot a glance at Ruth, who only raised her chin and gazed out over the water.

The attendant was back at his chess game. He didn't look up as Helma reentered his domain.

"Where's the pay phone?" Helma asked.

"Isn't one on the island."

"I must call the Gull Rock Inn."

"You can use mine, I guess," he said, pointing to a black desk phone. "It belongs to the state."

"I'll be gentle with it." Helma removed the Gull Rock Inn's card and dialed the number. It rang six times.

"Yeah?" a man's voice answered.

"Is this the Gull Rock Inn?"

"Yeah."

"This is Miss Helma Zukas. We have reservations for twenty-three for the weekend and we're here at the ferry dock waiting for transportation."

Helma finally broke the ensuing long silence by asking, "Have we been disconnected?"

"I'll get my wife."

While Helma waited she glanced around the small office. A thick-haired yellow dog lay on top of a blue diving suit, head on paws, seriously regarding Helma. A stack of western paperbacks leaned against the leg of the desk next to a six-pack of Coke, and a dusty radio sat on the shelf above the desk. The attendant rocked back in his chair, watching Helma, blatantly listening to every word.

"This is Diana Scott," a slow, measured—Helma would have thought sleepy if it weren't the middle of the afternoon—voice said in her ear.

Helma explained the situation again, listening to Diana Scott's steady breathing and another, barely audible conversation leaking through the line like buzzing bees.

"This is confusing," Diana Scott said. "We had a cancellation of your reservations last week."

Helma was so stunned she could only repeat, "Last week?"

"Mm-hmm. We were very disappointed since we'd prepared the rooms for you, laid in food and all."

"Canceled? By whom?"

"I took the call myself. The person was most apologetic and offered to compensate us for our trouble."

"But who? Who was it? A man or a woman?"

"Oh, it was a man. He said he was your husband. I thought it was a little odd, you calling yourself miss and all, and the other woman making the reservations in the first place, but who am I to judge? I'm really sorry."

"But we're all here, down at the dock."

"We're in the midst of packing up the place. It's coming down, you know."

"But . . ."

"I'm sorry. Truly."

✺ chapter nine ✺

GULL
ROCK INN

"When's the next ferry?" Helma asked the dock attendant.

He scratched his head. "The interislander at four-thirty will get you to Orcas Island and you can catch an eastbound from there."

"That's it?"

"Going east, it is. Until tomorrow. Saturday Island's not exactly on the island freeway."

"Does the county have a branch library here?" Helma asked, wondering what they would do until the next ferry.

The man laughed shortly and the dog wagged its feathery tail. "Library? We don't even have a post office."

Helma left his concrete building, slowly walking back to the group. Her classmates stood in a semicircle, silent, all eyes on her, their faces expectant. It was similar to a dream she'd had of standing in front of the entire student body to give a speech on the electoral college, then suddenly realizing she'd forgotten to research the topic.

"There's a problem," Helma announced. A breeze of murmurs went through the group. Ricky put a hand on his hip, a smile of satisfaction on his face.

"Through a miscommunication our reservations at the

Gull Rock Inn have been canceled. They can't accommodate us. We'll have to return to Bellehaven on the four-thirty ferry and find accommodations for everyone. We can arrange a dinner at the Sun Break Motel, in the Orca Room, or . . ." she trailed off. She'd *wanted* to cancel, hadn't she? But not like *this*.

"Bellehaven is a beautiful setting," Mr. Westright said, turning the crowd's attention from Helma to himself. "I say if we must go back, a little get-together in the Sun Break would be just as enjoyable."

"Canceled?" Ruth asked Helma in a hushed voice. "Who canceled our reservations?"

"My husband."

Ruth grinned. "That dog."

"This is like canceling our whole reunion," Lolly complained, her lower lip protruding. "And I thought it was going to be the best time in my life. All of us together and everything."

Ruth frowned and Helma knew she was thinking the same thing: whoever had canceled the Gull Rock Inn reservations had to be the same anonymous letter-writer who'd warned them against holding the reunion in the first place, who might have been involved in two murders, who might have intended harm against Miss Higgins. And worst of all, it was possibly someone standing right here at the ferry dock, someone taking pains right up to the last minute to make sure this reunion didn't take place.

Dora unzipped her suitcase and pulled out a yellow sweater. "It's getting cold," she said.

"It's just shady," Fiona said, looking up to where the sun had passed behind the dense trees.

"And damp."

" 'So dim so dank so dense so dull so damp so dark so dead,' " Wilson Jones said.

"Why, Wilson," Ruth said, smiling at him. "That's unlike you."

He shrugged modestly. "It's a Chinese poem. I memorized it 'cause it makes me feel like I've been dropped in a hole."

"And that's good?"

"It reminds me how bad things can *really* get."

A seagull landed on top of the ferry building, strutting and studying the group. Then, deciding no food was forthcoming, it flapped away.

"Not so efficient as you thought, huh cuz?" Ricky's voice came from the crowd. "Can't organize people like you do library books?"

"Oh, can it, zucchini-face," Wilson Jones answered. "It isn't her fault."

"*Que sera sera*," Sister Bea said, and Miss Higgins patted Helma's arm.

"Yeah, then whose is it? I canceled a trip to a gun show in Detroit to come out here."

"The choice was completely your own," Helma reminded Ricky.

"And how much did it cost you to get here?" Ruth asked. "Didn't Helma make sure you didn't have to spend a single frigging precious dime?"

"That's beside the point," Ricky said. "I want to know . . ."

Ricky was interrupted by a beat-up yellow pickup truck rattling around a bend. The driver headed straight for them, hood jouncing, muffler popping, bearded face visible through the cracked windshield.

They scattered to either side, parting so the truck could get through. The pickup stopped in their midst and the driver lazily stepped out. He was lanky and loose and wore bleached-out jeans and a wrinkled plaid shirt. His reddish beard was touched with white and his deeply receded hairline exposed a scalp that gleamed on either side of a narrow blondish swatch. When he grinned, his whole beard moved, like all the hair and skin of his face were one piece.

"Hi!" he said, leaning against the hood of his truck and crossing his arms. "I'm Captain Larry from Gull Rock Inn. Diana sent me down." He stopped as if that were explanation enough.

"To apologize?" Ruth prompted.

He glanced at Ruth and the beard moved upward.

"Nah, she said to come on up to the inn. We can fix you up after all. The staff's gone but she went over to the store to get some food and see if she can round up a couple girls for the weekend. The menu'll be different than you wanted."

"She told me she'd purchased food," Helma said.

"Sure, but when you canceled, we had one hell of a party. Right, Jer?" he called over Helma's head. The dock attendant stood in the doorway and nodded, holding up one thumb.

"This isn't what I'd planned . . ." Helma began. She'd envisioned a nice clean powder blue van with "Gull Rock Inn" tastefully painted in script along the side and a driver in white shirt and dark slacks, with good teeth—maybe an anthropology major who'd entertain them with stories of island history while he drove them to an exquisite resort where the sun shone on colored umbrellas sheltering tables scattered about a perfect lawn.

"Sounds great to me."

"We're already here. Why not?"

"But it won't be . . ." Helma tried again.

"C'mon, Helm," Ruth said softly. "You gonna let this anonymous twirp ruin the reunion?"

"Is the band still available?" Helma asked Captain Larry.

Captain Larry shrugged. "Canceled. But hey, we'll get another one together no problem." Again he called over Helma's shoulder. "You seen Stony go off today, Jer?"

"Nope."

"What about Ernestine?"

"Here, as far as I know."

"See, just that easy," Captain Larry said to Helma, his beard rising upward again.

Helma didn't see at all but everyone else laughed appreciatively.

"Let's do it!"

"I'm willing."

"Me too."

Helma considered the battered pickup. "How will we get to the inn?"

"The van's off-island already. Sold it, actually. But you've got your car and I've got my truck. We can make a couple of trips."

"Bet we could do it in one trip," Wilson Jones said, challenge deepening his voice.

"Think so?" Captain Larry asked, an answering challenge in his own. "I can come back and get your luggage."

"Sure. Sit on a few laps. Squeeze buns together. No problem."

"I get to sit on Forrest's lap," Lolly announced, wrapping her pink-nailed hands around Forrest's arm.

Before Helma could protest, her classmates were gaily jumping into the bed of the pickup, giggling and laughing, squeezing into the cab and filling Helma's car. Miss Higgins and Sister Bea sat up front with Helma. Six more, including Roman and his wife, crowded into her backseat.

"Follow me," Captain Larry said.

"Wagons ho," Helma muttered as Captain Larry pulled away from the pile of luggage, his pickup loaded with near middle-aged classmates, twittering and screeching.

"Oh, look," Miss Higgins said. "Can you believe what that silly Lolly is doing!"

"Are they singing?" Sister Bea asked.

Sure enough, over the rattling of Captain Larry's pickup and the sound of the Buick's engine, Helma heard strains of "Ninety-six bottles of beer on the wall, ninety-six bottles of beer. Take one down . . ."

The pickup traveled up the hill through the dark shadowed trees on a narrow, bumpy, but paved road. Then the forest opened onto a small treeless plateau that swept toward the sea like a wing. Three buildings occupied the plateau. Captain Larry waved out the window toward the largest building, which didn't have a sign but appeared to be a store. A red-haired woman loading bags of groceries into the back of a station wagon waved back, laughing. The young boy helping her watched the pickup and Helma's car pass without smiling.

"That must be the commercial district," Roman said dryly from the back.

Then the road followed the curve of the shoreline, up a high bluff where the trees were windblown and bare on the side facing into the wind and water, as if under perpetual assault.

They passed a driveway shrouded by cedars and thick shrubbery, the house invisibly expensive and exclusive behind its padlocked wrought-iron gate. They continued past a mobile home with a tireless red Corvair on cement blocks in the overgrown yard. A hawk soared above them, following the shoreline, curious at their raucous passage.

The scenery changed with each curve of the island, microclimates of mossy shadowed trees and the dank smell of composting vegetation, then a treeless shoreline of rippling pale grasses and rocky outcroppings bearing up the land and forming tiny scallops and tide pools along the water. In a meadow thick with Queen Anne's lace, full-blown thistle, and bracken ferns already turning yellow gold, a rabbit leapt across the road, paws barely skimming the pavement.

They dipped low, close to mossy rocks and lapping water.

"That must be it, up there," Miss Higgins said.

A long driveway turned off the road and away from the rocks, stretching across a windswept plain to a sprawling white Victorian building. It was clapboard with molded cornices and carved scrolls at the corners. A round tower accented the center of the building, encircled by glass windows. Bay windows and multipaned casements sparkled in the long walls. There was an adjoining carriage house and beside the inn, the delicate gingerbread of a gazebo.

It was breathtaking. As they drew closer they saw how the inn occupied a level, treed promontory that protruded into a narrow bay, cliffs and water on every side except from their approach.

"It's like it sits on a little Rock of Gibraltar," Sister Bea exclaimed.

"Oh my, what's that?" Miss Higgins asked, pointing out the car window.

"I think it's the future," Mr. Westright said.

Helma slowed her car. Beneath a rise to their left crouched a silent army of heavy equipment, all engines turned toward Gull Rock Inn, awaiting the green flag. Bulldozers, tractors, earth movers and dump trucks, dirt and mud mottling their yellow sides and clinging to their gigantic tires. To one side stood a portable toolshed, portable toilets, and the construction trailer. The earth was scarred and rutted from the road to their encampment.

Even the riders in the back of Captain Larry's pickup fell silent, peering at the looming destructors of Gull Rock Inn.

Helma shook her head, forcing away the image of terraces of bright condominiums, grouped to take the best advantage of the view, all identical with duplicated balconies decorated by wind socks and pots of red geraniums. A clubhouse and a pool, maybe even a golf course. Most certainly a new road would be cut across the island and guarded by security gates.

"Progress," Miss Higgins sniffed.

"A development in a spot like this will return millions to the investors," Roman Fonsilwick said in admiration.

Captain Larry drove the pickup to the wide front doors and the truck shuddered to a stop. Helma pulled her Buick in close behind him.

It was completely silent, eerily still. The pinging of cooling engines, the breeze ruffling grasses nearby, and the water lapping at the rocks beneath the inn were the only sounds.

They whispered self-consciously as they left the vehicles and stood together on the gravel drive in front of the Gull Rock Inn. A mossy-roofed birdhouse stood in a garden of impatiens. Other plants were perennials: hydrangeas, lily of the valley, daisies; overrunning their borders, untrimmed, mixed with chickweed and nettles. An empty hummingbird feeder swung from the branch of a Bigleaf maple.

Close up, it was apparent that Gull Rock Inn had lived a long life. The foundation had settled, softening its roof and wall lines. Window glass had rippled, and here and there, white paint chipped and curled off the clapboards, exposing bare wood. Still, it stood grandly on its last legs, a dignified old structure that had outlived itself.

"It's so cute," Lolly said, breaking the spell, looking up at the high white walls of the inn.

"Beautiful maybe," Ruth said. "Impressive, yes. But cute. I don't think so."

"Go on in," Captain Larry told them. "I'll run back and get your bags." And he was off, driving at what seemed a breakneck, sacrilegious manner down the narrow drive.

Helma noticed a small bronze plaque hanging beside the door. "Gull Rock Inn," it read, "1912."

"We may as well go inside and look around," she said.

They entered like students on a field trip, through the tall wooden doors that reminded Helma of a church entry, into a large foyer of once elegant but now scarred woodwork and faded wallpaper. Couches and chairs were shrouded in white sheets and a stale odor caused Helma's nose to twitch: mildew. Boxes were piled three-high against one wall. "Towels," was written on the side of one in black crayon, "Guest soaps" on another. Curtain rods lay across the top of the boxes.

"Hello?" Ruth called.

"A riot! A riot!" a voice screeched, then burst into a whistled rendition of the "1812 Overture."

In a brass cage on a pedestal by the inn's desk, a gray cockatiel skittered from one end of his perch to the other, bobbing his head, his round black eyes watching them.

"A riot! A riot!" he screamed.

Helma, who believed birds belonged in trees, in the air, or on telephone wires—not in cages—stayed back while her classmates gathered around the cage.

"Pretty, pretty Polly want a cracker?" Lolly asked.

Wilson Jones thrust one finger into the cage and the cockatiel promptly bit him.

"Yow!" Wilson yelped. "Vicious bas . . . bird."

"His name's Harry," Ruth said, pointing to the sign above his cage. "And it says here, he bites."

"No kidding."

"What a riot," Lolly said.

Off one side of the foyer, glass doors led into a conservatory, an octagonal room completely constructed of glass and filled with outdoor light, where now only a few plants and a wrought-iron bench remained.

Connected to the foyer was a dining room with chairs turned upside down on tables, more boxes, some scribbled with "Water glasses," and "Coffee cups." Bright squares marked the walls where pictures had been removed. One side of the dining room was a wall of glass. As one, they moved to the windows, murmuring in delight and awe.

"Wow, I haven't seen a view like this since I was up by Frankfort," Joey Barnes said.

"Remember King's Canyon before Consumers Power put in the hydroelectric plant?" Sandy Snow asked.

"I feel dizzy," Lolly said, stepping back. "Heights make me feel like I'm supposed to jump, you know what I mean?"

The edge of the dining room hung out over the cliff. Looking down, Helma found herself gazing only into water swirling against the rocks below, catching in eddies and barely hiding, she suspected, even more boulders and dangerous obstructions.

"I'd like my condo right here, please," Wilson said.

"Hah!" Michael told him, "This is where the clubhouse goes, I bet."

"Are those clouds coming in? Are we going to get some of that famous Northwest rain?"

"Maybe," Ruth replied. "It's kind of hazy. Hard to tell."

"Look what I found!"

Everyone turned from the window to look at Ricky. In a cove at the far end of the dining room was a lounge the size of a small-town establishment. A gleaming wooden bar with a rolled edge and leather bar stools stood against one wall. Bottles of liquor sparkled in ascending rows in front of the wall mirror, untouched by the packers. The window in the lounge was a giant porthole that shadowed the bar area to soft intimacy.

"Ricky, you may have justified your existence," Wilson Jones said.

"Why?" Ruth challenged. "Are you saying we couldn't have discovered the bar without him?"

"Psst," Michael Petronas caught their attention, nodding toward the dining room door.

A large woman with wiry gray hair pulled straight back into a bun stood in the doorway holding a box marked "Single sheets." She might have been thirty or she might have been fifty. She didn't smile. She didn't move.

"Are you Diana?" Helma asked. "We had reservations."

"Cornelian," she said. "You're the folks who changed their minds. I've come to work."

"Is Diana here?" Helma asked Cornelian.

"Not so I've seen her. I've come to work."

"Let me help you," Dora Durbas said, bustling forward and taking the box from Cornelian's arms, amiably following after the silent woman.

"It's Mrs. Dudley," Michael said. " 'I leave before dark comes. So there won't be anyone around if you need help.' "

" 'If you scream in the night,' " Helma added.

Ruth looked at them blankly.

"Shirley Jackson," Helma provided. "*The Haunting of Hill House.*"

"You mean this place is *haunted*?" Lolly asked.

"Woooo!" Ricky moaned, holding his arms above his head and swaying over Lolly.

"This would be *my* favorite vacation haunt if I was a ghost," Ruth said.

A woman in shorts and a red t-shirt entered the dining room, her round face shiny with perspiration. She carried two bags of groceries and behind her a sullen teenage girl, with hair cropped on one side like a boy's, carried two more.

The woman chewed gum and every few chews, cracked it like hot grease. "I'm Diana. Meet Kiki. I just drafted her to help in the kitchen. You guys find your way around okay?"

"We just arrived," Helma explained. She waved toward the upturned chairs and the packed boxes. "It doesn't look like you can accommodate us at all."

Diana cracked her gum. "It'll be okay. I couldn't get much of a staff but we can handle it, right, Kiki?"

The teenager shrugged. Five tiny gold hoops festooned one ear and each of her fingernails was painted a different color.

"We'll put this stuff away and show you your rooms.

I passed Captain Larry so he'll be here in a few minutes with your luggage."

"Is there a TV?" Ricky asked.

"No," Diana said. "The stereo's already packed, too. Sorry. Just . . . I don't know, have a drink or something." And she and Kiki departed through the swinging doors to the kitchen.

"She talks my lingo," Wilson Jones said, heading for the bar.

Captain Larry carried in their luggage, dropping it barely inside the foyer, then leaned against the desk and watched them sort it out. Diana joined him, handing him a frosted chocolate donut, which he broke in half and ate in two bites.

"The dealers are coming next week to strip the place," Diana told them, waving a hand at the wall fixtures, the carved bannister, and the rosewood paneling, "and as soon as they're finished the walls come tumbling down."

"What about you?"

"We're spending the rest of our lives in Mexico," Captain Larry said, "where it's warm."

"And cheap," Diana added. "Your rooms are on two floors, all facing the water. Cornelian might not have made them all up yet. None of the doors lock so you can leave valuables in our safe if you want."

"Two floors?" Helma asked. "One for men and one for women?"

Diana regarded Helma uncertainly. "Is that what you had in mind?" she asked doubtfully.

"Hell-mah!" Ruth groaned. "You're reverting to high school chaperone mentality. This is twenty years later, remember? We're bona-fide grownups." She pointed to the lines at the corner of her eyes. "See? Wrinkles to prove it."

"You made your point, Ruth. You can stop now."

"Well, you're welcome."

Helma and Ruth shared a room with white wainscoting and sun-streaked blue wallpaper. The drapes had already been removed. Mildew spotted the window frames and a Joan Hess paperback someone had left sitting on the bureau was swollen and warped to ripples, the cover curling backward.

"Don't worry about the drapes," Ruth told Cornelian, who was making up the beds. "Who's going to look in up here, anyway?"

There was a sink in each room but the bathrooms were on either end of the hall. Helma removed her can of disinfectant spray and a sponge from her suitcase and set them on the sink.

"Which bed do you want?" Ruth asked after Cornelian silently left.

"The one that's not so close to the window."

"Suits me. I'm not planning on spending much time here, anyway." Ruth held up her hand. "Good clean fun, that's all, Helma. Make every minute count, you know."

Helma checked to be sure the door was completely closed behind Cornelian. She turned to Ruth. "Someone tried to cancel this reunion and I suspect they're here on the island with us."

Ruth pulled an oversized orange t-shirt from her gym bag, not bothering to pick up the black underwear that spilled onto the floor. "Well, they failed, didn't they? So maybe they'll lay off now."

"That doesn't change what's already happened."

Ruth flopped on her bed. "Yeah, I know. I've had my suspicious eye on everybody, really. Aside from your cousin Ricky's general pig's butt personality, the whole gang looks clean to me. What do you think?"

Helma sighed and sat on her own bed. "The same," she agreed. "But we can't relax our vigilance. Whoever it is, he's bound to misjudge the limits of his deception. Criminals always do."

Helma tapped on Miss Higgins's door. Sister Bea answered. On one of the beds, a black suitcase sat open, and beside it, two tidily folded stacks of black clothing. Helma paused before entering the room, quickly absorbing the "feel," scanning its simple details for anything out of place.

"Is your room comfortable?" Helma asked. "Do you need anything?"

"Aren't you sweet?" Miss Higgins said from the closet where she was hanging a pink dress. "We're fine, dear. What a fabulous view."

The towel rack was secure; there were no suspicious obstacles on the floor; the windows were too far above the floor to trip through.

"I wish more of my classmates could have attended," Helma said. "It would be fun to see Susan Stamas, or even David Morse."

Miss Higgins paused, one hand raised toward the closet pole. "Poor David. So young."

"Did you have him in Latin class?"

"Oh no. I don't believe David was Latin material. He was in my study hall. My, how the girls buzzed around him."

Helma lifted a blue dress from Miss Higgins's suitcase and shook it out. "He had a fiancée, Patty Anne Sands, from Hopkins."

Miss Higgins frowned. "I don't believe I knew her."

"Was David ever a problem student? Did you have to give him special attention?"

"He was never a problem, but he was a little full of himself; a little sad, too."

"Why do you say that? Did he confide in you?"

Miss Higgins took the blue dress from Helma and slipped it on a hanger. "No. But once, not long before he died . . . well, remember that old water tower by the teacher's parking lot? I saw him sitting up there, on the very edge. It was dangerous, high like that, and in winter, too."

"What did you do?"

"I ordered him to come down that very moment. He did, and I got in my car and drove home. That was all."

❧ chapter ten ❧

EVENING
APPROACHES

Helma and Ruth strung crepe paper streamers in the dining room while dishes clattered and voices rose in the kitchen. Dora Durbas had marched boldly into the thick of it, her sleeves rolled up to her elbows, a butcher's apron tied around her body. She cooked, set tables, directed Kiki, commented on the decorations.

"That woman should run an old people's home," Ruth said.

Listening to Dora's industriousness, Helma realized that since telling Dora on the ferry that she wanted to discuss Patty Anne Sands, Dora had managed to be organizing either Gull Rock Inn or Miss Higgins and Sister Bea whenever Helma appeared.

"Ouch," Ruth said, pulling a thumbtack off the tip of her finger.

"Have you seen Miss Higgins and Sister Bea?" Helma asked Ruth.

"Safe and sound, taking a nap," Ruth told her, and stuck her finger in her mouth.

Their classmates were outside. She'd seen Roman, golf bag over his shoulder and *Jean* by his side, heading for a slope of the lawn that edged the cliff.

Captain Larry had disappeared into the manager's

apartment off the foyer, leaving the Scoop River class in charge of themselves. "Give a shout if you need anything," he said. Diana meandered through the inn, amiably smiling at whatever they did. "Let me know if you need anything," she said.

The class unshrouded furniture, took chairs down from the tables, and unpacked enough dishes and cutlery for the Scoop River group. Wilson and Michael searched the rooms until they found pictures to hang over the bare spots on the walls. Helma hung Ruth's door prize painting—slashes of purples and yellows she hoped she hung right side up—by the dining room doors. Lights were turned on, and finally there was an illusion of an operating, if slightly shabby, grand old resort.

Elsewhere in the inn, rooms were empty of furniture and boxes were piled behind doors. Holes gaped on either side of the entrance where rhododendrons had been dug out. An air of transience permeated Gull Rock Inn, an awareness of impermanence and termination, as if the wrecking equipment just beneath the hill stealthily ground forward a few feet each time they turned their backs.

"I bet you'll miss living here," Ruth said to Diana, who slouched in a bar chair, eating a Hershey's bar and watching Ruth and Helma hang crepe paper.

"Not really. The inn needs too much work, taxes are going sky high, and people want luxury anyway. They're disgusted if they have to share bathrooms and they want room service, so they don't have to come down and eat what's on the menu." Diana smiled. "Besides, we're making out like bandits."

"More to the left, Ruth. Speaking of menus," Helma began, but Diana anticipated her.

"Dinner won't be quite what you had in mind. Mac's is the only store on the island and I cleaned him out. Your friend's doing her best. It's a good thing she cooks because Bootie's gone and I'm sure no Julia What's-her-name. If we'd known sooner . . ."

Helma glanced at Ruth who'd stated scornfully that

confirming reservations was "too anal retentive to mention."

"Relax, Helm. This has taken on a life of its own. It'll be all right, you'll see."

"It's two-thirty now. Mr. Broder's coming in by private plane at five. Dinner's at seven. I trust the music's been arranged?" she asked Diana.

"Captain Larry talked to Ernestine and Stony. They'll be here."

"I'm afraid to ask," Ruth said, "but what do they play?"

"Stony plays the concertina and Ernestine's brilliant on the hammered dulcimer."

"An interesting combination. Do they do any Rolling Stones? Beatles? Alice Cooper?"

"They can play anything you have a mind for," Diana said with certainty.

"Have you seen my screwdriver, Di?" Captain Larry asked, entering with another chocolate donut in his hand.

"It was on the top of the box of serving trays by the desk."

"Isn't there now." He grinned, his beard twitching upward. "Guess I can't take off those doorstops after all." He bit into the donut and ambled out of the dining room.

"I'd better go find it," Diana said, rising from her chair. "We've got a buyer who's paying big bucks for all those old brass doorstops, can you believe it?"

As she left the dining room, Diana stopped and studied Ruth's painting. Ruth paused, watching and waiting expectantly. Finally Diana turned. "Thank you for painting this picture," she said with no indication of approval or disapproval, and left the dining room.

Ruth's eyes widened. She stuck out her tongue at Diana's back. "Oh, you're quite welcome," she called after Diana. "It was nothing. Thank you for thanking me."

A moment later, Ruth held up empty hands. "Whoops, Helm, we're out of blue crepe paper. Guess we'll have to quit now."

"There's another roll upstairs in our room."

"It looks good to me the way it is," Ruth said, leaning on the top step of her ladder.

"It's not even," Helma told her. "I'll be right back."

"Even? Don't you know 'being even' is death on artistic expression?"

Helma ran up the staircase to the second floor and down the scuffed hallway carpeting to the room she shared with Ruth. They were nearly finished; why did Ruth always give up so easily?

She took an extra roll of gold crepe paper from the cardboard box marked "Decorations," just in case.

Helma was nearly to the stairs when she heard an unidentifiable soft sound behind her. She stopped and turned around. The hallway, with its faded walls and sloping floor, was empty from one end to the other. She listened. A murmur of voices came from outside where the others were exploring. A tinny banging that sounded like pans being knocked together came from downstairs. But nothing else. No movement, no sound. The doors to the rooms were all closed; the second floor was silent, close, almost expectant.

"If someone is there, please reveal yourself at once," Helma said.

There was no answer. Light slanted in through the window above the steps. She swallowed and, breathing evenly, walked calmly to the staircase and down the steps, ignoring the disturbing sensation that she was being watched.

"A riot!" Harry the cockatiel called as she passed through the empty foyer.

"That was fast," Ruth said, resignedly holding out her hand for the crepe paper.

"I knew where it was," Helma told her.

Kiki opened the door from the kitchen, her face a study in deadly boredom.

"What's up, Sunshine?" Ruth asked.

"Phone call for the library lady," Kiki said, and stepped back into the kitchen.

"Phone call for the library lady," Ruth repeated in a robotic monotone, pointing a spectral finger at Helma.

It was Eve at the Bellehaven Public Library.

"Oh, Helma. I'm sorry to call you during your party,"

she said, her voice muffled as if her hand was cupped over the mouthpiece. "It's one of our . . . 'behaviorally unpredictable' patrons. He's insisting you're the only one who can help him. He won't leave. Do you think . . . Could you talk to him? He's threatening to set up camp in front of the desk. Please," Eve pleaded, sounding close to tears.

"Which one is it?" Helma asked. There were more "behaviorally unpredictable," as Ms. Moon called them, every year. Men and sometimes women who were disruptive, odd-eyed, and who the staff treated with an exaggerated courtesy, firmness, and whatever worked.

"Buggy Man."

Helma would never refer to him by that name but she knew who Eve meant. Instead of pushing a grocery cart along the streets of Bellehaven, Buggy Man pushed a shiny black and chrome baby carriage laden with neatly folded brown paper bags and two beagle dogs.

Buggy Man had an intense and abiding interest in the sinking of the *Titanic*, a tragedy which Helma had mistakenly told Buggy Man that she too agreed could have been avoided, making Helma Buggy Man's instant and intense confidante.

"Put him on," Helma told Eve.

"Miss Zukas," a voice roared in Helma's ear.

"We have an excellent connection. Please don't disturb the other library patrons."

"Where are you?" he demanded.

"I'm right here. Now what is your question?"

"There was a hearing," he whispered. "I just found out. Did you know?"

"Do you mean after the *Titanic* sank?"

"Yes. No one told me."

"It was in 1912."

"But no one told me. I should have been informed. I need to read it at once. It could answer our questions."

"I'd recommend you inquire at the college library," Helma said. "They have a government documents department. Ask for it there."

"I'll make a report to you when I've studied the material," he said earnestly.

"That will be fine."

Eve came back on the line. "Oh, thank you, Helma. I owe you. I'll bring you pizza every day for a month."

"Once will more than repay me," Helma assured her and hung up, feeling only a twinge of guilt that she'd passed Buggy Man on, picturing him pushing his buggy full of bags and beagles up the steep sidewalks to the local college.

"Everything okay?" Ruth asked.

"It was just a specialized research problem."

"Well, thank you for being a librarian," Ruth said, her speech lazily slow in an uncanny imitation of Diana's 'Thank you for painting this picture.'

Lolly burst into the dining room, her face rosy. She'd changed clothes again, to a one-piece playsuit it was really too cool to wear. "Hurry! Hurry! I've been sent to get you. We're going to play a game outside."

"A game?" Helma asked. "Already?" She'd brought an entire folder of games suggested as ice breakers: "Name my animal." "Pass the orange." "Who do you look like?" Ruth had said the reunion was taking on a life of its own, and it was: an as-yet unshaped life, but one that disregarded well-laid plans and order.

"Oh goody," Ruth said, dropping her crepe paper streamer too eagerly.

Everyone stood on the lawn, surrounding Wilson Jones, who held pads of paper and several pencils, all marked "Gull Rock Inn." A breeze had come up and it ruffled their hair and swept the long grasses into waves.

"The idea is," he announced, "that we break the 'nice ice' around here. Everybody take a piece of paper. On it you write one thing about somebody here. It can be something good, something rotten, something hilarious. Two rules: you have to name a name and you have to be anonymous."

"All right!"

Enthusiastic cheers rose from the group.

"This is potentially dangerous," Helma said to Ruth. "There's no point in dredging up old incidents."

"Why do you suspect anybody'd 'dredge up' slime? We can all confess to our good deeds." Ruth's gaze eagerly moved from face to face, speculating.

Helma doubted the number of good deeds that would be mentioned, not from the glances covertly passing between classmates, not from the way people were shading their paper from one another.

But she tore off a piece of note paper and waited her turn at a pencil, thinking intensely, wondering why her mind spun toward dark memories: dateless proms; sadly eager and unintelligent Hope Guptimas, who the boys had called "Peanut butter legs"; Geoff Jamas.

Lolly pressed her bright pink lips together and coyly hid her paper from Forrest. Roman Fonsilwick smiled in satisfaction and showed his wife his entry.

Wilson held up an argyle sock. "Okay, put them in here and all will be divulged at dinner tonight."

"Is it clean?"

"Only wore it a week."

The sock was passed through the group.

"Hurry up, Helm," Ruth said, holding out the sock.

"Helma," Helma corrected and quickly jotted her memory on the slip, folded it in half, and dropped it in the sock that now crackled with its paper burden.

"Okay," Wilson said. "Witness me tying the sock closed with this here piece of string, inserting said sock in my breast pocket, and buttoning said pocket for safe keeping."

"You look a little sexually confused," Ricky taunted.

"Then you ain't never seen me in the locker room, boy," Wilson said.

"Yeah," Ruth shouted out and when everyone turned to look at her she grinned. "I haven't either. Seen Wilson in the locker room, that is."

"Hey, you guys," Lolly said, raising her arms. "Have you noticed? There aren't any *bugs* here!"

Everyone looked around, squinting for small game.

"Now that you mention it," Michael agreed, "where are the mosquitoes, black flies, piss ants, deer flies, sand fleas? What's the challenge of living in a place without pestilence?"

Fiona stood in the midst of the group, unnoticed except by Helma. The left side of her mouth twitched but she was smiling, watching her classmates search for bugs, happily smiling. Lolly, as she had since their arrival, had placed herself far from Fiona. Helma sensed that like bats with highly developed radar, they each knew the other's location at all times.

Captain Larry's pickup rattled up the driveay toward the inn. A second person sat in the cab. "Must be bringing reinforcements," Fiona said.

"Well, I certainly could use more help in the kitchen," Dora said. "It's no wonder they're going out of business."

Captain Larry got out of his pickup with the most enthusiasm Helma had seen thus far and crossed to the passenger side to open the door, holding it like a chauffeur.

An elegant creature, slender, graceful, light brown hair in a timelessly stylish chignon, large sunglasses obscuring her face, emerged from the pickup as if it were a limousine. Captain Larry pulled a small leather suitcase from the bed of the truck.

"Is that one of us?" Lolly asked. "She's too gorgeous."

"I hate her already," Sandy Snow said.

"I believe it's Amanda Boston," Helma told them.

Michael Petronas stepped up to the pickup first. "Amanda?" he asked.

Amanda smiled and held out her hand. "Michael," she said. She turned toward the rest of them, her eyes invisible behind the dark lenses. "Ruth, Helma, Wilson, Lolly," she acknowledged. "I'm sorry I'm late. I had to catch the later ferry and then the interislander. How amazing to see you all again."

"Are you a movie star?" Lolly blurted out.

Amanda laughed, not unkindly. "No, but I did some modeling a few years ago, if that counts. It improved my posture."

They stood there, smiling, at a loss what to say next, suddenly as tongue-tied as awkward teenagers. Amanda seemed unperturbed, standing poised and beautiful beside Captain Larry's disintegrating pickup.

Diana emerged from the inn to welcome Amanda and they gratefully transferred their attention to her. "All the rooms on the water side of the inn are taken," she said. "Unless you want to share a room."

"You're welcome to share mine," Dora offered.

"Mine, too," Wilson Jones added.

"Thank you," Amanda said in her soft voice. "But a room without a view is fine."

"I'll have Cornelian get it ready."

"I'd like a glass of water and then, if no one minds, I'll rest for a while. I'll see you all at dinner tonight."

They watched Amanda enter the inn, looking expensive and stylishly understated. Even Roman Fonsilwick's wife stared after Amanda in a mixture of envy and admiration.

"Wilson should ask her to submit her high school memory," Ruth said.

Michael was looking at the door where Amanda had disappeared. "I'm afraid of what she might say," he said, half to himself and so low only Ruth and Helma heard him.

"What memory did you pen, Helma?" Ruth asked as they carried the detritus of their decorating efforts back to their room.

"It was difficult to make up my mind."

Ruth snorted. "Okay, so I won't tell you either. I *did* almost write about your dad's bomb shelter."

"What about it?" It had been her father and Uncle Tony's summer project when Helma was six. Every evening their Lithuanian jokes drifted into her window, the sibilant language blending amiably with birdsong. Digging, drinking, pouring cement, taking pictures of each other.

"He never locked it."

"I know. For expediency if a bomb fell."

"It was convenient for some of us."

"You mean you went into *our* bomb shelter?"

"We didn't hurt anything. Except once when I was dating Hoagie Stolinas: he ate a can of sardines."

"You went into our bomb shelter and didn't even tell me?"

Ruth raised one eyebrow. "What would you have done? Joined us or told your father?"

"I certainly wouldn't have joined you."

"I rest my case."

When it was nearly time for Mr. Broder's arrival, Helma and Ruth left their room together. "He looked good on TV," Ruth was saying. "A skinnier Ted Kennedy type. Well, younger, too, and better looking, maybe shorter. But you know what I mean." Ruth took two steps down the hall and stopped, tipping her head and listening.

"What's that?"

Helma listened, too. The sounds—hissing and buzzing—came from the women's bathroom at the end of the hall. At first, Helma thought it was plumbing gone amiss. Would there be anyone on Saturday Island to repair it?

Ruth grinned and put her finger to her lips. She beckoned Helma to follow her.

The bathroom door was ajar. Through it they had a partial view of Lolly and Fiona facing each other in front of the sinks. Bodies stiff, necks taut, heads foward, arguing in whispers that stretched and shaped their mouths like pantomime. Lolly's face was bright red; burgundy circles spotted Fiona's cheeks.

Ruth took another step toward the bathroom, her eyes lit in anticipation. Helma pulled her back. Ruth tried to shake off Helma's hand but Helma wouldn't let go and rather than make a fuss, Ruth was forced to accompany Helma to the stairs.

"What did you do that for?" Ruth demanded. "It was Lolly and Fiona. We could be missing the Big One."

"It's none of our business, Ruth," Helma said. "It's a private matter between Lolly and Fiona."

Ruth groaned and stomped down the stairs. "How can you be so frigging boring, Helm?" she asked over her shoulder.

"Helma," Helma corrected.

They heard the sea plane before it came into view, the sound of its motor reverberating off the rocks and between the islands.

A path descended through the rocks from the inn to

a long dock in the little harbor beneath the Gull Rock Inn, where Captain Larry had said, "A year from now there'll be a hell of a marina here."

Captain Larry, hands in his pockets, stood on the dock and watched the sea plane circle to improve its approach.

"Gotta be good to land here," Captain Larry observed. "Better be. We don't have any boats left to do a rescue if he screws up."

The red and white plane lightly touched down on its pontoons, spraying up water, cutting its engine. The pilot's door immediately opened and an arm vigorously waved.

"I think that's Broder piloting," Ricky said. "Our own little god has descended into our midst."

Despite his sarcasm, anticipation lightened Ricky's face. Helma looked at him curiously and Ricky's expression reverted to scowling smugness. "What are you staring at?" he demanded.

"You're happy to see Mr. Broder," Helma said, surprised.

"Now you can read minds?" And he turned and headed back toward the inn.

"Ricky!" Helma called after him, but Ricky kept walking, his stride angrily tight.

"Tsk, tsk," Ruth said, looking after Ricky. "You caught your cousin exhibiting a normal human emotion. He's humiliated."

"He's being childish."

"My dear, is this the first you've noticed?"

Mr. Broder exited the plane and stepped from the pontoon onto the dock, trim and athletic, his blond hair now stylishly silver, wearing chinos and a cotton sweater, his hand already out, smiling.

"How are you?" "Wilson, you're looking good." "There you are, Helma. Thanks for inviting me." The professional politician, the campaigner, his handshake strong, warmly greeting each of his former students. "This is an uncommonly beautiful spot you've found for this reunion."

"That was a pretty good landing," Michael said, shaking Mr. Broder's hand.

"Thanks. If there's time, I'll take you up tomorrow."

Mr. Westright stepped forward. "Don," Mr. Broder said, clapping his shoulder, almost too heartily, Helma thought. "How are you?"

"Good, Wayne. How's the political hero?"

Mr. Broder laughed. "I'm hardly that—yet."

The two men stood facing one another, the embodiment of two worlds: politics and education. Mr. Broder outgoing, worldly, and Mr. Westright, reserved, more narrowly self-assured.

They trooped up the path to the inn, Mr. Broder the undisputed center of attention, exhibiting the uncanny skill of including them all while seeming to single each of them out for his undivided attention.

"I'm in love," Ruth whispered to Helma.

"Again?" Helma asked, and Ruth wrinkled her nose at her.

Outside the inn, Mr. Broder stopped to chat with Miss Higgins and Sister Bea who sat facing the sea. They were bundled in wool afghans on wooden deck chairs Captain Larry had pulled from the inn's storage earlier in the day.

"You certainly missed a sight," Sister Bea told them. "The screws were loose on Ellie's chair and it collapsed underneath her. She could have rolled right down the lawn and over the cliff."

Ruth and Helma exchanged quick glances. "Are you all right, Miss Higgins?" Helma asked.

"Don't be silly. Bea's exaggerating. Of course I'm all right. A tender posterior, is all. I don't have the padding I used to." She turned her attention to Mr. Broder.

"You haven't changed much," Miss Higgins said, "except for that silver hair. Is it natural?"

Sister Bea elbowed her but Mr. Broder laughed. "All my own. Do you think it makes me look distinguished?"

Miss Higgins squinted at him. "It would if there weren't so much of it."

"I wish I'd brought my slingbacks," Ruth said, on her knees, pawing through her gym bag.

"You should have packed more than ten minutes before the ferry left," Helma told her.

"Hah! And you accuse *me* of exaggerating?"

Helma studied Ruth's sweater and skirt ensemble. "Ruth," she pointed out, "we never wore poodle skirts in high school. That was before our time."

"We never wore poodle skirts like *this*, you mean," Ruth said, lifting her skirt so Helma could see the design.

Helma recognized the likeness to a poster she'd seen years ago: a poodle with a Mohawk haircut, a vicious expression, and a studded collar.

"Charming," Helma said.

Ruth dropped her skirt. "Sarcasm can't hide your envy, my friend. I can't find my comb. Can I borrow yours?"

Helma was uncomfortable sharing toiletries but if Ruth didn't find her comb she'd be in a snit for half the night. Instead, Helma opened her purse and reached inside for her extra comb.

She felt a slash of pain and, gasping, jerked her hand out of the bag. Blood ran down her palm, dripping off her fingers onto the floor.

"Geez Louise!" Ruth said. She snatched a towel from the sink and threw it at Helma, then grabbed Helma's purse and dumped the contents on her bed.

Helma's wallet, keys, comb, checkbook, address book, a square of aspirins fell onto the bed, and in their midst was the bottom two inches of a brown beer bottle, broken, its jagged edges lethally sharp.

"Cute. Really cute. What rat's ass did this? Are you okay?"

Helma pressed the towel tightly against the gash in her palm. Red seeped through the white. It didn't hurt; it tingled warmly, as if she'd plunged her hand into hot water. "I will be. There's a first-aid kit in my suitcase."

"Why aren't I surprised?" Ruth asked, unzipping Helma's tan suitcase.

"Do you know what color blood is?"

"Yeah, beany brain. It's . . ." Ruth's eyes widened. She sat back on her heels with the open first-aid kit in her hands. "The last anonymous letter! 'Do you know what color blood is?' My God, do you think that's who did this?"

"Who else?"

"Where's your purse been?"

"Either with me or here in our room." She pulled away the towel. A deep cut an inch long was sliced into the lower edge of her palm, blood turgidly welling in it.

Ruth opened a sterile gauze pad and handed it to Helma. "And the rooms don't lock. It could have been *anybody*."

"I hope this is 'real proof' enough for you," Helma said. "Put this together with Miss Higgins's collapsing deck chair and we know one thing for certain." Helma said.

"What's that?"

"The letter-writer is definitely here on this island with us."

🌿 chapter eleven 🌿

HOME COOKING

Dora Durbas, her cheeks flushed pink, her short hair curling in damp tendrils around her face, beamed as her Scoop River classmates entered the crepe paper and balloon decorated dining room. She stood, still in her apron, next to the wooden podium and the space cleared for the musicians, who had yet to arrive.

Ruth waved to Wilson Jones and followed Helma to the circular table, where Roman and his wife and Michael Petronas sat with Mr. Broder and Mr. Westright. "I'm sitting with the grownups tonight," Ruth called to Wilson.

To Helma she whispered, "I'll watch your back if you watch mine."

Helma peered around the dining room, verifying that every classmate was present. Had anyone awakened Amanda? Yes, she sat at the far table, too far to take advantage of the view of the approaching sunset. Yet Helma noted how eyes in the room were continually turning toward Amanda's fair face. Miss Higgins and Sister Bea sat with Fiona at the next table over from Helma, within easy reach and sight.

Diana and Captain Larry, who'd been invited to join the class for dinner, had declined, retreating instead to their apartment. "I only eat when I'm hungry," Captain Larry said.

"It looks like everything's under control," Diana said. "I think I'll take a bath."

By each plate, one of the tiny blue and gold paper flags Helma had brought was stuck into a sparkly pedestal. "I made them out of egg cartons," Dora confided to Helma. "You'd never guess, would you?"

Dora held up the program with the original menu printed in it. "There had to be a few changes in the menu," she announced. "Don't forget this is an island and we had to work with what was available on short notice."

"Oh oh. That sounds like a warning," Michael said.

Ruth raised her program and squinted, reading aloud the original menu Helma had planned. "Seafood bisque, spinach salad, scallop provencale, baby carrots, raspberry cheesecake. Sounds scrumptiously Northwest."

Under Dora's watchful eye, Kiki and Cornelian each carried a tray of food into the dining room. The group silenced in anticipation.

"What happened to your hand, Helma?" Mr. Broder asked.

Helma removed her bandaged hand from the table to her lap. "I scraped it on . . ."

"She cut it with her scissors when we were hanging all this crepe paper," Ruth said, kicking Helma under the table. "Clumsy, isn't she?"

Helma turned her attention to the window. The sun lowered toward the horizon, but it appeared to be dropping into dense shadow, distorting as it fell. The earlier haze of the day had thickened, forming wisps of low clouds over the ground that obscured the view of the next island and condensed in tiny droplets on the dining room windows. Mr. Broder saw Helma looking out the window and said, "The weather report said possible fog."

"They were right."

"I didn't think it would come in so fast. It's a little early in the year."

"It could dissipate just as quickly," Helma reminded him.

"A high pressure system is stalled to the northwest,"

Jean Fonsilwick said. "With a low pressure system inland, trapping moist cool air beneath a layer of warmer air, causing possibly dense fog. That's also why we're experiencing light northerly winds."

The words had issued from *Jean*'s mouth in complete self-assurance, beautifully modulated and enunciated. Roman beamed at his wife, stroking her slender wrist above her diamond bracelet.

"You're a weather girl!" Ruth said.

"I'm a meteorologist for WTRU," *Jean* said.

"On the five o'clock evening news," Roman added proudly. "*Jean* studies the weather wherever we go."

Jean smiled shyly. "I have a keen interest in meteorology."

"Is the fog likely to last long?" Mr. Broder asked *Jean*.

"Fogs are very difficult to predict but it'll probably be with us into tomorrow."

"It shouldn't be a problem for us leaving on the ferry tomorrow afternoon," Helma told Mr. Broder, "but it may be a hindrance to your flight out."

"I can't think of a more enjoyable place to be fogbound," Mr. Broder said. He turned to Mr. Westright. "Are these kids still calling you, 'Mister,' too, Don?"

"It was too ingrained during our formative years," Helma told the two men.

"Yeah," Ruth agreed, "even though you guys aren't as old as you used to be."

"Even with this?" Mr. Broder asked, touching his stylishly cut silver hair.

"I know women who pay to have their hair that color," *Jean* said.

Helma glanced at Mr. Westright's light brown hairpiece, the hairs almost—but not quite—blending where artificial met authentic.

Mr. Westright caught Helma's glance and quickly asked Mr. Broder, "What made you abandon education for politics?"

"It didn't take me long to realize I wasn't cut out for education." He nodded to Michael and Mr. Westright. "Although the experience gave me inestimable respect for teachers like you two. I decided to go into politics after watching years of gridlock. I'm not so naive to think *I* can change the situation but the more people like me who are elected into congress, the better our chances of change. What about you? Still teaching history?"

"That and a few other subjects. I'm a dean at a private school."

"And progressing to higher glories?" Mr. Broder asked.

Mr. Westright laughed and pulled his pipe from his pocket. "Maybe before I retire, but I won't count on it."

"After a lifetime teaching history, you must know it inside out," Ruth said. "At least history doesn't change."

Mr. Westright shook his head. "You're wrong, Ruth. History is actually fluid. We historians anticipate the future. With each new phase of consciousness we can look back from a new angle and reinterpret the events of history."

"You're saying that time is a kind of job security," Michael said.

"Is that what's called historical revisionism?" Helma asked. "Isn't that changing the rules after the game is over?"

"I don't believe so," Mr. Westright told her. "It only broadens our understanding, making it multifaceted."

"The players are all dead," Ruth said, "so who can argue, anyway?"

"Speaking of players," Helma said, "does everyone here remember when David Morse, the basketball player, was killed?"

"This is the second time you've brought him up, Helma," Michael said, glancing at Kiki and Cornelian, who were serving food two tables away. "Do you have a special interest in his death?"

"Seeing us all together again reminds me of him," she said.

Roman looked at his perfectly manicured hands. "David Morse liked to give a rough time," he said quietly.

"Like maybe to you?" Ruth asked.

Roman nodded. "Forrest Stevens took his share from David, too. But that was a long time ago."

"David's fiancée was murdered a few weeks ago," Helma said.

"I heard," Michael said. "I think Patty Anne was headed for trouble from the get-go. Speaking from hindsight, of course."

"I wasn't aware you knew Patty Anne," Helma said.

Michael shrugged. "I didn't, really, but Dave talked a lot in the locker room."

"Yeah?" Ruth asked eagerly. "What'd he say?"

"Guy stuff."

"C'mon Mikie," Ruth teased.

"Petty things back then. Shoplifting, drinking, fooling around."

"Do you mean with other guys?"

"That was my impression."

Helma followed Mr. Westright's gaze. Lost in thought, he peered across the room at Amanda. She, in turn, seemed to be studying their table, most specifically Mr. Broder.

Michael leaned closer to Mr. Broder and Helma heard him ask, "Do you feel you were a good counselor?"

Mr. Broder looked at Michael. "I did my best, Michael," he said after a moment. "That's all I could do."

Michael sat back; neither man smiled.

Finally, Kiki set a tray down beside their table and began serving their food, doling it out haphazardly, some from the right, some from the left. Helma could only stare.

Meat loaf, mashed potatoes, a puddle of corn, plain white bread rolls.

"This is uncanny," Ruth said. "We might as well be in the Chat & Nibble in Scoop River. I didn't even know you could get pickled apple rings west of the Mississippi."

Roman Fonsilwick's wife bit her lip, making no move to pick up her fork. Mr. Broder smiled gamely, while most of their Scoop River classmates dug in.

"The only thing that can help this is more booze," Ruth said.

Dora beamed over the tables and bowed to the scattered applause before she removed her apron and sat down between Fiona and Sister Bea.

"Do you have a family?" Helma asked *Jean*, who sat politely beside Roman, her eyes moving from one speaker to another in the manner of people who felt they had little to contribute.

Jean smiled and her face grew animated. "A four-year-old son. His name is Dunston Roman, after my father and Roman."

"Do you call him Dunn?" Ruth asked and laughed heartily.

Jean's smooth forehead wrinkled.

"Get it?" Ruth asked. "Dunston Roman? Dunn Roman?"

Roman smiled but Helma had the feeling that beneath the table, he silently tapped the toe of his loafered foot. Impatient, unable—or unwilling—to relax.

"What's that?" Sister Bea asked, tipping her head.

A distant electronic tone sounded, one single note held for a second, then cut off to silence.

"It's a foghorn," Ruth said.

"Pretty wimpy," Ricky commented.

"Yeah," Michael agreed. "Remember the old foghorn on Lake Michigan?"

As one, they imitated the deep voiced old horn of their childhood, before it too had been replaced by a single tone, back when it sounded like the Wicked Witch's guards in the Wizard of Oz.

"B . . . O."

Drawing it out, laughing together as they had when as children, they'd first understood the joke.

Ernestine and Stony, the musicians, arrived halfway through the meal. "Pea soup coming in," Stony, who was a burly man in his sixties with scarred hands and a thick neck, said. He competently went about the business of setting up. Ernestine, who was the same general age as the Scoop River class, pulled her dulcimer into the room on wheels. She might have stepped out of a time capsule, with her fringes and headband holding back waist-length straight hair, dark ends fading to salt and pepper near her face, and long flowered skirt and the bell on her ankle. Helma caught herself craning to see if she was barefoot but no, she wore Birkenstocks.

When Stony pulled his concertina from the battered case and squeezed it a few times, Helma had the strangest sensation of being in the Scoop River Fire Hall at the Harvest Banquet, listening to Stanley Rybauskas warming up with a polka on his accordion. Her neck prickled as if her father and grandfather and that whole zealous family were sitting behind her, impatiently waiting for the first note to break into the room and set it on fire.

"You okay?" Ruth asked.

"Just thinking."

"Thinking we might as well have held this thing in Scoop River after all?"

"Something like that."

Ruth nodded toward the gigantic window. "Even the view's gone."

The fog swirled against the window, impenetrable, insulating and isolating. It wasn't quite dark yet but it was a different kind of night, one without shadows or hope of illumination.

"All we need is the Hound of the Baskervilles howling on the moors," Michael said.

Helma resolutely looked away from the window toward the musicians. She'd never gotten used to Northwest fog, the way it hid the world so much more unyieldingly than the blackest night, defeating sunshine, headlights, and landing airplanes.

Ernestine led off with "My Bonnie Lies Over the Ocean," and Stony joined in on the chorus and so did most of the room, swaying in their chairs.

They moved from one song to the next, from old chestnuts like "Roll out the Barrel," to songs of their own teenage years: "Where Have All the Flowers Gone?" and "Blowin' in the Wind" and "You're so Vain."

Once when Ricky forgot himself and stood, raising his glass to Ernestine and Stony's skill, Helma gasped, struck again by his similarity to those who were already gone.

"It's corny but I love this kind of stuff," Ruth told Mr. Broder.

He nodded. "I'd forgotten how entertaining it could be."

"Helma, you're crying!"

"I am not."

"Are too."

Helma touched her cheeks. They were wet. She didn't know what from but she certainly hadn't been crying.

When Ernestine and Stony took a break, Wilson Jones stood, holding high his argyle sock, his heart tattoo shining in the light. "Remember this?" he asked. "Are you ready?"

"Another round of drinks before we do it," Joey Barnes called out.

"I second the motion."

Amanda raised her hand. "I'd like to be part of this. What is it?"

Wilson Jones explained and Mr. Broder asked, "Can I add something as well?"

"Sure." Wilson handed them each a paper and pencil and they both, without hesitation, jotted a memory on paper and gave the slips to Wilson.

Wilson shook the sock and stuck his hand deep into the toe. "Here we go!" he shouted, as if he were priming himself to announce bingo numbers. He unfolded the paper and looked around the room, grinning, silent until Ricky and Lolly began stamping their feet, the way they used to when the projectionist mistimed a new film reel.

"The secret," he said, "is in the presentation. Let the bait roll with the current. It takes perfect weight and impeccable timing to pull in the big ones."

"Wilson, do *you* want the hook?"

"Okay, okay. 'I remember,'" Wilson read from the slip of paper in his hand, "'the time Wilson Jones, Davy Raspinas, and Toby Winsett put Lolly Kuntritas's Volkswagen on top of the fountain in front of the funeral parlor.'"

Lolly squealed and jumped out of her chair. She pointed a scolding finger at Wilson. "*You* did that?"

Wilson frowned and studied the audience. "Who told?" he demanded in mock anger.

"Wasn't there a bra tied to the antenna?"

When the laughter subsided Wilson pulled out another slip. "'Was Fiona Kamden telling the truth when she said the grains of rice in the cafeteria soup were actually maggots?'"

Fiona stood. "I swear it's true."

Miss Higgins held her hand to her heart and the room resounded with groans.

"'I saw Roman Fonsilwick moon Mrs. Sartori, the typing teacher.'"

Roman's wife pulled back and considered her husband. Roman actually blushed and ducked his head.

Wilson read the next one to himself, paused, then looked up and said, "This one says, 'We were all nicer than we think we were.'"

There was silence, and Wilson asked, "Anyone care to add to that?"

No one did.

Ruth leaned close to Helma and whispered. "And someone here doesn't qualify as 'nice' at all."

Helma looked around the room. Everyone was intent on Wilson, everyone except Amanda, who also slowly scanned the room, her expression bland and inscrutable. Helma turned her eyes back to Wilson just as Amanda focused on Helma's table.

Wilson held up the next note. "'Why didn't Geoff Jamas come?'" he read. "'Which one was he scared of: Ruth or Helma?'"

Helma felt every eye in the room turn toward her and Ruth. Her hands went icy and she bumped her wine glass clumsily against her dessert plate. It rang out like the single toll of a bell.

"Oh yeah, that big fight in the hall," Lolly said into the silence. "I can't remember who won."

"It was a doozie. And people think *guys* fight?"

"Did you write that?" Helma demanded of Ruth.

Ruth raised her chin. "N-O. But you never did tell me why he wasn't coming."

"He didn't answer the letters."

"That's what you say."

"Are you accusing me of lying?"

"You accused me."

"That was over twenty years ago, Ruth."

"You thought I was sneaking around, trying to steal your little boyfriend."

"You had a crush on him."

Ruth shrugged. "He was tall. It seemed a shame to waste that height on someone as short as you."

"I'm not short."

"No. You're not. You're average, completely average."

"You're overbearing and pushy and . . . undependable."

"Hah!" Ruth half rose from her chair. "Hah! *You're* paranoid. Geoff and I were just having a Coke, that's all, and you know it. You got bent out of shape and ruined it for yourself. By the time you finished your tantrums and screeching and making a *total*, complete and undeniable ass out of yourself, he didn't care if he saw either one of us again."

"Ricky said . . ."

"And *you* believed *him*? Did Ricky *ever* tell you the truth in his *entire* life?"

The dining room was completely silent, except for Ruth and Helma. Everyone avidly listened. Not even a fork clattered against a plate. Ricky rocked back and forth in his chair, smirking. He was having the time of his life.

"I don't want to discuss it anymore," Helma said.

"Then don't, but learn to live with it."

Helma sat back, folding her hands tightly in her lap. Ruth drank a half-glass of wine in one swallow.

"Well," Wilson said, clearing his throat and reaching into the stocking. "What do we have next?"

Helma sat stonily at her place, leaning as far from Ruth as she could, unable to understand the words Wilson was saying, her perceptions as fogged as it was outside, remembering Geoff Jamas. They'd been neighbors, friends from childhood and then during the summer between their sophomore and junior years, Geoff Jamas changed. He grew tall, less clumsy, funny, turning into something other than the boy next door. And Helma's interest had changed from childish friendship. Maybe Geoff's had, too. And Ruth's definitely had, no matter what she claimed.

It was Ricky who'd told her Ruth was dating Geoff: "Stealing him from under your nose, cuz." Ricky who said he'd heard Ruth tell Geoff that Helma was a bore and wasn't interested in boys yet, anyway.

And Helma had believed Ricky. There'd been a confrontation in the hallway and Helma closed her eyes against the memory of it. Still, she saw herself and Ruth screaming at one another, accusing each other while the rest of the school, including Geoff Jamas, watched in shock and delight.

Helma couldn't bear sitting there one moment longer. "Excuse me," she said, avoiding any glance toward Ruth, and left the dining room.

She wandered through the silent foyer and into the conservatory, realizing she was alone, exactly as she and Ruth had planned not to be. But, mysterious criminal or not, she wasn't going back in the dining room.

The only plants left in the conservatory were a few ferns, a ficus, and a single large palm tree. Rings marked the cement floor where other pots had stood, probably for years. Above and around her fog and darkness closed in on the glass room, nudging against the glass like unheard murmurs. It was a comforting place. An old plaid jacket lay across the wrought-iron bench by the palm tree and Helma sat down, draping the jacket across her shoulders. It smelled of gardens and sea air.

❧ chapter twelve ❧

VOICES

Helma was awakened by voices. She opened her eyes and saw fronds of overhanging branches. It was dark, the only light seeping through an open door. How had she gotten outside?

Then she remembered: the conservatory at Gull Rock Inn, the plaid jacket, her embarrassed and humiliating retreat from the dining room.

"But you must know," a woman implored.

"I'm sorry," a man answered.

"What about the Starlight Motel? Certainly that meant something?"

Helma quietly raised her head and peered between the fronds of the palm. It was Amanda Boston and Mr. Broder, the outlines of their bodies only inches apart against the light from the open door. This was not idle conversation, but entreaty and sad denial. Helma didn't move. In fact, she held her breath and strained to hear their low voices.

"Believe me," Mr. Broder was saying.

"You're refusing to help me."

"That's not it at all. I simply . . ."

They paused as a figure passed outside the door. Cornelian carrying a stack of towels.

"I can't listen to this anymore," Amanda said. "I'm going for a walk."

Her graceful figure turned away and headed for the door.

"Wait!" Mr. Broder said, hurrying after her.

For several minutes, Helma remained where she was, her breathing quiet in case they returned. She wiped the sleep from her eyes. What time was it?

Mr. Broder had left the conservatory door open and laughter still came from the dining room, punctuated now and then by a whoop. She wasn't going back in there, no matter what.

The foyer was empty, even shabbier by the single light burning on the desk, illuminating the packed cardboard boxes and exposing bare wood where the varnish had worn off the desk top. Harry's cage was covered by a denim work shirt.

"Oh no!" someone shouted from the dining room, followed by more laughter and muffled voices of encouragement.

Moving swiftly and silently, Helma climbed the stairs to her and Ruth's room, closing the door on the partying voices in the dining room. She didn't expect Ruth to be there and she wasn't. Helma changed into her flannel nightgown, brushed her teeth, and opened the window wider, allowing the salt air to freshen the musty room. Since she couldn't lock the door she leaned her Scoop River annual against it so the annual would fall forward when the door opened, and if that didn't wake Helma, it might warn away an intruder. She climbed under the covers, turning her back to Ruth's bed.

But sleep eluded her. She tossed, first to one side, then the other, bunching the pillow under her head, then discarding it. Ruth had probably already forgotten their quarrel, once again performed in front of the whole school.

Helma rarely thought about Geoff Jamas anymore, at least not in the way she had as a teenager; it was the memory of the whole silly incident that haunted her. She and Geoff hadn't spoken again after that day, had avoided even meeting each other's eyes.

It had been her own fault, believing her cousin Ricky. When had Ricky *ever* told her anything without a nefarious motive? He'd gleefully taken up her persecution as if it were his mission in life, her due for having been born a month before him, in the same town with the same last name, the first grandchild. And for keeping her father when he'd lost his.

Uncle Mick, dead when they were both nine, the deed completed by looping a rope around his neck and over a tree branch and then driving his tractor out from under himself. In a part of the country where suicide was viewed as an acceptable solution, Uncle Mick's had been deemed truly noteworthy.

And the reunion: *nothing* had gone as Helma planned. All her menu planning, her careful research into entertainment and music, even the weather.

She cradled her bandaged hand against her stomach. The broken glass had been one more warning, just like the letters, the cancellation. She pictured her classmates again, overlaying on each of their images the guise of a criminal, maybe a murderer. Instead of making Helma fearful, it weighted her heart with a sadness akin to grief.

It wasn't any of Helma's business but that *had* been a curious exchange between Mr. Broder and Amanda. She'd been half-asleep; had she truly heard it or had her mind supplied her with some made-up new intrigue? Amanda had been pleading. Mr. Broder had sounded regretfully sympathetic.

She'd only spoken to Mr. Broder in private once and that was after her mortification when her father and Aunt Aldona had been sent to Scoop River First National Bank to pick up a donation for the Scoop River Park fund and had chosen to arrive at the bank on Suzie and Betty, her grandfather's old workhorses, disguised as robbers, demanding the exact amount of the donation be put into a paper bag. They'd been fortunate it was Scoop River.

Helma lay on her back and crossed her arms over her chest. She breathed slowly, in for a count of four, hold for four, exhale for eight. She imagined calm blue water and pale green light. Her eyes were open because it was as dark outside as it would be if they were closed, a velvety black without a trace of reflection from city lights or streetlights. With the fog, the night had weight and texture, even a kind of sound, like in that old song: the sound of silence, as complete as the darkness.

Helma Zukas lay in her bed, arms crossed, ankles together, a slender figure beneath the covers. She breathed deeply and slowly and floated, a troubled heart suspended in the inky, tranquil night.

Loud keening broke the night, a scream that rose like a high wind and then fractured into sobs and rose again, a noise so terrifying Helma awoke to find herself standing in the middle of the room. The throbbing of her heart melded with the screaming like primitive music.

"My God, what is it?" It was Ruth and they banged into each other in the darkness. "What is it? What in hell is going on?"

"We'd better turn on the light," Helma said. But there was no definition of shapes in the room. Helma felt Ruth next to her, could touch her but she couldn't see her. Ruth shook as if she were freezing. "Make it stop. It sounds like somebody's dying. Helm! Where'd you go?"

Ruth stumbled against something of substantial size and heft and burst into fluent cursing. Helma held one hand lightly against the wall and the other in front of her as she worked her way around the room. "I'm looking for the light switch."

The screaming paused, then began again, so shrill it became mechanical. "Faulkner!" Helma said, searching vainly for the light. Doors banged. Helma made out sudden faint light glowing around the cracks of the door and with that to orient her, immediately put her hand to the light switch.

She squinted against the garishness of the overhead bulb. Ruth stood in the middle of the room, hands to her mouth, hair wild, wearing only a man's t-shirt. "Something's happened."

"I agree."

Outside their door, voices questioned, called to one another.

The scream deteriorated to a series of breathless cries.

"It's coming from outside," Ruth said. "I'm going out there."

Helma was already pulling on her slacks and reaching for a sweater from the closet. "I'd put something on if I were you," Helma said as Ruth grabbed the doorknob.

Ruth looked down. "Right." She grabbed jeans from her still unpacked gym bag and stuck her bare feet into a pair of loafers. "If this is Lolly making it with one or all of our male classmates, I'll kill her."

"If it is, it doesn't sound like she's having much fun."

The hallway was lit by only the light shining through the open bedroom doors.

Miss Higgins and Sister Bea clung together outside their door, watching former students tumble from their rooms and race down the hall. "Careful! Be careful," Miss Higgins called. "The hall lights are burned out. Careful on the stairs!"

"Stay here," Roman was saying at the door of his room. "I'll be back as soon as I know." He wore a velvety piped robe and carried a length of curtain rod.

"It came from outside," he said when he saw Helma and Ruth.

"We thought so." Helma turned and called back to Jean, "Stay with Miss Higgins and Sister Bea."

They dashed down the wide staircase into the foyer. The front doors of the inn stood open to the night. The outside light had been turned on but it was swallowed to a pinprick in the fog. Wisps of damp fog slipped inside like ghostly fingers.

The screaming stopped but voices came from the side of the inn, distorted by the dense mists. Ruth and Helma, with Roman close behind, took a few cautious steps toward the voices.

"Hello!" Helma called. "What's happened?"

"Stop," a woman called from behind them. "Stay on the path. Wait 'til I get there."

They stopped and waited, unable now to even see the lights above the door of the inn, stranded in nothingness. Sounds were magnified, ominous. Quiet sobbing. Gravel crunched as footsteps neared.

"I've been here before," Ruth said.

"What do you mean?" Helma asked the misty shape beside her.

"This is the one where the thing that usually lives under my bed is waiting in the fog and when I try to run away my legs won't work."

The circled beam from a flashlight loomed out of the fog.

"It's me, Diana," the figure said. She flashed the beam at herself and they saw her round face. "Stay with me. It's too easy to go off the path into the rocks."

"Do you know what it was?" Helma asked.

"Screaming, that's all I heard."

A second circle of light, its center ringed, bobbed out of the night toward them. It was Wilson Jones, his figure thrown to gigantic proportions. "There's been an accident," he said.

"What kind of an accident?" Helma asked. "Who?"

Wilson hesitated. He shone the light on Helma and she blocked its beam with her hand. "You'd better go back to the inn and wait," he said.

"We're *not* returning to the inn," Helma told him firmly. "Lead us to the scene, please. We'll decide what's to be done next from there."

"Let me go first," Diana said. "Stay close together. The path follows the cliff."

The gentle lapping of water and the odor of rotting seaweed rose from the unseen shore. The foghorn cried out.

Figures emerged from the fog, standing close to large rocks, Cornelian sobbing. Mr. Broder bending over a figure on the ground. Ruth gasped.

"Who is it?" Helma asked, afraid to look at that prone shape, so ominously still.

"Amanda," Wilson Jones said, his voice too loud, harsh.

"Amanda?"

"Is she . . . " Knowing already.

"Yes. She must have lost her way in the fog and fallen."

Silence followed their first gasps, the protestations and disbelief. Helma raised her hand and touched the smooth coolness of stone. Finally, Diana said, "The trail through the rocks here is tricky."

"Where does it go?"

"To the old staff's quarters," Cornelian said, her voice ragged and raspy from screaming. "I stay there when I work at the inn. I know this path with my eyes closed. I set up for breakfast after you all went to bed—and I tripped over her. I stepped right on her . . . " Cornelian broke into sobs again.

While Diana comforted Cornelian, Helma took Diana's flashlight from her hand and shone it on the body.

Beautiful Amanda lay on her back in the worn path, her eyes closed, her face gentle and serene, a smudge of dirt darkening one cheek. Her arms were crossed over her chest, as Helma's had been when she was trying to fall asleep, as Amanda's might be in her casket. Her slender skirt was smoothed over her legs. In the uneasy light, she truly looked as if she'd just fallen asleep. The flashlight in Helma's hand wavered, began to shake, and Helma turned it off.

She moved closer to Wilson. "Remember how you found her for the police," she told Wilson quietly. "It was thoughtful of you to arrange her like this, to give her dignity. You probably shouldn't have moved her, though."

"I didn't," Wilson whispered. "This is how she was. Laid out just like that."

"Who found her?" Helma asked, louder.

Mr. Broder stood just outside the light, his features indistinguishable. "Wilson was here first, after Cornelian."

"I didn't touch her," Cornelian said. "Only to step on her. She was lying right in the . . . "

"Shh, shh," Diana soothed.

A tense silence descended, separating them from one another, each isolated in the fog. Either someone had found Amanda and arranged her so lovingly or someone had killed her and then ghoulishly removed all traces of the horror of Amanda's last moments.

Helma wished she dared shine the flashlight on Mr. Broder's face. Had he heard Helma and Wilson discussing the position of Amanda's body?

The amplified sounds of feet on gravel reached them and a light bobbed out of the mists. It was Michael Petronas. Michael dropped to his knees beside the beautiful corpse and said, his voice catching in a sob, "Oh, sin."

Lights blazed inside the inn when they returned, having cautiously made their way back in a silent single file. First, Diana, leading the others and lighting the path as best she could with her flashlight. Next, Wilson Jones, carrying Amanda's body. Michael was last, behind Helma.

Somehow in the fog, they'd lost Roman Fonsilwick, but there he was in the foyer, minus his curtain rod, *Jean* held close to his side, waiting with the others, all of them in their nightclothes or haphazard dress.

Miss Higgins cried out when she saw Amanda, extending her hand tenderly. Sister Bea, looking like Miss Higgins's twin without her veil, made the sign of the cross and bowed her head.

"Oh no," Mr. Westright said. "What happened? I'll call an ambulance."

"It's too late for that," Wilson said. He stood uncertainly, looking around the foyer, Amanda in his arms, her head against his chest.

"There's no ambulance on the island, anyway," Diana said, pulling down the elastic leg of her shortie pajamas.

They surrounded Wilson and his tragic burden, gazing at Amanda in wonder. Death. A tear slipped down Fiona's cheek.

"Oh," Diana said, realizing what Wilson was looking for. "We can put her . . . the body . . . "

"What'll we do?"

"This is a nightmare."

Cornelian began to sob in gasps again. Feet shifted. Hands helplessly gripped nothing. Desperation seized the group, threatening to erupt in panic.

Helma struggled to remember her crisis center training, but instead, all that came to mind was her class in "Serving the Difficult Reference Patron." It was imperative for the professional librarian to project a calming demeanor, to be reassuring and provide factual information in order to defuse potentially disturbing situations.

She stepped forward and pointed toward the conservatory. "There's a wrought-iron bench in there you can lie her on." Somehow it didn't seem right to put Amanda in a bedroom, and certainly not to keep her in their midst.

Wilson carried her into the conservatory and Helma turned to Forrest Stevens, who, wearing a pair of striped flannel pajamas, stood beside Fiona. "You should go with him and write up a report."

"A report?" Forrest asked.

"Yes, for the coroner. I'm sure he'd appreciate the benefit of a colleague's observations. And . . . it may be a while before one can get here."

Forrest stood dumbly looking after Wilson Jones and his burden.

"I'll find paper and pencil for you," Helma said. "You'll want to examine her, describe her wounds."

"Touch her?" Forrest asked.

"Yes, you idiot," Ruth broke in angrily. "That's what doctors do. You're a doctor, aren't you?"

Forrest didn't answer. Ruth towered over him. "Aren't you a doctor?" she demanded.

"Not exactly." He refused to meet her eyes.

"So what are you, 'exactly'? An EMT?"

Forrest seemed to grow smaller as Ruth grew taller, his shoulders slumping, his neck compressing.

"I work in a doctor's office," he said in a low voice.

"And just what do you do in this doctor's office?" Helma asked.

"I dispose of biohazardous waste," Forrest said in an even lower voice.

"You're a *janitor*?" Ruth fairly shouted.

"This accomplishes nothing, Ruth," Helma said. "We should call the police immediately."

"There aren't any police on the island, either," Diana told them. "We call the county sheriff if there's a need. We don't call them much. We usually take care of things ourselves here on the island. There's a nurse on Fox Bay: Barbie Bell. She can set bones."

"This is beyond Barbie Bell's capabilities," Helma said.

"We'll call the sheriff." She picked up the phone on the desk in the foyer. There was no dial tone. She did what they did in the movies: she pressed the button several times. But still the phone was unresponsive.

"It's dead," Helma said, holding out the headset.

Diana gasped. "Oh. They must have turned it off already. I'm sorry. With the excitement of your arrival I forgot to put in a stop order."

Ruth frowned and opened her mouth. Helma gave a quick shake of her head, which fortunately Ruth saw. She looked quizzical but she said nothing.

"I'd send Captain Larry out to find a phone," Diana said. "But he's . . . he drank too much."

"I'll go," Mr. Westright volunteered.

"Not in this soup," Diana said. "It's too dangerous if you don't know the island."

Roman raised his hands helplessly. "This is the first vacation I've taken without my cellular phone."

"I begged you to leave it behind," *Jean* said sadly.

"It doesn't matter," Helma said. "In this fog they couldn't get here tonight anyway. We can call from the store in the morning."

Diana nodded. "That makes more sense."

"But what'll we do?" Fiona asked, waving her hand toward the conservatory.

"Ruth and I will take care of the preliminaries," Helma said, ignoring Ruth's shocked gasp. "Do you have a lamp that doesn't use electricity?" she asked Diana.

"Sure. The electricity can be undependable out here. I've got a battery camp lamp."

To Dora Helma said, "We'll need a couple of blankets, and Roman, find us pencil and paper. The rest of you may as well have a drink or a snack or go back to bed. There's nothing else we can do tonight."

It was as if a held breath had been released from the surrounding group. Everyone gratefully scattered from the foyer, given a task, a moment of meaning in the midst of horror and uncertainty. All but Forrest, who walked alone to the dining room, dejected and ignored.

Wilson Jones came out of the conservatory, a stricken look on his face. "Now what?" he asked of no one.

"Ruth and I will take care of Amanda. Can you . . . "
She nodded toward Michael Petronas who sat slumped
in a chair, staring blankly at the wall.

Wilson gently shook Michael's shoulder. "Hey Guy,"
he said softly. "Let's go get a beer."

When Wilson and Michael left the foyer, Ruth fairly
pounced on Helma. "Have you gone mad? What in hell
are you doing? What are *we* doing?"

Helma turned away from Ruth as Diana entered the
foyer from a door behind the desk.

"Oh, Diana. Thank you," Helma said, taking the plastic-
shaded lamp.

❧ chapter thirteen ❧

IN THE CONSERVATORY

Helma closed the conservatory door. A single wall light shrouded by a pink art deco shade cast a feeble rose glow, overpowered by the darkness and fog looming on the other side of the conservatory's glass walls and ceiling. On the long bench behind the palm, where Helma had dozed off and heard Amanda and Mr. Broder's urgent conversation, Amanda's light brown hair shone, a lengthy lock undone from the chignon and curling over the edge of the bench.

Ruth leaned against the door. Her voice was low, like in church, like in a funeral parlor. "I can't do this, Helm. I can't. Please." She rubbed her arms, avoiding glancing toward the bench.

"We had to talk immediately," Helma said. "I couldn't think of any other way."

"Amanda. She didn't just trip over a rock out there and have the time and forethought to compose herself into a tasteful funereal pose before she died, did she?"

"No. And I don't think the phone was turned off by the phone company as Diana suspects, either."

"Yeah, that's what I thought, too," Ruth agreed. "It was in fine order for library business this afternoon and since when does the phone company work on Saturday night?"

Helma nodded. "That's right. And another thing: I don't know of the significance, but Amanda and Mr. Broder were here in the conservatory tonight, holding an emotional discussion."

"Mr. Broder? What were they talking about?"

"She was asking him whether an incident had 'meaning.' I remember her saying, 'Didn't the Starlight Motel mean anything?'"

"The Starlight Motel? Wasn't there a Starlight Motel on Lake Michigan?"

"I don't remember."

"I do. I was there once with . . . well, never mind. Amanda and Broder at the Starlight? You don't think? Not *together*?"

"I was half-asleep. The nuances escaped me."

Ruth looked above their heads at the fragile glass ceiling holding back the night.

"If the phone's dead, then somebody did it."

"Somebody here."

"The same person who put glass in your purse, maybe collapsed Miss Higgins's chair, then killed Amanda and laid her out in the middle of the path?"

"I would suspect so."

"And you still think this is connected to David Morse? I'd swear Amanda and David barely recognized each other on sight. They were both too involved in their own little worlds, which I can't believe had a point of convergence."

Tapping sounded on the glass door behind Ruth. She jumped and spun around, staring at the man's outline on the other side, his face in shadow.

"It's only Mr. Westright," Helma told her, opening the door.

"Roman's comforting his wife," Mr. Westright said. "So here's a pencil and paper." His voice was hushed, like Helma's and Ruth's. "Would you like me to help you? I know this isn't easy; I can at least keep you company."

"You *could* help," Helma said. She nodded toward the

door to the dining room. "Everyone's upset. If you and Mr. Broder could reassure them this was a terrible accident, that might help soothe everyone's nerves."

He looked past Helma toward Amanda, his eyes sorrowful. "I can do that. Call me if you need anything."

Helma gently reclosed the conservatory door. The latch clicked, sharp, like a retort. Ruth took a deep breath. "You have an idea, Helma, I can tell. What is it?"

It was chilly standing on the concrete floor. Helma tucked her hands in her pockets. "We're going to call the police."

"Did I miss something? The phone is dead."

"We'll find another phone."

"Helm. Weren't you just in the foyer with the rest of us? Didn't you hear Diana? It's the proverbial pea soup out there. We don't know our way around this island. Ask Diana to pour some coffee down Captain Larry and shove him out the door. He'd at least know which direction to stumble off into."

"What do we know about Captain Larry?"

"You mean if he's the killer?"

"What if the perpetrator were to follow him? We couldn't take that chance. No, we have to leave the inn, find a phone, and return without anyone knowing."

"We can't. We'll be missed. We won't know where we're going. It's ridiculous."

"Ruth," Helma said patiently, nodding toward the bench. "There's been a murder."

"A kinky one."

"You might say that. Whoever's responsible will have no compunction about killing again to keep his secret. It's a mistake to wait until morning before we call the police."

"Then why'd you suggest it in the foyer?"

"To put the killer at ease. Whoever it is, he or she won't expect us to leave the inn."

"And following your line of reasoning, will simply trundle off to bed and wake up to discover a policeman slapping on the cuffs."

"That would be the ideal scenario."

Ruth dared a glance at the wrought-iron bench. She sighed. "Why Amanda?"

"Lolly's right. None of us really knew Amanda, not in high school and not now, either. She arrived at the inn late, and after her arrival, she managed to sidestep any questions about her personal life or what she'd done since she left Scoop River. We don't even know if she was married or had a family or where she worked."

"But you think Mr. Broder does?"

"I believe he knows *something*."

"Let's get out of here and go ask him."

Helma put her hand on Ruth's arm. "That's not a good idea. Not yet. He isn't aware he and Amanda were overheard."

"You think he'd . . ." Ruth made a cutting motion across her throat with her finger.

"We won't take any chances. Three people are dead already."

"Three?" Ruth frowned. "Oh. You're counting David Morse and Patty Anne Sands, too. I can't believe Amanda had any connection with Patty Anne Sands, either. If none of *us* knew Amanda, why would a student from another school know her any better?"

"Maybe they didn't know each other; maybe they just had knowledge of the same incident."

"Like in that movie where innocent people get offed because they witnessed a death and didn't realize it was really a murder?"

"It might be."

Ruth broke a leaf from the dying ficus plant beside her and rolled it between her fingers until it crumbled. "And by extension, Miss Higgins must know, too."

Helma nodded. "We can't leave Miss Higgins or Sister Bea alone until the murderer is apprehended."

"That shouldn't be too difficult," Ruth said. "When Dora's not cooking or mopping up, she's got them both firmly tucked under her wing."

Helma explained how they were going to phone the police while Ruth alternately nodded and rolled her eyes. When she was finished, Helma turned on the battery-operated lamp and headed toward the bench.

"Why do we need that lamp?" Ruth asked, panic rising in her voice. "What are you doing, Helm?"

"Helma. We needed a battery lamp because there aren't any outlets in here. Bring the blankets, Ruth."

Amanda lay peacefully on the bench. Wilson had refolded her arms across her breast and she was like a pale, exquisite effigy carved over a tomb, her perfection marred only by the dirt on her cheek and the hair that had slipped from her chignon.

Helma bent beside her, set the lamp on the floor next to the bench, and readied the pencil and paper Mr. Westright had delivered. Then, while Ruth stood above her holding the blankets, Helma described the condition of Amanda's body.

❧ chapter fourteen ❧

IN A FOG

The he majority of the guests of the Gull Rock Inn had, by general and unspoken consensus, gravitated to the dining room, brought together by the need for company, and the reassurance of order and normalcy. Blankets and pillows had been carried down from rooms, chairs pulled together to lie across, tables moved nearer to other tables.

The lights were on in the kitchen and Dora Durbas, in curlers, a plush blue robe, and matching slippers, pulled containers from the cupboards and constructed trays of pickles, beets, crackers, and peaches. A cart, loaded with glasses and bottles from the bar, slowly migrated from one corner of the room to another.

Helma felt the group's expectant, even . . . yes, *trusting* attention. She longed to blurt out everything she knew: the letters, the other deaths, Miss Higgins's floor and deck chair, the broken glass in her purse, her suspicions. But *no*, one person in this room had performed foul deeds, had taken a life, possibly even two or three, and who knew what else they had done or would yet feel driven to do next?

An empty bottle of whiskey sat on the floor between Wilson Jones and Michael Petronas, and Wilson had a precarious grip on another half-empty bottle. He took a swig and passed it to Michael. Had they realized the significance of the positioning of Amanda's body? Had they told anyone?

"How did Amanda die?"

At first Helma didn't recognize the questioner without makeup, her bright hair pulled back into a low, severe pony tail. It was Lolly. Dressed in a pink peignoir, she sat at a table with Sandy Snow and Joey Barnes; Forrest had been abandoned. Looking at Lolly, Helma again experienced the uneasy shifting of time and place, only instead of the young Lolly Kuntritas, she saw Lolly's mother in Bundtberger's Grocery pushing a wire cart while she tried to keep track of too many children.

Helma hesitated. "She fell on the cliffs in the dark and hit her head. Her head . . . well, there's evidence."

Let whoever felt compelled contradict her. But no one did. Wilson Jones looked at her as intently as his alcohol-fuzzed mind allowed and Mr. Broder was definitely frowning, but neither spoke up.

"What are we going to do?"

"There's nothing we can do now except go to bed. When it's daylight we'll call the authorities and take it from there."

"Why not now?" Ricky asked.

"Because of the fog," Helma explained to her scowling cousin. "It's dangerous because we're unfamiliar with the island."

"You're going to let a little fog stop you? I didn't think anything stopped the Wonder Cousin."

"Go ahead, Ricky," Ruth challenged. "You just get your tail on out there and find a phone in this stuff. We'll all be right here waiting for you."

"I think . . ." Ricky began.

"Think?" Ruth interrupted. "You think so rarely, Ricky Ticky, that you can't do it without moving your lips."

"No one is taking any more risks tonight," Mr. Westright interjected, rising from the table where he sat with Mr. Broder, his voice rich with authority. "It's two now; a few more hours won't make any difference. Even if the fog doesn't lift by daylight it'll be easier to see then."

"What about Amanda?" Lolly asked.

"She'll remain in the conservatory," Helma told her.

"If she doesn't we're in real trouble." It was cousin Ricky again. No one laughed; his comment was met by silence, but everyone turned to look at him slouching against the wall, his face as sullen as a thwarted ten-year-old's.

"Okay, so I'm sorry," he said, and took another long drink from his bottle, holding it by the neck.

"I'd rather stay down here than go back to my room," Sandy said.

"Me, too," Lolly agreed.

"Some reunion," Ricky griped

"We should have stayed in Scoop River. There aren't any cliffs in Scoop River."

"Can we get off this island tomorrow if it's still foggy?" Sandy asked.

"The ferries run in the fog," Helma assured her.

Helma nodded just perceptibly to Ruth and the two separated. "Is Cornelian all right?" Helma asked Diana, who was passing with a plate of cold meat loaf.

"Her niece is with her," Diana said.

"Her niece?" Helma asked, puzzled.

"Kiki. Most everyone around here is related."

Helma sat with Fiona and Forrest, and Ruth joined Mr. Westright and Mr. Broder.

Forrest slumped in his chair, light emphasizing the round, thinning circle on the top of his head. Fiona, who'd been speaking quietly to Forrest when Helma sat down, straightened and smiled slightly. "This has been a long night."

Helma nodded. "Did you talk to Amanda this evening at all?"

"Briefly, on the stairs before dinner. I asked her if she had a family, and I didn't even realize until later that she managed to turn the conversation around and hadn't answered me."

Helma wasn't surprised. "And now her life is over," she said, half to herself.

Fiona regarded Helma. "Living," Fiona said slowly, "isn't always a privilege. Sometimes it can be a sentence."

Helma paused, wondering, then asked, "Do you remember if Amanda and David Morse knew each other very well?"

"David and Amanda? They might have. I wasn't aware of it—but that doesn't mean they didn't. The only boy I ever saw Amanda with was Michael." They both glanced over at Michael and Wilson sitting on the floor.

"You and David dated each other, didn't you?"

Helma watched Fiona's face closely. Her gaze was steady, untroubled. "Briefly. We went out twice and on our third date, he walked out on me at Donna Torkas's party."

"With Lolly," Helma supplied.

"That's right. He grew tired of girls very quickly, even Lolly, until he met Patty Anne Sands."

"You knew her?"

"Just what I heard. He was very possessive, I understand, and Patty Anne liked to tease him, or as Lolly called it, 'turn the screws.'"

"You and Lolly never got along. Why?"

The corner of Fiona's mouth twitched. "It's been silly. Mostly it's bad chemistry. It happens between some people; you'd love to tear each other apart. But I'd like to clear it up before ... before the reunion ends."

Forrest raised his head, noticing Helma as if she'd just sat down. "I never really lied," he said, his voice choking, turning his glass back and forth between his hands. "I only said I was *in* medicine. People took it from there. I just didn't stop them, that's all. I would have gone home after the reunion and none of you would have thought of me again, except maybe to believe I'd been successful in my life."

"I never thought otherwise," Helma said. "There's no reason to be ashamed of your occupation."

Forrest looked sadly over Helma's head. "Remember what a whiz kid I was in school? Everybody expected me to go into science of some kind. But for some reason, I just couldn't ever get it together. Being smart is a trick of Mother Nature, like being good-looking, or tall."

He sighed. "And I didn't want people to know how I'd failed. I didn't want *you* to know."

"*Me?*" Helma stared at Forrest in surprise.

Forrest nodded. "You were always so sure of yourself. Everything about you was neat and certain. You reminded me of an elegant physics formula: $E = mc^2$. Or $v = d/t$."

Helma closed her mouth. "I . . . I didn't know," she finally said.

"You never noticed me hanging around wherever you were? I even joined the Library Volunteers to be near you." He sighed. "I couldn't have told you then. I only came to the reunion because you were here. Now, it doesn't matter."

Helma touched Forrest's arm. "When you return to Florida, none of this," she waved her hand to encompass the dining room, Gull Rock Inn, and the entire reunion, "is going to matter. It'll be as if it didn't happen."

"It matters to me."

"I'm sorry, Forrest."

Forrest pushed his glasses further up his nose, took a drink, and grinned morosely at Helma and Fiona. "There's a lesson here, I guess, but I'd rather not learn it this way."

"Excuse me. I'll see if Dora needs any help," Helma said, and left the table.

Dora had rolled up the sleeves of her blue robe and was fishing peach halves out of a gallon can and arranging them in bowls, cut side down like giant egg yolks.

Helma stood beside her and opened a package of saltine crackers and fanned them evenly on a glass tray.

"I know what you want to talk about," Dora said, turning to Helma and wiping her hands on a striped dish towel.

Helma waited and Dora provided, "About Patty Anne Sands."

"Did you phone her?"

Dora nodded. "After you asked about David Morse's death, I was curious. I didn't mean anything by it. She was nice at first, but then she just exploded at me."

"Do you remember what she said just before she became angry?" Helma asked.

Dora bit her lip. "Not word for word. I told her our class was having a reunion and we'd been discussing David's death. Then I said, well, I kind of lied. I told her David had told me all about her. When I said I hoped she could give me more information, she started calling me names before I'd even finished the sentence. She said I wasn't getting a cent."

"A cent?" Helma asked. "She thought you wanted money?"

"I couldn't believe it either. Why would I want money?"

"Then what did you do?"

"I decided she must be drunk and I hung up. I really didn't think any more about the call until you wanted to discuss Patty Anne with me." Dora faltered and rolled the sash of her robe into a spiral. "Then it hit me." She looked at Helma beseechingly. "Did *I* have something to do with Patty Anne's death? Did my call put events in motion?"

"No," Helma hastily and emphatically told Dora. "For whatever reason she died, it had nothing to do with you."

Dora's shoulders relaxed. She dropped the sash. "You're sure? Then why were you curious about the call?"

"Because I called her, too, and received a similar response. I suppose we'll never know the reason now."

"Patty Anne's death seems long ago, now that Amanda . . ."

Helma placed one of the dishes of peaches on her tray of crackers, added napkins, forks, and small plates and lifted the tray. "I'll take this out," she told Dora.

As Helma set the tray on Fiona and Forrest's table, she wondered, as Dora had, if *her* call had set in motion the events that led to Patty Anne's death.

Conversation ebbed and flowed through the dining room, low voices revealing secrets and sharing confidences.

"No, you were damned good on the field," Michael was telling Wilson in alcoholic earnestness. "You just sucked on the basketball court."

"No cheap solution exists," Mr. Broder told Mr. Westright. "The package has to contain both tougher punishments and more money for violence prevention."

Helma noticed Fiona's eyes close, then snap open. "You should get some sleep," Helma told her.

"I don't want to miss anything," Fiona said. "It'll be over so quickly."

Helma bit into a saltine from the tray. It was stale, without any "crisp" to it. She longed for the comfort of an overly salty, mealy piece of *kugelis*. She glanced at Ricky, who'd eaten the *kugelis* Aunt Em had sent. Ricky sprawled in a padded chair, asleep, a bottle of beer wedged between his legs, his head back and mouth open.

Michael, still sitting on the floor beside Wilson, stared across the room, frowning, his lips tight. Helma followed his gaze. He was unmistakably staring so intensely at Mr. Broder, who was deep in political dialogue with Mr. Westright.

A few minutes later, Helma yawned. "I think I'll go to bed," she said, loud enough for people at the surrounding tables to hear.

"How can you sleep after this?" Lolly asked.

"I'll function better in the morning if I have some rest."

A few half-hearted "good nights" followed her as she left the dining room.

In the empty foyer, Helma brushed against a lampshade balanced on one of the boxes. It fell and rolled across the floor asymmetrically, turning in a circle as if it were coming back for her. She swiftly returned it to its place, glanced through the closed conservatory door, and hurried up the stairs to the second floor.

The hallway was dark. Light shone from the open bathroom doors at the end of the hall. Miss Higgins had said all the wall lights were burned out. All of them? At once? Helma reached up and felt behind the dark sconce of the light closest to the top of the stairs. She wasn't surprised to discover the bulb was loose. She twisted it twice and the light came on. The same with the second light, and the next.

Someone had deliberately darkened the hall. Why? In hopes they'd all pile on top of one another and fall down the stairs in the dark to lie in a broken heap in the foyer? "How sophomoric," Helma commented aloud.

The walk to her room seemed inordinately long. The doorways off either side loomed darkly, a few of the doors ajar into the inky rooms.

She wouldn't have been shocked to find their room altered, affected by the events of the night. But no, everything was unchanged: her bed which she'd automatically smoothed even as she leapt out of it; Ruth's bed with blankets on the floor, clothes scattered around her gym bag.

Helma quickly pulled on the light green jacket she'd bought at Eddie Bauer for the reunion and grabbed Ruth's. Her address book and her keys she removed from the bureau top and shoved in her pockets. Then she left the room, silently closing the door behind her.

At the bottom of the stairs she stood behind the carved balustrade for a moment, her hand lightly on the newel post. A murmur of voices came from the dining room, quieter now, dozy, like evening birds settling in. Helma crept across the worn carpet and took the flashlight from behind the desk where Diana had left it.

And then she did it. She slipped through the heavy front door into the foggy night.

The bulb above the door was still on, forming a feeble circle of light unable to penetrate beyond the doorstep.

Keeping to the wide front entry, Helma stepped to the side of the door, out of the meager illumination. She should have brought her hat, too. Droplets adhered to her hair like a fine spray. Dense fog fingers swirled lazily into the light, forming eerie shadows that took shape and then, just when she thought she recognized them, dissipated. Nothing was visible beyond the front step. Helma shifted her feet, put her hands in her jacket pockets; July or not, it wasn't *that* warm. What was taking Ruth so long?

A rustle sounded to Helma's right, like tiny feet in leaves. She froze, peering into cotton wadding darkness, listening so hard her heart whooshed in her ears. Who had been in the dining room and who hadn't? She mentally went around the room, trying to match faces with her mental reunion roster.

Beside her the door opened and Ruth slipped through, a shape made taller by the fog than Ruth actually was, not two feet from Helma. "Helm?" she whispered.

"I'm right beside you," Helma said.

"Geez!"

"Shh," Helma cautioned her.

"I hope you have x-ray vision," Ruth said, taking her jacket from Helma and pulling it on. "This could be our last ride together. End up in the drink."

"All we have to do is follow the road," Helma assured her. "No turns, just stay on the road."

"A bigger problem might be finding the car."

"I know exactly where it is."

Five minutes later, Helma accidentally bumped into the rear fender of her Buick.

They climbed inside. "Open your door and give us a little push," Helma told Ruth.

"What?" Ruth squawked.

"Shh. It'll be easy. We're on a hill. We don't want to risk anyone hearing us start the engine."

"Easy, sure," Ruth said resignedly.

Helma took off the brake and put her Buick in neutral. Ruth strained against the door frame.

Gravel crunched beneath the tires and the car began to roll, first slowly, then alarmingly fast. Helma left the headlights off and steered by the sound of gravel and the feel of the tires in ruts.

Ruth threw herself inside, grabbing desperately for the back of the seat. With one hand, Helma clutched the sleeve of Ruth's jacket. The passenger door swung wildly back and forth. Ruth's eyes were huge in the car's dome light.

"Stop the damn thing so I can get in!"

"I don't want to lose momentum. You're okay. You're nearly in."

Ruth struggled until she'd pulled her feet completely inside and then reached out and slammed her door closed.

"Did you have to slam it?" Helma asked. "Somebody might have heard."

"I'm not even going to answer that. What are you trying to do, get even and kill me? Are we still on the road?"

"We're not on it yet. Can't you feel the ruts? This is the driveway."

"Slow down, damn it."

The sound beneath their tires changed and Helma hit the brakes. Ruth braced herself against the dashboard. "Now what?"

"We're at the road. You have to drive."

"I'm not driving."

"You have to."

"I can't. Why do I *have* to?"

"Because I left my driver's license in our room."

"Oh, for pity's sake, Helma. That's the least thing in the world we have to worry about. There are no police here, remember? And if there were, we'd be *grateful* to see their little flashing lights behind us, believe me."

"I'd feel better if you drove."

"I don't drive without my glasses."

"I thought those were just sunglasses."

"Well, they're not 'just sunglasses,' okay?"

Helma turned on the engine. "It wouldn't matter. You can't see anyway."

Helma bent close over the steering wheel, staring futilely into the foggy night. The windshield wipers arced without effect. They cautiously crept along the road, gratefully passing through spots where the fog lightened and gave the headlights some length. Ruth hung her head out her open window, watching the road, saying now and then, "A little too close to the edge." "Turn coming up, I think."

The sensation was like driving on ice, the feeling that the steering wheel was superfluous, that remaining safely on the road depended on the whims of the elements, not on Helma's own skill.

Two pallid street lights shone above them like distant moons. "Must be Mac's store," Ruth said.

Helma pulled into the store's parking lot and winced as something metallic scraped beneath her car.

"Where's the pay phone?" Ruth asked.

"The dock attendant said there wasn't one on the island but I can't believe that."

"Oh, but I do," Ruth told her. "This is an *island*, Helma."

"And?"

"My humble experience is that people who live on islands don't appreciate amenities like pay phones, alarm clocks, and navigable roads. Right now I don't believe anybody lives on this island at all. It's like a deserted movie set. The help's all gone home and we're locked inside."

"Let's check anyway."

They climbed out of the car and felt their way carefully around the building's exterior, hands in front of them, bumping a trash can, stumbling on a cage from which emitted a bird's squawk. "Fresh eggs," Ruth muttered. And around to the front door where they'd begun.

"Told you," Ruth said.

"There has to be a phone inside."

Ruth picked up a brick that outlined a flower garden beside the door. She held it up. "Ready?"

"Don't. There's a phone at the ferry dock office."

"It'll be locked, too."

"I know but I feel better about breaking into state property than a private building."

"C'mon Helm. We're talking about another mile's drive in this crud. We're lucky we've made it this far."

"I think I've got the knack of it."

They returned to the car and got inside. "You can leave that brick behind," Helma told Ruth, nodding toward the brick still in Ruth's hand.

Ruth opened the door and tossed it out, cringing at the sound of the brick hitting metal.

Helma carefully maneuvered back onto the road and continued toward the ferry landing.

"Hey, Helm," Ruth said.

"Mmm," Helma answered.

"Are you still mad about Geoff Jamas?"

"That was a long time ago."

"Are you?"

"No. Well, yes, to be honest, I am, a little."

"I *did* have the hots for him," Ruth said. "I *would* have stolen him if I could have."

"You *would* have?"

"Sure. Back then, anyway. I'm older and wiser and have a more highly developed sense of loyalty now, of course."

"So Ricky told the truth?"

"Only if he could see into my heart and we knew even then he couldn't see so much as the writing on the wall. I never dated Geoff or did *anything* sneaky."

"Honest?"

"I swear." Ruth paused. "But only because you went ballistic in the hallway and forever killed my chances." Ruth snickered. "You called me a whore, only you pronounced it 'war.'"

"I read it in books. I hadn't heard it pronounced."

"That's what happens when you read about life instead of live it."

"Well, you said I was a 'Lugan mackerel snapper,'" Helma countered.

Ruth giggled, then Helma joined her and soon they were both laughing hysterically.

"Watch out!" Ruth cried.

Helma slammed on the brakes and the Buick shimmied to a stop, knocking over the barricade that blocked the ferry ramp.

"I believe we're here," Helma said.

"Ten more feet and we'd be here permanently."

The brick building was directly beside the car, so close Ruth couldn't open her door all the way.

"Careful not to scrape my car door," Helma warned her.

"Ssss," Ruth hissed back.

The foghorn was closer, more shrill. Danger. Danger. By the dock a sea bird near shore sleepily "gronked" in answer. There was another noise, too. Helma stopped and listened: it sounded like something gliding through the water beneath the raised ramp. It's the tide changing, Helma told herself, that's all.

While Helma held the flashlight, Ruth picked up a rock and hurled it through the window of the ferry building's door. Breaking glass chimed into the fog like music, singing over the water and back to them, even louder. Ruth reached through the broken window and then laughed.

"You won't believe this. I was a law-breaking vandal for nothing. The door wasn't even locked. They probably never lock it."

"I'm surprised," Helma said. "Surely there's a state rule that requires they keep it locked."

Ruth turned on the inside lights. The bright light was jarring, but even inside, there was a haze, like smoke. "Oh look. Here's why they don't have to lock the door. They keep an attack dog on the premises."

The yellow dog Helma had seen inside earlier cowered on a blanket in the corner, watching them, shivering, his tail thumping nervously against the floor.

"Poor pooch-a-roni," Ruth crooned. "Did we scare you? All shut up inside. Mean old people." She half sang: "If we'd a known you were alone we'd a brung you a bone."

Helma pulled her address book from her jacket and sat beside the phone.

"Your address book, Helma? To call the police?"

Helma flipped the pages to the *B*'s. "I'm calling Amanda's parents first."

Ruth crouched beside the dog and rubbed its golden head, allowing the animal to slurp its tongue all over her face. "Do you think that's a good idea? Let the police do it, okay?"

"Her parents should know at once," Helma said. She remembered how she'd been at a play when her father died, having *fun*, not knowing for four hours that her father was dead, horrified that she hadn't somehow sensed his leaving.

"Don't, Helma. It's none of our business."

"How can you say that? It's the humane action to take."

She dialed Amanda's parents' number in Pennsylvania and charged it on her phone card. It was three hours later there. They might already be up.

"Yes?" a sleepy woman's voice asked.

"Mrs. Boston, this is Miss Helma Zukas in Bellehaven, Washington and I'm afraid there's been an accident involving Amanda."

There was silence and then the voice, wide awake and filled with rage, blasted into Helma's ear. "How dare you be so cruel? How dare you?" And the receiver was slammed down.

"What happened?" Ruth asked.

"I approached it incorrectly," Helma said. "I was too blunt. I'm calling them back."

"Don't, Helma. Really. Call the police."

"I have to repair the damage I've done first." Helma redialed the number, checking each digit against her address book before she pushed the corresponding button.

"Hello," a man answered. Definitely awake, suspicious and angry.

"I'm sorry," Helma said, explaining who she was again. "I didn't mean to upset your wife but there's been an accident."

"Involving Amanda?" the man asked coldly.

"Yes."

"I don't know who you are or why you've upset my wife by pulling this sick stunt. Amanda's been dead for eighteen years."

"Eighteen years?" Helma repeated, stunned.

"Yes, she killed herself. Are you happy to hear that? Now leave us alone, you sick bitch." And he hung up.

Helma stared at the phone in her hand.

"Helma! What's wrong?"

Helma carefully replaced the receiver and turned to Ruth. "He said Amanda killed herself eighteen years ago."

"That's impossible. Amanda's at the inn."

"Or someone we *think* is Amanda."

The yellow dog raised his head and looked toward the door. He bared his teeth and growled.

Ruth rubbed her hands through her wild hair. "Call the cops, woman. Do it now."

Helma nodded and flipped to the *G*'s, where she kept Chief Gallant's home phone number, which was unlisted, but which he'd given her a year ago during a rather sensitive time.

"Shh, puppy," Ruth told the growling dog. She leaned over Helma's shoulder. "*Now* what are you doing? *Chief Gallant*? You know we're out of his jurisdiction. Call the county sheriff."

"Chief Gallant will know what to do. He can alert the proper authorities for us."

"We're capable of alerting the proper authorities, too. This is the weakest excuse you've used yet to get his attention."

Helma ignored Ruth and carefully dialed Chief Gallant's number.

"Gallant here," he answered, wide awake, officially alert.

Helma pictured him sitting up in bed, his hair tousled. She didn't know but she doubted he wore . . . She cleared her throat. "This is Helma . . ."

And the line went dead. She pulled the phone away from her ear. "Oh, Faulkner," she whispered to Ruth. "It's dead."

"And here we sit like two ducks in a shooting gallery." Ruth reached for the light switch and flicked off the lights.

"Should we try the radio?" Ruth asked.

"We'd better get out of this place now," Helma said, surprised how calm she felt, how *purposeful*.

"Hell, yes, I'm for that," Ruth agreed. "We might want to 'stay low,' as they say."

They crouched, Helma leading the way, opening the door, stepping on broken window glass that crunched into the night.

They felt their way to Helma's car. "Oh damn," Ruth said. "I dropped the flashlight. Just a sec."

"Leave it," Helma said. Ruth cried out and Helma

stood, forgetting herself. "Ruth! What's wrong?"

"Oh deary deary deary," Ruth's voice shook and rose to a higher pitch. "I just tripped over something. No, *somebody*."

Keeping one hand on her car, Helma made her way toward Ruth, and stumbled against the shape on the ground.

"Is he dead?" Helma asked. "Where's the flashlight?"

"Against his leg. You get it."

Helma picked up the flashlight and shone it on the body sprawled in front of her car. It was the dock attendant.

"Is he?" Ruth asked.

Helma touched his neck, then felt his wrist. "He's dead," Helma affirmed, "but not very long."

"What'll we do? Should we put him in the backseat? Who killed him? God, Helma, we nearly ran *over* him."

"We can't move him. Only the authorities should move a body. This is a crime scene."

"No lie." Ruth grabbed Helma's arm. "Shh. What's that?"

"What?"

"Over there. Is that somebody standing there?"

"Get in the car, Ruth," Helma ordered. "Quickly." Helma scrambled back to the driver's side and jumped in just as Ruth slammed the passenger door.

Helma backed up her car, tires spinning. Through Ruth's open window, as they sped away, she heard barking from the yellow dog.

chapter fifteen

LIES AND
BEARS

Helma pulled off the road at the bottom of the driveway to the Gull Rock Inn. "We have to walk from here. Everyone inside the inn would hear my car straining up the hill."

Ruth didn't answer. She sat slumped against the car door, her head against the glass.

"Are you asleep, Ruth?"

"More like catatonic. I thought we were going to die."

"We don't really *know* there was anyone at the ferry dock," Helma reminded her. "We couldn't actually discern a figure. And we don't know yet how the dock attendant died."

"I don't mean then. I'm talking about just now, driving back here. You can't *see* in this stuff, Helma. You were driving like it was frigging mid-sunshiney-day."

"It seemed wise to return to the inn as quickly as possible."

"You were all over the road."

"I stayed on it, didn't I?"

"Only through divine intervention."

"Well, we're here. All's well that ends well."

They climbed out of the car and waded into the fog, walking side by side in vehicle tracks. The feeble beam of Helma's flashlight didn't pierce the fog, only transformed it into a solid moist wall in front of them.

"Let's hurry," Ruth said. "I want to be back inside the Inn of Death."

"The murderer is there, too."

"At least we'd see him—or her—coming. Whoever did in Amanda probably zapped the dock attendant, too. Do you think the killer was trying to get off the island?"

"He'd be giving himself away if he left," Helma said. "It's more likely he was trying to cut the island's communications and the attendant surprised him."

"That poor dog. I hope he doesn't have to go to the pound."

Helma stumbled and caught herself. The flashlight beam arced into the gloom. The foghorn sounded and Helma tipped her head, unable to tell which direction it was coming from.

"If that's not Amanda," Ruth asked, "then who is it?"

"I'm not certain, although I have a suspicion."

"I know, I know—which you won't divulge until you're dead certain you're right. She had me fooled. I really believed her."

"It's been twenty years," Helma said toward Ruth's shadowy figure. "We were *prepared* to believe her. People often see only what they expect to see."

"This fog is damn irritating," Ruth said, her voice rising in bravado. "Feels like Halloween."

Helma had an unbidden memory of her eighth Halloween when she and her cousin Varonni went trick-or-treating and Ricky trailed them, hiding behind trees and houses, emitting burps and body noises he could gleefully perform at will, scaring Varonni into dropping her bag and forcing them to cut their night short.

"You remember how Wilson and I used to go at it like minks back in high school?" Ruth asked in the darkness.

"I'm not sure 'remember' is the right word, Ruth. I only heard rumors."

"Well, they were all true, every one of them. It's funny how different it is now. I mean, I *like* him."

"And you didn't before?"

"Well, *yeah*. Sure I did. But I was . . . you know, not thinking about it."

"You mean you were more immature?"

"That's not . . . Wait," Ruth whispered. "I hear something."

They stopped, listened. Water dripped somewhere, irregularly, like a leaking faucet. Without thinking, Helma raised her hand as if she could physically part the fog. The harder she listened, the more indistinct the sounds. Directionless, distorted. The rustling of leaves? Or footsteps? Waves turning on themselves? Or the murmuring approach of voices? Fog hovered thickly between her and Ruth. Beyond the flashlight's pitiful stream of light there was nothing.

"No one's there," Helma said firmly. "You're just jumpy."

"You're damn right I am."

Helma turned off the flashlight. There was no sense advertising their position.

Helma's stride was reduced to a shuffle as she struggled to stay in the tire track, one foot in front of the other, the rut occasionally so narrow she balanced with her arms like a tightrope performer. She didn't recall the driveway to the Gull Rock Inn being so deeply rutted.

"Shouldn't we be there by now?" Ruth asked.

"It seems to be taking overly long because we're anxious."

"Is that what we are, *anxious*? You don't know this island. Maybe you stopped at the wrong driveway."

"I stopped at the correct driveway," Helma told her.

"It feels like we're going the wrong way to me."

"Ruth, you're whining. We're nearly there."

They had to be near the inn by now. Any second they'd discover themselves at the big double front doors of Gull Rock Inn. In a minute they'd be back inside four walls, where it was light, where there were friends. Friends and murderers.

"Ouch," Ruth cried. "Turn on that damn flashlight."

Helma turned it on and shone it toward Ruth's voice.

Ruth's veiled figure grew visible, flat against something tall, looming.

"Shine it right here, would you?"

Helma did. "Caterpillar" was printed on the metal above Ruth's head. "It's a bulldozer!"

"We're in the wrecking crew's camp."

Helma turned in a circle, holding out the flashlight. Heavy machinery, indistinct, hunkered in front of them, beside them, circling them like menacing prehistoric beings. The low-tide smells were overpowered by the odors of diesel and oil.

"Did you ever see *Christine*?" Ruth whispered. "These things could come to life and grind us up like peanut butter."

"We just need to backtrack," Helma whispered back. "We veered off the driveway, that's all. At least now we know where we are."

"I thought you knew all along."

"I knew we were in the right area."

"Sure you did," Ruth snarled.

A breeze rose. The wind moaned through the intricacies of the machinery, barely audible, first a pressure in the ears, rising in decibels but still so low it could be felt in the chest, as if it were reaching inside their bodies. Then another higher-pitched moan, accompanied by the tinkling of metal.

"I want my mother," Ruth said. She took panicked steps away from Helma and her misty outline disappeared into the fog.

"Ruth!" Helma called. "Come back here."

Ruth's shaky voice came from somewhere to Helma's right. "I guess I lost it. Sorry."

Helma turned the flashlight toward her voice. "Can you see the light?"

"No."

"Stay where you are but keep talking. I'll come toward you. Just keep talking."

"I don't know what to say."

"Ruth!"

"Okay, okay. Here we are lost in the fog, dodging murderers. I'm having such a fine time at this reunion. A-B-C-D-E-F-G."

Sibilance, like breath through bared teeth, sounded

close to Helma's ear and she jumped ahead into the darkness, crashing into oily machinery.

"Helm, you still there?"

"Yes." Helma bent down and wiped grease from her hand onto the grass. "I ran into a pump or something."

"Go to the light. Go to the light," Ruth moaned.

"Cut it out, Ruth."

"I see you!" and in an instant she was beside Helma. Her voice trembled. "Now let's get the hell out of here."

They hurried back along the construction road, watching the ground for the turn onto the driveway to the inn, hearing the chorus of low moans and whistles from the wrecking crew's camp, wondering what lay hidden by the fog, known and unknown, benign and evil.

At the door to the inn, Helma told Ruth, "If we're seen coming in, say we heard a cat outside and went to look for it."

"You don't like cats."

"No one else knows that."

"What about the dock attendant?" Ruth asked. "We have to tell someone."

"No," Helma told her firmly. "Not until we contact the authorities."

"But . . ."

"Think of the consequences, Ruth. We'd have to explain why we went to the dock."

"Yeah, I guess," Ruth said in resignation.

The foyer was empty. The lamp still glowed on the desk, the dining room doors were closed, the conservatory remained dimly lit.

They hurriedly climbed the staircase, slipping off their jackets as they went. Helma couldn't believe their luck; no one was in the second floor hall either.

"Allie, allie oxen free," Ruth said as she opened the door to their room and turned on the light.

Wilson Jones lay sprawled on his back across Helma's bed.

"Oh no!" Ruth cried, her face going dead white. "Oh no. Not Wilson! Is he . . ."

A snore burst from Wilson's lips and Ruth slid down

the wall to the floor, closing her eyes and shaking her head.

Helma was appalled. Drool dribbled from Wilson's lips onto her pillow. His big bare feet, the soles dirty as charcoal, rested on her bedspread. In one hand he clutched the argyle sock, which still held a slight bulge where the remaining slips of paper rested.

"Wilson," Helma said, shaking his shoulder.

Wilson's snore gurgled and halted, then resumed.

"Wilson Jones," Helma said in her silver-dime voice.

Wilson's eyes flew open. He stared around the room and wiped his wrist across his mouth.

"Huh?"

"Wilson, you're lying on my bed."

He focused on Helma, struggling to sit up. "Looking for you."

"Why?"

Wilson held up the argyle sock. A sweaty lock of hair stuck to his forehead in a giant comma. "We didn't read all the memories."

"Now is hardly the time. Go back to your room, Wilson."

Wilson shook his head. His vision cleared. "No, no. Want to show you one." He opened his hand, then searched around himself on Helma's bed. "Where'd it go?"

Ruth picked up a folded slip of paper from the floor beside the bed. "This what you're looking for?"

"That's it. Read it."

Ruth handed the slip to Helma. "You do it. At this stage I'm not sure my simple brain can take any more."

Helma unfolded the paper. " 'Who killed Amanda?' " she read aloud.

"That's what it says?" Ruth demanded. She took the slip and read it for herself. " 'Who killed Amanda?' "

Wilson nodded. "It was in the sock and the sock's been in my pocket since dinner."

"So the note was put in the sock *before* Amanda died?"

Wilson nodded again.

"But Amanda's been d . . ." Ruth began.

Helma pinched Ruth and put her finger to her lips.

"Huh?" Wilson asked.

"Somebody knew Amanda was going to die," Helma said.

"That's what I think," Wilson agreed. "Dja think the murderer wrote the note?"

"What murderer?" Helma asked innocently.

Wilson frowned at Helma. "Don't futz with me, Helma Zukas. Amanda didn't go outside in the middle of the night, lie down like Sleeping Beauty, and *die*."

"Have you told anyone how she was found?" Ruth asked.

Wilson shook his head. "Everybody's upset enough without that."

"Can we wait?" Helma asked. "Keep it to ourselves until the police get here?"

"Fine by me. But whoever did it knows that whoever found her knows somebody did it."

"You're thinking too hard, Wilson," Ruth said.

"Those of us who saw her lying on the path shouldn't be alone until we're off the island," Helma said. "Where's Michael?"

"Downstairs in the dining room."

"You and Michael stay together. Ruth and I will be down shortly."

"Let's go with him now," Ruth said.

"I want you to help me for a minute first."

"Okay. See ya downstairs later," Wilson said. He saluted vaguely from his forehead, and, stumbling once on Ruth's bag, ambled from their room.

"Help you do what?" Ruth asked.

"Inspect Amanda's room."

"What for?"

"To discover who was posing as Amanda."

They crept into the hall, looking both ways. Amanda's room lay beyond the staircase and across the hall.

"Don't *sneak*," Helma told Ruth.

"I can't help it."

A door clicked and they turned to see Mr. Westright emerge from the men's room, his face weary. "Ruth, Helma, that was a beautiful thing you did, taking care of Amanda. Your classmates are bearing up well."

"That's all we can do until the authorities arrive."

"One of my best memories of Scoop River was the way people pulled together in difficult times. It restores my faith a little to see that happening now."

"Many primitive tribes do that very thing," Ruth said.

Mr. Westright smiled at Ruth. "Your hiding your emotions with sarcasm is another of my memories."

Ruth shrugged. "I hate being so transparent to grownups."

"I tried to sleep but it's useless so I'm going back to the dining room. Are you?" Mr. Westright raised his hand to beckon them ahead of him.

Helma hesitated. Ruth suddenly raised her hand to her shoulder.

"Oh!" she cried, her eyes widening. "My bra strap broke. Helma, can you help me fix it? I can't stand being uneven."

"We'll be downstairs in a few minutes," Helma told Mr. Westright, following Ruth back toward their room.

Inside, Ruth guffawed. "Am I a quick thinker or what?"

"I wouldn't have thought of that," Helma said.

"Of course you wouldn't have. Is the coast clear?"

Again, the hallway was unoccupied. Helma stepped out, followed closely by Ruth, and together they walked down the hall to Amanda's room. Helma put her hand on the doorknob, suddenly reluctant to open it.

Ruth nudged her. "Go on!" she whispered.

They stepped inside Amanda's dark bedroom, which felt colder, danker, more oppressive, than their own. So dim so dank so dense so dull so damp so dark so dead.

Ruth turned on the light. "Surprisingly messy, wasn't she?"

Helma experienced that sensation again, like she'd felt in Miss Higgins's room: of disorder and violation. Amanda's suitcase sat open on the floor, expensive clothing spilling from it. Her makeup case lay on the sink, unzipped. Her bed was unmade. A stuffed teddy bear, its fur worn smooth and one eye missing, sat on the bed pillow, poignantly alone.

"I wonder," Helma said.

"Wonder what?"

"Whether Amanda was the one who was this untidy, or . . ."

"Or whether someone has been here?"

Helma nodded.

They searched Amanda's room, at first looking without touching, then lifting up clothes with their fingertips and finally simply rifling through her possessions.

A Scoop River High School annual sat on the bureau, beside it the reunion program. A Donna Karan leather purse lay on the bed, the flap open.

"There's no identification in here," Ruth said. "Think it was swiped?"

"Or else it wasn't found. Maybe the woman pretending to be Amanda, hid it."

Ruth tipped up the mattress and felt beneath it. Helma examined the makeup case and checked the drawers of the nightstand.

"We were beat to the punch, I guess," Ruth said. She picked up the annual and began flipping through it. "Young and innocent," she murmured. "Right now, it's painful to see these bright and hopeful faces, isn't it?"

Three small pages, densely covered with tiny, narrow handwriting, fell out of the annual and drifted to the floor. Helma picked them up. The long edge of each page was ragged, as if it had been torn from a book.

"Three pages from a diary," Helma said.

"Amanda's?"

She read a few lines aloud. "'B' will help but wants to know more. There's too much at stake.'"

"What's the year?"

"There isn't a year, only dates. May tenth, this entry is."

Ruth took a page. "'I've been afraid, ever since D.M.'s death after the SR/H game.' That's the Scoop River/Hopkins game, Helm, the one where Dave died. D.M. is David Morse. These have to be from Amanda's diary." She read further. "'He won't talk to me. I don't know what to do.' Oh, Helm, listen to this: 'No one knows me here. I'm so lonely.'" Ruth sat on Amanda's bed. "She's talking about us, isn't she?"

Helma read on. The diary was in fragments, the hand-writing cramped, then sprawling, panicked, sometimes incomprehensible, once the word: "no" written over and over again.

"'The results arrived—I'm not!—and I hid it in Corky,'" and further down on the last page, "'P.S. The Starlight!'"

"The Starlight," Helma repeated. "That *is* what I heard Amanda and Mr. Broder talking about in the conservatory. The Starlight Motel."

"He was there when Amanda's body was found," Ruth pointed out. "Do you think he . . ."

"I don't know." Helma looked around the room. "The teddy bear," she said, pointing to the threadbare animal on the pillow.

"Very good, Helm. The teddy bear did it."

"No. 'Corky.' That's a name you'd give a stuffed animal. She hid 'it,' whatever 'it' is, in Corky."

Ruth picked up the teddy bear and examined it. Between its legs under a flap of cloth was a tiny zipper. "Bingo." Ruth unzipped it and put her hand inside. "This feels a little perverted, like bear molestation."

What Amanda had hidden inside twenty years ago was gone but Ruth pulled out a driver's license and a credit card.

"Cynthia Boston," she read.

"Amanda's sister? Her poor parents." Helma dropped into the chair opposite Ruth. "I remember that Amanda had younger brothers and sisters, but I didn't pay much attention."

"Nobody did," Ruth said sadly. "They were outsiders, newcomers, remember?"

Helma did. Scoop River had been coolly polite. One year's residence wasn't long enough to become intimate members of the community. Helma remembered when Sandy Snow's family moved to town and she joined their kindergarten class. During their senior year, she'd heard Mr. Pincer at the drugstore refer to Sandy's family as, "the new family out by Barrows Corner." There hadn't been any malice in it; that was simply how it had been.

"So that's Cynthia in the conservatory," Ruth said.

"Do you think she wrote the 'Who killed Amanda?' note?"

"Probably. I'm guessing she came here to discover who killed her sister."

"But her father said she killed herself."

Helma studied the face on the driver's license. Not even the licensing bureau could detract from that lovely visage. "Maybe Amanda's diary made her suspicious. She was looking for whoever was responsible and she hoped the note would make them show their hand."

Ruth sat on the bed, smoothing the teddy bear's remaining fur. "From her diary, I'd say Amanda thought she was pregnant."

"But she wasn't," Helma said.

Ruth set the bear back on the pillow. "So now what do we do? The cavalry isn't on the way. We're fogged in, no phone, stuck here with a murderer or murderers."

"Well, we know whoever it is can't leave, either."

"I'm so happy to hear *that*. I hope knocking people off isn't his idle pastime. We could be the twenty-three little Indians."

"We do know Mr. Broder knows *something*," Helma reminded her. "Or at least Amanda's sister thought he did."

"Well, let's just waltz up and ask him if he gets his kicks killing sisters."

"It wouldn't do much for his political aspirations if he were the murderer."

"It would only hurt him if he got caught." Ruth yawned and held up her wrist. "It's nearly four o'clock. It'll be light in a while."

"Let's return to the dining room and sit where we can observe Mr. Broder," Helma said. She carefully folded the diary pages and slipped them into her pocket to read more carefully later.

"Murder or not, I can't keep my eyes open much longer, period," Ruth said.

❧ chapter sixteen ❧

MORNING BREAKS

Miss Higgins and Sister Bea sat side by side on two cushioned chairs from the bar, a single blanket over both their laps, eyes bright like two sentinel birds keeping watch over their dozing flock.

"Sleep isn't so important," Miss Higgins said, "*id est*, when you're as old as we are."

"Time's more important," Sister Bea added, "especially if you don't have much left." Then her face saddened as if she were thinking of the body in the conservatory.

Lights had been turned down and the atmosphere in the dining room beat with quiet respiration, marred now and then by a snore. Even those who weren't asleep, like Wilson Jones and Forrest Stevens, had sunk into a kind of somnolence, their breathing paced by that of the sleepers.

Mr. Broder sat by himself in the bar alcove, writing in a small notebook. Helma and Ruth occupied a table near the dining room door where they could watch who came and went.

Roman and his wife had returned to their room. At some point Lolly had reclaimed her makeup case and curled her hair. Even in the dim room, with her head on Joey Barnes's lap, she shone out in her bright pallet of colors. Somehow, Helma felt reassured seeing that Lolly had recreated herself.

She removed the pages of Amanda's diary from her pocket and unfolded them on the table. Ruth watched through heavy-lidded eyes, but shook her head when Helma offered her a page.

The three pages of crowded writing held more than just adolescent angst. Helma recalled the diary she'd kept briefly during her high school years and all its silly melodrama. No, Amanda spoke of a darkness Helma hadn't comprehended at that age: of "fanged and bloodied gargoyles watching outside my window"; or "slicing deep, my blood flowing until I am cleansed"; or "my body barely conceals the terror."

During high school, Amanda had already been contemplating suicide, that was now horribly clear. What had occurred in Scoop River that contributed to that urge? And "P.S. The Starlight!" as if she were reminding herself of the motel.

Cynthia had brought only these three pages to the reunion for a reason: they held what Cynthia must have believed were important clues to her sister's death.

But the picture was incomplete. If only Helma had known Amanda better, or if she possessed Amanda's entire diary.

"I'm going to talk to Mr. Broder," Helma whispered to Ruth.

Ruth yawned. "Go ahead. I have to close my eyes for a minute."

Helma threaded her way through the maze of her classmates in their various poses. Lolly raised her head from Joey's lap and sleepily waved her fingers.

"Helma," Mr. Broder said warmly, closing the notebook and clipping a pen to its cover, then slipping it into his pocket. "Sit down, please."

"I have a friend who carries a notebook like that," Helma said. "He's a policeman."

"I like to record my thoughts," Mr. Broder said. "No grand literature, no exposés, but you'd be surprised how many times I refer back to these jottings, just to check facts: what happened when, that sort of thing."

"And are you recording the tragedy that's taken place here?"

Mr. Broder nodded. "That and a few other thoughts."

"Tell me," Helma asked in a low voice, "what do you think happened to Amanda?"

He looked at Helma long and steadily. "You stated yourself she'd fallen and hit her head. Wasn't it obvious?"

"At first glance, perhaps."

"And now you feel Amanda's death is more complicated than a simple fall in the dark?"

"I believe it's related to incidents that took place long ago."

Mr. Broder didn't respond and Helma continued, "I heard you and Amanda talking in the conservatory. It sounded like you were disagreeing."

"We were discussing the past. Remember when I was your counselor? I've never betrayed any of your confidences and I wouldn't do so now." He spoke gently, without chastising but with an underlying core of firmness.

"I don't think she fell out there on the rocks."

"It might be wise to discuss your feelings with the police, Helma."

"I intend to do that," she said and left Mr. Broder's table.

Ruth was asleep, hunched over with her head lying on the table, her hair half hiding her face. Helma looked around the room. Wilson and Michael were sitting on the floor with a fresh bottle of whiskey. Miss Higgins and her sister's lips moved in unison. They were saying the rosary. Unconsciously Helma's thumb and forefinger rubbed together, as if the glow-in-the-dark rosary she'd won in third grade and kept beneath her pillow until eighth grade, was slipping between her fingers.

She was restless. She felt trapped. They were suspended, all of them, in a time period Helma suspected didn't really exist. The hours between two and five in the morning, the "death hours," her father had called them, when houses burned and loved ones died.

Unable to sit any longer, Helma rose and idly perused a stack of old books sitting on a box of glasses. By the light through the kitchen door she rearranged the stack in Dewey Decimal order. A Bible first, then a self-help, stop smoking book, followed by a vegetarian cookbook, a collection of Raymond Carver short stories, and a history of the Columbia River dams.

She left the books and wandered into the foyer, careful not to let the dining room door bang behind her. Mr. Westright sat on the couch by the desk, leaning his head on his hand.

"This must have been a showplace in its day," he said, raising his eyes to Helma, his voice husky from lack of sleep. "See the way those beams are joined above us? That's real craftsmanship."

Helma looked up where he pointed, noting more than the joints. The fine old wood, clear of knots, was of a quality not readily available anymore. "It's a shame it's coming down," she agreed.

"Time passes. Life changes," he said, sighing. "Don't we all wish we could turn back time."

"Do you?"

He waved a hand toward the conservatory, where the single light still glowed. "For some reasons, yes."

Helma nodded. "Amanda wasn't very happy, I don't think," she said.

"Why do you say that?"

"A feeling I have. I overheard her and Mr. Broder talking about the past."

"And she sounded unhappy?"

"Confused, perhaps."

"When you're at a reunion, the past is really all there is to talk about, isn't it? We don't have much else in common but memories."

"I don't know."

Mr. Westright looked up at Helma and smiled. "Now you don't think your beloved Mr. Broder has been up to some bad business, do you?"

"I don't know," Helma repeated and Mr. Westright's smile faded.

"You've always been very astute, Helma. I'll tell you what. I'll stick close to Broder until we leave the island, how would that be?"

"I can't ask you to do that."

"Certainly you can. Is he still in the dining room?"

"In the bar area."

Mr. Westright stood and worked his shoulders, stretching them first one way, then the other. "I think I'll have a glass of club soda." He winked at Helma. "Excuse me."

Helma sat on the couch in Mr. Westright's place. The cushions were warm from his body and she moved to the other end. In the distance a ship's horn blasted, warning other ships of its presence.

Why hadn't she trusted her instincts and heeded the anonymous warnings? She should have canceled the reunion. Cynthia would still be alive. And the dock attendant. So might Patty Anne Sands, for that matter. What had David Morse, Patty Anne Sands, and Amanda—or Cynthia—known that caused someone to extinguish their lives? And was anyone else in danger because they knew that same thing?

Helma shivered and crossed her arms. Movement caught her eye. A tiny brown mouse slipped beneath the dining room door and whisked across the foyer as smoothly as if it were on minuscule wheels. It disappeared behind the boxes and Helma pulled her feet up onto the cushion.

The aroma of coffee permeated the dining room like perfume. Even Helma, who didn't drink coffee, found herself deeply inhaling the rich, almost chocolatey smell. It worked like an alarm clock: movement stirred through the dining room, accompanied by a few groans and yawns.

"I'm too old to sleep on the floor," somebody said.

"Did I dream it or is Amanda . . . She *is*, isn't she?"

It was morning and it was definitely lighter but not a light caused by sunshine, only by the absence of night. Thick white fog still enveloped the inn.

"I don't believe we're on the planet earth at all," Lolly mused, looking out the window. "We've been abducted and we're on another planet so the aliens can perform experiments on our bodies."

Captain Larry entered the dining room from the kitchen, overcautiously carrying a tray of cups and spoons, wincing when the cups rattled together, his face pasty. "It'll burn off by noon," he said. "I can feel it."

"I hope you're right."

"Diana's just getting up. I'm driving down to Mac's to call the police."

"Good idea," Helma said.

Ruth raised her head. "Helma, if you're truly my friend, you'll bring that pot of coffee over here and just pour it down my throat."

Helma poured a cup of coffee and set it in front of Ruth. "Captain Larry just left to call the police," she said softly. "He's bound to find my car at the bottom of the driveway."

"Hope he doesn't hit it."

"I don't know how it got down there, do you?"

"Yes, you dum . . . " Ruth set down her cup. "Oh. No, I guess I don't."

"Sister Bea and I'd like to have a memorial for Amanda before we leave the island," Miss Higgins announced, "while we're all together."

"I could put together a lunch and make a cake," Dora Durbas volunteered.

"That's so Scoop River," Ruth said. "In times of crisis, everybody gathers around the food trough. Why do people do that?"

Dora answered immediately, facing Ruth with her considerable supply of severity, her tired eyes blazing. "Because eating is comforting and when people die, we need to be comforted. Besides that, Ruth Winthrop, I'm not a 'backyard pumpkin.'" And with that Dora turned and marched into the kitchen.

Ruth looked after Dora with her mouth open. "Where'd that come from?" she asked.

"Probably a little epithet you gave her twenty or more years ago," Helma said.

"I don't remember it."

"She obviously does."

"Oh yes, oh yes," Sister Bea said. "You don't forget. I remember my brother calling me 'Blubber Buns' when I was twelve."

"George said that?" Miss Higgins asked in surprise.

Sister Bea nodded gravely. "He denied it later, of course, but *I* remember."

"I'm glad *I'm* not that thin-skinned," Ruth said, shaking her head and still looking at the gently swinging kitchen door. "And stop looking at me like that, Helma Zukas."

The front door of the inn banged, then angry voices rose in the foyer.

It was Captain Larry and Diana, facing each other beside the desk, Diana in her shortie pajamas and her fists clenched. "I *didn't* leave the lights on. You know that."

"A riot! A riot!" Harry the cockatiel squawked.

"What's wrong?" Helma asked.

"My pickup's gone and Diana's car won't start," Captain Larry told her. "Can I use your car?"

More people entered the foyer, forming a phalanx behind Helma. "Certainly," she told Captain Larry. "Let me get my keys."

"Can't somebody muzzle that bird?" Ricky asked as Harry broke into his shrill rendition of the "1812 Overture."

"It took months to teach him that," Diana said indignantly.

"Life gets pretty desperate on this rock, huh?"

"Someone stole your pickup?" Mr. Westright asked Captain Larry.

"I doubt if little green men took it. I leave the keys in it. Everybody on the island does. At least it has to still be on the island somewhere."

"Who'd want that junker, anyway?" Diana asked.

"What happened?" Ruth asked, entering the foyer with her cup of coffee.

"Captain Larry's pickup's gone," Helma told her.

Ruth's eyes widened. She raised her cup in front of her mouth and muttered, "Think our murderer borrowed it last night?"

"That's a definite possibility."

It was a shock to everyone but Helma and Ruth when Captain Larry returned a few moments later and angrily announced that Helma's car was gone, too.

"Damn it. I'm walking down to Mac's to call the police. It looks like I've got a list of crimes to report." He glared at the tired group as if expecting confessions.

"Want some company?" Joey Barnes asked.

Captain Larry shook his head. "It'll be faster if I go alone. The rest of you might as well eat breakfast."

"When's the first ferry out of here?" Ricky asked.

"Two-twenty."

In the dawning gray light, the others returned to the dining room. Helma stood by the conservatory door, deep in thought, until she grew aware of someone beside her. It was Michael Petronas, staring sadly at the shrouded figure.

"How long did you know?" Helma asked.

"Know what?"

"That it wasn't Amanda."

Michael didn't seem surprised that she'd guessed. "Maybe from the beginning. I *wanted* it to be Amanda. I wanted to believe that her life had turned out successfully after all, that she'd straightened out her head. But she didn't, did she?"

"Her father said she committed suicide eighteen years ago."

Michael's face stilled. "She was so beautiful, but she was miserable. Now we'd label her 'troubled,' I guess, probably even mentally ill. And besides that, there were other problems, too."

"What were they?"

"I honestly don't know. She was secretive. I thought I was her friend but she was moody and sometimes irrational. She needed more help than Scoop River could give her, and people who had the power to help her couldn't see that."

"Is that why you've been feeling antagonistic toward Mr. Broder?" Helma asked. "Because you feel he didn't help Amanda when he could have?"

Michael nodded. "I know it's been twenty years and I'm looking at it from hindsight. But he should have seen what was happening. He was our counselor."

"The young can be remarkably adept at hiding their feelings."

"What did I know back then? After a while, being her friend was too much for me and I bailed out." Michael closed his eyes as if he were in pain. "Then she didn't have anybody."

"The rest of us didn't help either," Helma said. "I hardly remember even speaking to her. She must have felt isolated."

"Amanda's problems began before Scoop River. We can't beat ourselves up for acting the way we did. That was how things were back then, that's all." Michael hit his fist against his palm. "But I can tell you, if I ever detect anything similar in any of my own students, I'll demand help."

Helma remembered the first time she'd seen Amanda, her head high, eyes straight ahead. Snobbish, they'd pronounced. That wasn't what it had been at all.

"How did you figure out I knew?" Michael asked.

"In the fog, when you saw her body. At first I thought you were commenting on the morality of her death and then later I realized it wasn't, 'Oh, sin,' you were saying; it was, 'Oh, Cyn,' as in Cynthia."

Michael nodded. "She wasn't aware I knew. I thought she had to have a reason for masquerading as her sister."

"She suspected someone here was responsible for Amanda's death."

"There's no doubt someone here's responsible for *Cynthia's* death."

"I wonder which sister the killer thought he was murdering: Amanda or Cynthia?"

Michael shook his head.

"Have you discussed it with anyone?" Helma asked.

"Wilson and I danced around the subject a little. He still thinks it's Amanda."

Each of them held a piece of information. Wilson, the note asking who killed Amanda; Mr. Broder, the conversation in the conservatory; Michael, the knowledge that Amanda was actually Cynthia. And she and Ruth had the anonymous letters, the reservation cancellation, the glass in Helma's purse, the tampering in Miss Higgins's room, and the pages from Amanda's poor sad diary.

No, they had one more thing: the dead man lying by the ferry dock. It all made the whole elephant, but she still couldn't grasp how the pieces went together.

"Do I have time for a shower before breakfast?" Helma asked Dora, who was breaking eggs into a metal bowl in the kitchen, once again solidly cheerful.

Dora looked up at the wall clock. "Fifteen minutes?"

"That's enough time, thanks."

"Is Dora in there?" Ruth asked as Helma came out of the kitchen.

"Yes."

"I guess I'll see if she wants some help or . . . something."

On the way to her room, Helma met *Jean* coming from the bathrooms, a towel wrapped around her hair, no makeup on, looking small and surprisingly young. *Jean* stopped and smiled at Helma. "I know the reunion hasn't gone well, but I wanted to tell you how excited Roman was to come."

"He was?"

Jean nodded. "He talks about high school a lot, what a good time he had with all of you. I felt like I knew you all before we arrived. My high school years weren't as enjoyable as his."

In her room, Helma grabbed clean underwear and an unwrinkled skirt, thinking about Roman and *Jean*. Roman had been smugly disdainful of his classmates in high school, rarely joining in—not just overlooked as Helma sometimes was, but rarely asked—overly dependent on his mother, a tattletale. Yet he'd shared only happy memories with his wife. It was curious.

There were two showers in the women's restroom at the end of the hall. The restroom was empty but as Helma hung her towel outside the first shower stall she heard a noise from the second stall. She froze.

"Who's there?" she demanded.

"Can you help me?" a voice, definitely feminine, asked.

"What do you need?"

"If you could hand me a towel and help me up. I slipped."

"Are you hurt?"

A small laugh. "No, just embarrassed."

Helma pulled a towel from the rack and handed it through the shower curtain.

"Okay, I'm ready." The curtain was pulled back to reveal Fiona sitting on the floor of the shower stall, her shower cap tipped over one ear. She grinned up at Helma. "Is this old age or what? I can't seem to get off my butt."

Helma reached in and helped Fiona stand. She was shockingly light. Her bones strained against her flesh. The long veins of her arms showed blue and her knees were the thickest part of her legs. Fiona wobbled and clutched at Helma's arm, gasping, her face gray.

"Let me call someone," Helma said in alarm.

"No!" Fiona told her firmly.

Tightly gripping Helma's arm, Fiona stepped from the shower. The towel around her body slipped and Helma saw the scar on the left side of her chest, where her breast had been. Fiona released Helma and jerked up the towel. She stood on her own, straight, gazing fiercely into Helma's eyes.

"Don't you say one word, Helma Zukas, not one single word."

Helma stood beside the shower, silent, and watched while Fiona, with studied dignity, pulled on a terrycloth robe and left the bathroom without another word.

❧ chapter seventeen ❧

BREAKFAST

Even if it hadn't been accompanied by champagne, the breakfast Dora prepared, eggs, potatoes, juice, and toast, was greeted with enthusiasm by the exhausted, sleep-deprived guests at Gull Rock Inn.

"You should cook in a cafeteria," Lolly told Dora.

"Thank you," Dora replied, smiling and adding an extra bit of scrambled egg to Lolly's plate.

It was eight-thirty in the morning but because of the fog, the intensity of daylight hadn't changed since dawn. The dining room lights remained on and the Gull Rock Inn felt as isolated and timeless as the night they'd just passed through.

Helma looked down at her crisp twill skirt and blue cotton pullover, then around the dining room at her classmates, several of them rumpled and in need of a comb. Helma had yet to be in a situation where it wasn't possible to tidy up if one *sincerely* desired to be presentable.

After breakfast, the class remained in the dining room, drinking coffee and champagne. Another case of champagne sat on the buffet table, the cardboard box soft and swollen from the cooler.

There really wasn't much else to do now except wait. Helma thought of the folder of games in her room. They

192

were completely inappropriate with a body lying in the conservatory and another at the ferry dock.

"Shouldn't it be lighter by now?" Dora Durbas asked. She sat, still in her apron, but momentarily at rest, her feet on the chair opposite her.

"The fog keeps it in a state of twilight," Helma told her. "Captain Larry says it'll burn off by noon."

"Well, I suppose he should know."

Helma had drunk two glasses of champagne herself and the night's horror was receding, losing its edge. By now, Captain Larry had certainly found a way to contact the sheriff, who would arrive soon to take charge. Once Helma told the authorities what she knew, they'd question the guests and solve the mystery by the time the ferry arrived. The reunion would conclude and they'd all go home. And that would be that.

"Helm, want to join us?" Ruth asked. She held a pitcher of orange juice and pointed to the bar where Wilson was demonstrating casting to Lolly, Michael, and Ricky, using a curtain rod as a fishing pole. "Ten o'clock, two o'clock, twelve o'clock," Helma heard him say. "Ten, two, twelve."

"No thank you."

"You sure? Instead of a champagne headache I can promise you a real kick."

"No thank you," Helma repeated.

"Okay," Ruth said. "Enough with the daggers. Suit yourself."

Mr. Broder stood and stretched. He still wore the sweater and slacks he'd worn the night before. "I think I'll step outside for a few minutes and clear my head."

"Don't get lost," Dora warned.

"I won't go out of sight of the inn."

As the door swung closed behind him, Mr. Westright got up and stopped behind Helma's chair. "I'll keep an eye on him," he said quietly. "Make sure he stays on the island."

"Come here and sit with us for a while, Helma," Miss Higgins called, patting the chair next to her. She and Sister Bea, their cheeks flushed pink, sat at a table for four, a bottle of champagne between them. Sister Bea had yet to reclaim her veil and her white hair was ridged where the band normally rested.

Helma moved to their table, carrying her cup of tea cradled in a napkin. Across the dining room, Ruth stood behind the bar mixing orange juice and various alcoholic beverages with intense concentration.

"But then," Miss Higgins was saying, eloquently accompanying her words with her hands, "everyone in the teachers' club had their own way of doing things. Heaven knows it wouldn't have been fair for me to force my ideas on other people, but still, I *was* the president."

"Heaven knows," Sister Bea repeated, chuckling. The two sisters affably bumped shoulders and Sister Bea said, "You can kiss a nun but don't get in the habit," and they burst into a paroxysm of giggles.

"Private joke," Miss Higgins told Helma, wiping her eyes. "Bea's such a card."

Helma nodded politely, wondering if Mr. Broder might really try to fly off the island, even in this fog. And what would Mr. Westright do if he *did* try?

" . . . and they've just grown so mistrustful over the years," Miss Higgins said, onto another subject. "People *expect* ulterior motives these days."

"Mm-hmm," Helma agreed. Fiona had joined Lolly at a table in the bar. They smiled warily at each other and Fiona leaned across the table toward Lolly, earnestly speaking.

" . . . so I said," Miss Higgins went on, "of course Donald Westright was always very fond of his students, and why are you asking such ridiculous questions."

Helma set down her cup and turned to Miss Higgins. "I beg your pardon; who was asking about Mr. Westright?"

"Those people from that private school. I heard it costs as much to send your child there as it does to attend Bryn Mawr, can you imagine? With uniforms and little wool hats. The parents are Anglo- or Francophiles, if you ask me. It's hardly American."

"Hardly at all," Sister Bea agreed.

"But why were they asking about Mr. Westright?" Helma asked.

"My dear, were you woolgathering? That's unlike you."

"Is Mr. Westright being considered for a position?" Helma prompted.

"Only the headmaster," Miss Higgins said proudly. "He's one of three finalists." She shook her finger in emphasis. "In a school like that it's necessary to be *very* careful about who's at the helm. He'd most likely make as much money as the president of the United States."

"No!" Sister Bea said.

Miss Higgins nodded knowingly. "The president doesn't make *that* much, you know. Not like baseball players and those musicians with the hair."

"Did school officials phone you?" Helma asked Miss Higgins.

"Yes, because I was president of the teachers' association when Donald Westright taught at Scoop River. But that was just the beginning. Those were the preliminary interviews. When we return to Scoop River, two representatives from the search committee are coming to interview me—in person." Miss Higgins nodded her head in approval. "It's all very professional."

"Did Mr. Westright know the search committee had contacted you?"

"He did. He was in Scoop River shortly after they called me, and stopped by—a little late for my tastes—but I forgave him since he brought a box of those nice chocolates, the dark kind with creamy centers. Wasn't that sweet?"

"But," Sister Bea told Helma, leaning in front of Miss Higgins, "Ellie won't set mousetraps so we had to throw it out."

"I beg your pardon?" Helma asked.

"The candy," Sister Bea explained. "It was on the couch all night and a mouse nibbled on the corner of the box, so out it went."

"And we didn't get to eat a single one," Miss Higgins said.

"Mr. Westright was in Scoop River?" Helma asked. "When was this? What date?"

Miss Higgins looked at Sister Bea, frowning. "Why, a month ago. That's right, the week before the Fourth of July because the next Saturday Bea and June Johnston and I went to Ludington on the senior center bus to watch the fireworks over Lake Michigan. I think it was their best display ever, don't you, Bea?"

Sister Bea giggled and nodded. "Lots of my favorite ones . . . you know, where little fireworks explode out of the big one and go twirling off, whistling like tea kettles."

"I wonder why Mr. Westright hasn't mentioned he's a finalist for such a prestigious position," Helma asked Miss Higgins.

"He asked me not to tell anyone; he thought it would be bad luck." She covered her mouth and slapped her hand on the table. "But now I've spilled the beans, haven't I? *Fiat lux.* But wasn't that silly of him? He should be proud as punch." And she punched the air. Sister Bea playfully punched back.

"You mentioned how close he was to his students," Helma said, carefully choosing her words. "Do you recall if he was close to Amanda?"

Miss Higgins and Sister Bea slipped into solemnity. "That poor girl," Miss Higgins said. "And here we are, laughing."

"Was he?" Helma asked again.

Miss Higgins studied the champagne remaining in her glass. "I never saw anything."

"Miss Higgins," Helma urged gently, hearing the unspoken "but."

The elderly woman swallowed the last of her champagne and pushed her glass across the table. "Her parents went to Stanley Carson, the principal—he died six years ago, you know—concerned that Amanda had developed an unusual attachment to Donald Westright."

"How did Mr. Carson deal with it?"

"He and I talked to Donald, who stated he was totally unaware of any infatuation. Then we spoke with Amanda who admitted she'd fabricated the story. We sent her to Wayne Broder for counseling."

Miss Higgins sighed and held her hand to her heart.

"To think I'd be here twenty years later and see that lovely girl dead."

"Helma!" Ruth called from the bar. "Come here. You've got to hear this."

Helma stood and excused herself as she distractedly pushed in her chair. Why would Amanda have fabricated a story about Mr. Westright? she wondered, while she walked across the room.

Ricky sat on a bar stool beside Ruth, a self-important grin on his face.

"Tell her," Ruth said.

"About the Scoop River/Hopkins game? You shoulda asked me, cuz. The fight afterward involved one of our dear Scoop River faculty."

"Who?"

Ricky shrugged. "Hard to say. I was getting a hit after the game and heard them going at it behind the gym. By the time I showed up, some Hopkins guys had broken it up, the cops had been called, and everybody was hightailing it out of there."

"Didn't you hear anything?"

"Maybe. What's it worth to you?"

"Are you serious, you cretin?" Ruth asked.

"Okay, okay. Can't blame me for trying. There was some macho talk about our teacher fooling around with a Scoop River jock's girl. He took her to some motel."

"The Starlight?"

"Mighta been. I don't remember."

"Could it have been Mr. Broder?"

"Nah, Broder gave me a ride home. I was suspended from the team bus."

Ruth turned to Helma. "Do you think it could be the same person? A *teacher*? Two different girls, one from Scoop River, one from Hopkins?"

"What's this about?" Ricky asked. "What girls?"

"P.S. The Starlight," Amanda had written. P.S. Not "Post Script." P.S. stood for Patty Sands. Patty Anne Sands had been at the Starlight Motel.

"Are you positive Mr. Broder gave you a ride home?"

"Yeah, Stretch. We stopped at Zack's for a burger. He paid."

"And was Mr. Westright at the game?" Helma asked.

Ricky shrugged. "Maybe. I don't remember. He went sometimes."

"Ruth, we'd better go outside," Helma said.

"Outside? Why?"

"Just come with me."

"So, cuz," Ricky called after them. "Since I was so cooperative, can I get a little loan?"

"I never loan money to strangers—or relatives," Helma assured him.

In the foyer Helma told Ruth what Miss Higgins had said about the interviews for Mr. Westright's possible new job. "He told me he hadn't been back to Scoop River in seventeen years."

"What else did she say?" Ruth asked.

"I haven't had time to decipher it yet, but Amanda's parents were concerned in high school about Amanda and Mr. Westright."

"And now Westright's outside keeping an eye on Mr. Broder?"

"Right."

"Is this the equivalent of the fox watching the henhouse?" Ruth asked.

"I believe it may be," Helma concluded.

They stepped into the foggy morning. A bird chirped tentatively. The dewy fragrance of flowers hung in the moist air.

"We can't just wander blindly around in this stuff," Ruth said. "Should we call?"

"No. Just wait."

They stood silently, the inn at their backs, ghostly shrubs nearby, slight sounds they couldn't place. High above their heads a hint of light shone through the fog; the sun was finally making headway.

"Do you hear voices?" Helma asked.

"No. Yes!"

"Can you tell where they're coming from?" Helma turned, trying to ascertain the direction of the sound.

"Somewhere in the fog," Ruth told her.

"I'm aware of that, Ruth."

"Help! Help!"

Ruth grabbed Helma's arm. "Somebody's in trouble. But where in hell are they?"

"By the cliffs, I think," Helma said. They took cautious steps into the white mist.

"Where are you?" Helma called.

The voice was panicked. "On the rocks. Be careful. But hurry, please! Help me!"

Helma and Ruth, heads lowered to watch their steps, crossed the lawn and hurried toward the voice. "I swear I'm moving to Arizona," Ruth muttered.

The lawn ended and they found themselves stepping onto rock. They stopped, finally able to see who was calling.

Mr. Westright hung half over the edge of a cliff, his face dirty, his hands frantically clutching for purchase on the smooth rocks.

"It was Broder," Mr. Westright told them, his voice cracking. "He tried to kill me. I managed to fight him off but he went over the rocks."

Ruth and Helma gripped Mr. Westright by the arms and pulled him back on solid ground.

His legs wobbled. He ineffectually brushed at his clothing, hands shaking. "Could you help me inside?" he asked, reaching for Ruth's arm.

"Why would Broder try to kill you?" Ruth asked, stepping back from his outstretched hand.

Mr. Westright patted his hair, realigning his slightly askew hairpiece. "Because I guessed he killed Amanda. He was trying to save himself from a political scandal. Amanda came here to get even. She could have ruined his career."

"How?"

"He had an affair with her when she was a student. She became pregnant and if she would have told, he'd be finished in politics."

"Really?" Helma asked with real interest. "How do you know?"

"She confided in me last night. He was making certain neither of us would ever tell."

"You didn't tell me that in the foyer a few hours ago," Helma reminded him.

"I suspected then but I didn't want to put you in danger, too. Who knows what Broder might have done to you. After Amanda . . . "

"Oh, you misguided man," Ruth said, clicking her tongue against her teeth. "You've been seeing ghosts. Amanda's been dead for eighteen years. That's her sister Cynthia who's lying in the conservatory. You of all people should have known that."

Westright's mouth fell open. "Cynthia?"

"Theater, not history would have been a better vocation for you," Helma told him. "And Amanda never was pregnant. She kept your secret. You did all of this for nothing. You took lives for a *job*."

"So it was you, Westright," Mr. Broder said, stepping out of the mist and brushing sand from his pants. His cheek was scraped raw, the knee of his pants torn. "Lucky for me the fog hadn't lifted or you'd have seen the rocks here are only ten feet above the shore."

Westright took a step backward and Mr. Broder followed after him. "When Cynthia read in her sister's diary that Amanda was frightened after David Morse died, Cynthia believed I was the *B* who'd promised to help Amanda. She thought I knew who was responsible for her sister's death. That's why she came to the reunion. That's why she wrote to Helma and reminded her of her promise to organize the event."

"Cynthia wrote the first anonymous letter?" Helma asked. "Did *you* write the others warning *against* holding the reunion?" she demanded of Westright.

"But they were postmarked Scoop River," Ruth interjected.

"A postmark is no mystery," Helma told her. "People send letters to post offices for their postmark all the time, like Santa Claus, Arizona."

"Or Hell, Michigan."

"You canceled our reservations here," Helma accused Westright.

"And put the glass in Helma's purse?"

"And tried to harm Miss Higgins so she wouldn't tell. You didn't call me from Denver that night, did you? You were already in Bellehaven."

"And the dock attendant . . . " Ruth added.

"The dock attendant?" Mr. Broder repeated, puzzled.

Westright's eyes narrowed. He studied the three people in front of him. Helma felt him speculating, surmising how great a threat they were. He looked Helma in the eye, challenging her.

"If you'd listened to me," he said with a tone of authority that made Helma cringe, "Cynthia would still be alive. If you hadn't gone out last night . . ."

Ruth guffawed. "*Helma* forced you to kill? Uh uh, I don't think so."

"I didn't kill Amanda," Westright said. "She left Scoop River right after graduation. I never saw her again, never heard from her."

"No, you didn't kill her directly," Mr. Broder said quietly, "but you took advantage of her. She was too fragile to overcome what you did to her. Cynthia came here to find answers, and peace for her sister."

"We know you took both Amanda and Patty Anne Sands to the Starlight Motel," Helma bluffed.

"Tacky, tacky," Ruth said.

"You killed Patty Anne's boyfriend, David, because he found out about you and Patty Anne and was ready to tell. Then, twenty years later, you wanted that job so badly you tried to sneak back into Michigan, to discover what Miss Higgins remembered. You didn't want her to bring up that old story about you and Amanda, did you? Miss Higgins hadn't forgotten it. She was still uncomfortable and even suspicious it might be true. Tell me," Helma asked, "if Miss Higgins had eaten those chocolates you brought her, would she have lived to attend this reunion?"

"The old biddy. I should have . . ." Westright stopped.

"And then you killed Patty Anne Sands. Why? After twenty years? The search committee never would have talked to her."

"Patty Anne and I stayed in touch for a time after her boyfriend's death. I helped her out occasionally."

"And then, knowing how to take advantage of a situation, Patty Anne resurfaced to blackmail you," Ruth surmised.

Westright closed his eyes for a long moment. "Patty Anne told me a woman had called her, claiming to know the truth about the dead boy. I believed it was Amanda, and she and Patty Anne would join together to ruin my life."

"You mean ruin your chance to become a headmaster, don't you?" Helma corrected. "To finally reach the pinnacle of your career before you retired."

"You must have been passed over a few times along the way to get so desperate," Ruth said.

Westright looked at Ruth, Helma, and Mr. Broder in entreaty, raising his hands in supplication. "I made a mistake. I was young. It was as much their fault as mine."

"I believe you're speaking of historical revisionism again," Helma said.

"You *killed* them," Mr. Broder pointed out. "That qualifies as more than a simple mistake."

The rumble of a boat engine sounded through the fog. They turned toward the sound and when they looked back, Westright held a gun in his hand. "Get back," he shouted.

"Uh-oh," Ruth said.

They held their ground, not moving.

"This is unreasonable," Helma pointed out to Westright. "We're on an island. You're not going to kill us. And you're not going to get away with this, either."

"You might have, though," Ruth said, as if suddenly struck, leaning toward Westright. "Why'd you arrange Cynthia's body the way you did? *That* was weird."

Westright faltered. "She was so beautiful. After . . . when it was over, she was pitiful, broken. I couldn't leave her like that."

"Where will you go?" Broder asked. "You can't get off the island."

"I can fly a plane."

"In this fog?"

"If I have to. Now stay back. Don't move or I'll shoot you. I mean it."

The rumble of the boat grew louder, nearer. Westright took two more steps backward, then turned and disappeared into the fog. Mr. Broder threw himself into the murk after him. Helma heard the smacking of their bodies together, the grunts and curses. She leapt after their shadowed figures.

"The gun!" Mr. Broder shouted. "Get the gun."

Helma dropped to her knees, tearing her stockings, and groped desperately along the rocks until her hand touched the cold steel. Ruth, meanwhile, jumped too close to the men, nearly catching a punch herself.

"Cease and desist! I'm holding the gun," Helma said, gripping the handgun in both her hands, bracing herself. She'd never held a pistol and it felt repulsive, vile, and most horrible of all, too beguilingly easy to pull the trigger. "Get up. Put your hands in the air."

Westright slowly stood, raising his hands above his head. Helma kept the gun pointed at the center of his forehead. He stared at her, his gaze piercingly cold. She held his eyes with her own until he finally looked away.

A beam suddenly swept through the fog, crossed over them, and came back to rest on the group, momentarily blinding them. It came from the direction of the water, too bright to face directly.

"Helma Zukas, is that you?" a voice called through a loudspeaker.

"The cavalry, at last," Ruth said.

"Yes," Helma called back. Despite herself, despite the situation, she smiled.

"This is Chief Gallant. I'm coming ashore."

Chief Gallant hadn't brought the designated cavalry; he'd come on a Coast Guard cutter, but with Westright already subdued, the cutter's crew was perfectly adequate to assist him until the county sheriff arrived.

"How'd you find us?" Ruth asked after Westright was securely stowed aboard the cutter and they sat in the dining room of the Gull Rock Inn. Diana and Dora were in the kitchen with Mr. Broder, cleaning and bandaging his abrasions. The rest of the class stood by, bright-eyed and curious, absorbing these latest developments in their twentieth reunion.

Chief Gallant smiled at Helma. "I knew you wouldn't be calling me in the middle of the night on a trivial matter," he said. "So I tracked down your reunion. It looks like I could have saved myself the trip. You had it under control."

"We all did our best," Helma said modestly.

"I told you it would all come out in the wash, didn't I?" Ruth said.

"The story might have been different if I hadn't supplied the critical information," Ricky interjected.

"Where were you when we were out there on the rocks wrestling guns from killers?" Ruth asked.

"Preparing alternative plans," Ricky said.

Even Helma snorted at that.

❧ *chapter eighteen* ❧

TIDE POOLS

By noon the fog had dissipated to a light haze, burned away in the open areas, just like Captain Larry had predicted, but still clinging stubbornly to the shade in coves and glades. The class left the Gull Rock Inn to the converging authorities and clambered over Saturday Island's glistening rocky shore at low tide.

Although the seashells they found were mainly fragments, the tide pools pulsed with barnacles and urchins and sea anemones. Ricky chased Lolly with a giant purple starfish. Dora and Sandy followed a tiny crab scuttling toward the water. Wilson Jones stood on a rock and cast an imaginary line into the salt water.

"Ten, two, twelve," Michael called to him.

Rarely did they look above them at the gleaming white inn where things were being "tended to."

"Now, *this* stuff doesn't live in Lake Michigan," Forrest said, holding the luminous golden bladder of a six-foot strand of bull kelp.

"But *we* have alewives and zebra mussels," Michael said, naming two of the most hated species of the Great Lakes, destructive invaders who'd slipped in from the wider world through the St. Lawrence Seaway.

Bundled up in a heavy jacket while everyone else was in shirtsleeves, Fiona sat on the rocks above the tide pools, huddling over Helma's marine life identification book, and providing details for whatever creature was described or held up to her.

"It's a sea cucumber and if you upset it, it eviscerates."

"What does that mean?"

"It pukes out its guts."

"That shell that looks like the forehead of Worf on 'Star Trek,' is a dried chiton shell; a seagull ate the soft parts," she told Wilson, who then pressed the imbricated shell between his eyes.

Ruth showed Dora and Sandy how the back of a tiny empty crab shell they were clucking over sympathetically could lift like the trunk of a car. "It's not dead," she explained to their relief. "It just molted. You know, backed out of its shell, like those loud, buzzing bugs in Michigan."

"Cicadas?"

"Right."

Helma watched Chief Gallant descend the path from the inn to the shore, his hands in his pockets. He stood for a moment, breathing deep, jingling coins and looking toward the distant islands. Then he stepped from rock to rock to where she had resumed gazing at barnacles gracefully feeding in a tide pool, their feathery legs sweeping up plankton.

"You're welcome to take the boat back to Bellehaven with me," he invited.

With the stick she carried, Helma turned over a broken crab shell partially buried in the pool. "Thank you but I'd better stay with the reunion. I appreciate your going to the trouble to discover where we were."

"I'm honored you thought to call me. And even more honored you kept my home phone number all this time."

"I . . . It was . . . in my address book. What will happen to Mr. Westright now?" Helma asked.

"I imagine there are people in Michigan who are very interested in talking to him, as well as here. He'll be busy for a long time."

"Did you contact Cynthia's parents?"

The chief nodded, looking to the west again, over the water. "The sheriff did. That's one of the hardest parts of this job. If criminals were forced to face . . . well," He smiled at Helma. "Don't get me started."

Roman Fonsilwick, his pant legs rolled to his knees, gingerly lifted an object from a tide pool and held it out in his palm to his wife, *Jean*. She bent her head over his hand and then touched Roman's cheek. Helma turned away, feeling as if she'd pried.

"I *liked* Mr. Westright," Helma told Chief Gallant, surprised at the anger rising in her voice. "He was a good teacher. Why didn't we see through him? Even in high school, after David Morse died, I don't remember him acting suspiciously."

"It's our nature to trust, I think. Westright probably didn't see himself as guilty so you didn't either."

"And four people died because he believed they were in his way."

"But no more will. In a few hours, Helma, you solved what might have become four unrelated deaths. That's quite an accomplishment."

"I didn't accomplish it by myself, but thank you. Did Westright confess to David Morse's death?"

The chief nodded. "David confronted Westright after the basketball game. Westright followed him and ran him off the road."

"And the dock attendant?"

"Just as you suspected. He surprised Westright. Westright might have gotten away with it all if he hadn't killed the attendant." The chief grinned at Helma. "Of course, he hadn't counted on your inquisitive nature." Chief Gallant looked at his watch. "I have to go back up to the inn. Enjoy what's left of your reunion. I'll see you in town."

"Goodbye."

Helma watched him climb up the rocky path, surprisingly graceful for his size. Halfway up he turned and smiled, then briefly waved. Helma raised her own arm.

"Go on. Go after him," Ruth said. "Say you've changed your mind and you'd *love* to ride home with him."

"You were listening, Ruth."

"Of course I was. Go on. You can still catch him."

Helma shook her head. The chief was at the top of the path, disappearing over the crest. "I don't want to leave everyone yet."

Ruth gazed around at their classmates, as curious as children, poking around in the tide pools and stomping on seaweed air bladders along the shore. "Yeah, now that the dirty business is over, this is kinda fun."

Forrest Stevens, sitting on a rock and pulling apart a piece of seaweed, looked up the path after Chief Gallant. He turned and nodded to Helma, a wistful smile on his face.

Ricky walked by, still holding the purple starfish. He looked up at Ruth, who stood on the rocks above him. "How's the weather up there, Stretch?"

Ruth pursed her lips and spit a bubbly blob, neatly landing it on Ricky's forehead. "It's raining," she said. "How's the weather down there?"

❧ chapter nineteen ❧

REVENGE

When Helma entered the library workroom on Monday morning, the staff was waiting for her beside her cubicle.

"We *heard*, Helma," Roberta said. "It was on the radio this morning."

Patrice rose up from her side of the bookshelves. "They made it sound like you were running wild all over that island."

"I saw it on TV last night," Eve added. "That cute newscaster on Channel five, he said it was the biggest news in the islands since the Pig War."

"Only a pig died in that incident," George Melville pointed out. "And that was a hundred years ago."

"It was a tragedy," Helma said.

"Yeah, even pigs have a right to life," Eve replied compassionately.

"I think she speaks of her own more recent tragedy."

Eve clapped a hand over her mouth. "Oh. Sorry. But was it fun? I mean, if nobody had died? Did you fight over old boyfriends and stuff like that?"

"We're all beyond that," Helma assured Eve. "You forget those silly quarrels when you get older."

As she always did, Helma attended Ruth's opening in Seattle, but only for a glass of alcohol-free sparkling cider and just long enough to be certain Ruth saw her.

She traded her Friday night shift at the crisis center for a Saturday night. "Friday's grown quieter since you came aboard," the supervisor had told Helma. "A lot of our regulars have quit calling."

"Perhaps they've found more meaning in their lives," Helma had suggested.

Ruth's autumn opening was at a trendy art gallery a block from trendy Pioneer Square, filled with trendy people who rarely smiled and wore a lot of black and earrings in other body parts besides their ears.

The gallery was crowded. Voices echoed between the high ceiling and the wooden floor and all the white walls hung with Ruth's brilliant paintings. Knots of people stood around the gallery blocking her view of Ruth's artwork, even if Helma had been determined to inspect them.

Spotting Ruth wasn't difficult. She stood by the reception table, her bushy hair pulled severely back without even a wave to soften it, her dress a surprisingly plain black sheath and wearing black stockings and heels. As usual she wore too much makeup, but what was really too much, even for Ruth, was the amount of jewelry she wore. From her distance, Helma couldn't make out the details but Ruth was certainly "laden": silver and bronze necklaces, dangling copper earrings and clanking bracelets. Ruth fairly glittered with metal.

Helma couldn't get close to Ruth but finally she caught her eye and Ruth waved one long arm above the crowd. "Helm!" she called.

Helma waved back, saying, "Helma," to herself.

"Vigorous paintings, aren't they," a man in a black shirt and a Mickey Mouse tie commented to Helma. "Pulsing with the elemental urges that obviously pour from the artist's belly and bowels."

"Excuse me," Helma said, taking the cracker smeared with paté away from her lips, and edging toward the trash bin disguised as a fire hydrant.

She left not long after and drove two hours back to Bellehaven in the cool evening, watching the rose-purple light of the sunset fade over the Olympics and distant humps of the San Juan islands.

She supposed the Gull Rock Inn was gone by now and sleek condominiums sprouted in its place, the uneven shore soon to be tamed and prettified. Captain Larry and Diana were in Mexico, no doubt telling stories about the last guests they entertained at the Gull Rock Inn.

She'd had a scattering of notes from the reunion attendees. Sister Bea had enclosed a holy card of Saint Cecilia, Roman Fonsilwick a brochure on investments. Lolly's note was on pink paper and sealed with a red and gold sticker in the shape of a heart with x's and o's dashed liberally beneath it.

Dora had sent Fiona's obituary from the *Scoop River Herald*, saying that Fiona had requested her high school graduation picture illustrate her obituary. Helma had written a check for the remainder of the class's money to the Susan Komen Breast Cancer Foundation in Fiona's memory.

It was dark when Helma pulled into her parking slot at the Bayside Arms. She removed her mail from the box and carried it inside her apartment, ignoring the irritable meow from her balcony. A letter from Aunt Em, a Nordstrom bill, an ad, and a square white envelope with no return address. Helma swallowed past the sudden lump in her throat. Not again.

But when she turned this envelope over a return address was printed on the back flap: the Bellehaven City Police.

It was an invitation to an open house in celebration of the police department's renovations. At the bottom, in strong black penmanship, it read, "Helma, I hope you'll be here. WG."

Wayne Gallant, Chief Wayne Gallant. Helma smiled and stood the invitation in the middle of the table.

Ruth showed up while Helma was still eating breakfast and reading Saturday morning's *Bellehaven Daily News*. The paper was open to the engagements and anniversaries page. Helma liked to compare then-and-now photos of the fifty-year anniversary couples, speculating on which partner had changed the most and why.

Ruth wore the same clothes she'd worn at her gallery opening the night before, minus the jewelry and her hair gone wild again. Her face was lit by a satisfied smile and she cradled the Seattle paper to her heart.

"Have you seen this?" she demanded.

"Not yet. It must be laudatory though from the look on your face."

"Read it."

Helma took the paper, already opened to a review of Ruth's show. It was a long review that said things like, "Simplicity of shape doesn't always equate with simplicity of experience," and called Ruth's painting a "metaphor for spiritual states, with precisely tuned tonalities."

A short paragraph was highlighted in yellow but Helma read her way down to it, to Ruth's obvious impatience.

"Are you there yet? Read it out loud."

"'The one embarrassing element,'" Helma read, "'was the "art" worn by the artist herself which, in a blatant effort to promote the hobbyist, she announced as originals by a local Bellehaven hopeful. It makes this reviewer wonder about the supposed "art colony" they trumpet up there.'"

Ruth guffawed. Her eyes glinted wickedly.

"The reviewer doesn't name Kara Cherry as the 'hobbyist,'" Helma pointed out.

"No, but *she'll* know. That's all I care about."

"Remind me never to criticize your art, Ruth."

"Helm, I did nothing. Absolutely nothing. Justice has a way of seeking its own level, don't you think?"

"Something like that."